PRAISE FOR N

The Candid Life of Meena Dave

Center for Fiction First Novel Prize Finalist

"A thoroughly entertaining rendition of one woman's search for belonging."

—Kirkus Reviews

"Full of lively characters who will win readers' hearts and keep them thinking long after the book is finished, this book is a genuine, charming debut. Long-buried secrets and a journey of self-discovery will keep the pages turning."

—Booklist

"[A]n inherently fascinating and impressively scripted novel…"

—Midwest Book Review

"Namrata Patel's debut is a delightful exploration of identity, community, and growth. I was drawn into Meena Dave's captivating journey from the first pages and was rooting for her until the end. This poignant and witty story is perfect for book clubs!"

—Saumya Dave, author of Well-Behaved Indian Women

SCENT
OF A
GARDEN

OTHER TITLES BY NAMRATA PATEL

The Candid Life of Meena Dave

SCENT OF A GARDEN

A Novel

NAMRATA PATEL

LAKE UNION
PUBLISHING

Text copyright © 2023 by Namrata Patel
All rights reserved.

Published by Lake Union Publishing, Seattle

www.apub.com

Amazon, the Amazon logo, and Lake Union Publishing are trademarks of Amazon.com, Inc., or its affiliates.

ISBN-13: 9781542039086 (paperback)
ISBN-13: 9781542039093 (digital)

Cover design and illustration by Kimberly Glyder
Cover image: © jakkapan / Shutterstock

Printed in the United States of America

To Mike and Donna Grohol from #3

AUTHOR'S NOTE

What do we owe each other, and what do we owe ourselves? Over the years, it's a question I've pondered in many contexts. But in this novel, I wanted to explore how second- and third-generation immigrant families carve out their own paths while navigating familial expectations.

In *Scent of a Garden*, Asha Patel has spent most of her life pursuing her passions until her world changes in an instant. As she faces the challenge of what's next, she wrestles with whether she needs to honor the efforts of her parents and grandparents or choose for herself. As an Indian American and the granddaughter of immigrants, she understands that her family struggled so she could thrive.

I saw this internalized tension play out over and over again, particularly when I worked in the hospitality industry where immigrants worked twenty-four seven to make their businesses successful, then passed them down to their loved ones.

According to the Asian American Hotel Owners Association, Indian Americans own anywhere from 40 to 60 percent of hotels across the United States. It started in the early 1940s when Kanjibhai Desai, an immigrant of Gujarat, India, bought the Goldfield Hotel in downtown San Francisco. He found a way to build a future, not only for himself but for other Gujarati immigrants who followed.

I wondered what it might be like for descendants of such a lineage to hold the weight of this accomplishment. Asha's parents are hoteliers who are dedicated to preserving the generational legacy of what her grandfather built. This is the choice she is faced with as she struggles to balance her family's expectations with her individual aspirations. I hope you enjoy reading Asha's story as much as I enjoyed writing it.

Please note that while the surname Desai is used in this novel, this is a work of fiction, and it should not be inferred that there is even a tangential connection to the original. Additionally, I am using Goldfield only as a way to pay homage to the original hotel, but its description and location are not related to the original hotel in San Francisco.

CHAPTER ONE

Asha's future rested on the five vials in the center of the jet-black conference table. The room was quiet enough to hear the hum of office noise on the other side of the beige wall. Stomach in knots, she sat in a white swivel chair with her back straight, trying to project confidence she didn't quite feel.

The brief was aspirational—a fragrance that conveyed artist Paul Gauguin's Tahiti for luxury perfume brand Guerlain. It was the historical nature of the project that had drawn her in. The idea of immortalizing a person in a place in a 3.4-ounce bottle wasn't daunting but rather a welcome challenge. Especially because it would give her the blueprint for a scent close to her heart. She'd channeled all her creativity to build a perfume that was layered and unique and captured not only the sense of place and time but the artist and his volatile nature.

Yes, there were tropical notes, but she'd added smoke and earth to hint at the late 1800s. She'd included a touch of clove to convey Gauguin's fiery temperament. Asha's take had won the account because she'd personified the whole artist, his talent, and his problematic nature. She hadn't romanticized him, only evoked him. That's why she'd been named perfumer, much to her colleagues' surprise. At thirty-two, she was considered young, both in age and experience, for such a big responsibility, especially in France, the epicenter of the fragrance industry. To date, Asha had never played a large role; she'd merely assisted notable and talented perfumers. However, if she succeeded, she'd be that much closer to master perfumer—a goal Asha had set for herself and an expectation of her mother and grandmother, who had helped her get here, to this place and this moment.

If this didn't work . . . nerves buzzed in her chest. Asha stopped herself from shaking her knee or swaying in her chair. Instead, she subtly bit the inside of her cheek as Esme Moreau, the head of marketing for Guerlain, sniffed multiple fragrance strips. The brand was under the powerhouse LVMH corporation, an important client for her employer, International Flavors and Fragrances. Esme was known in the industry for having a nose that could instinctively sense whether a fragrance would be a hit or miss. There was no room for average at this level.

And Esme gave nothing away as she moved from one vial to the next. Her two colleagues—who, as Asha knew from past interactions, would support Esme's decision without question—made notes in their leather-covered folio. Asha pressed her black stiletto-heeled pumps into the tiled floor to keep her legs steady. It would work.

Scent had a memory component, and Asha had an encyclopedic knowledge of thousands of essences she'd used over the course of her career. Never in her life had she leaned into the label her grandmother, past professors, and colleagues had given her—"a natural talent." Yet in this moment, she had to fervently believe that her gift and all she'd done to nurture it would see her through.

"No." Esme dropped the final scent strip. The slim woman leaned back in the chair and crossed her arms over her sleeveless navy dress, her expression completely neutral as she rendered her verdict.

The two-letter word sat heavy in Asha's ears, refused to penetrate her brain. Asha didn't fail. Ever. Not in anything she tried. The only time she'd received a less than perfect report card was in kindergarten when she got a check minus in nap time. She'd cried in her grandmother Leela's lap for a full thirty minutes when she found out. Then she'd decided she would become good at napping until she got a check plus. It only took two months to improve the skill.

No. Esme had said *no.* And why not? The fragrance industry was not only competitive but cutthroat. It had been difficult enough for Asha to get here. Her boss, Celeste Martine, who was an institution at IFF, believed Asha's winning pitch had been a fluke. She'd questioned Asha at every turn, picked apart formulations, challenged ingredients, and generally pushed her to work under constant stress. But Asha hadn't let that defeat her as she spent every waking moment on this fragrance. But that was before . . .

The conversation around her continued, though Asha couldn't focus on a single word. It wasn't because of the rapid-fire Parisian French, which she spoke as well as any nonnative fluent speaker, but more that she had to figure out how to turn the no into a yes.

"The balance isn't there. The gardenia-to-alcohol ratio is wrong. The pepper is too strong."

Esme's voice jarred Asha out of her thoughts. "Clove, not capsicum."

Esme crinkled her forehead, which was prominent with her black hair tied up in a tight bun. "I am aware. *This* smell is like Gauguin dying of syphilis, not alive in Tahiti." Esme pushed away from the large conference table where they sat and rose to indicate the meeting was over.

It was harsh. Unnecessarily so.

"There is a hint of darkness in there," Asha offered. The artist, after all, had been the impetus for Van Gogh to slice off his own ear. "Gauguin wasn't exactly a jovial person."

"Yet this is coming across as rancid." Esme picked up her large leather tote from the floor.

Numb, Asha stayed in her chair. Two things that couldn't be faked were chemistry and creativity, both critical to developing a successful fragrance. When the perfume had more than sixty ingredients, nuance was key. Asha's leg shook as Celeste ushered the clients out of the conference room with assurance that she would handle things, make it right. She stilled it with her hand on her knee.

A few minutes later, Celeste paced the length of the windowless room. "That was a disaster. What happened?"

"I increased the head slightly and adjusted the base for balance," Asha said.

"The top was fine," Celeste said. "Esme wanted depth after the last round."

"She wanted more spice."

Celeste took the seat across from Asha, the one vacated by Esme. The two women were very different. Where Esme was tall, with the raspy voice of a recovered smoker, Celeste was diminutive, and no matter how she styled her short salt-and-pepper hair, it became mussed by noon. Celeste had been with the company for over forty years, and she was formidable. Well respected, she gave her life to IFF. The only personal thing Asha knew about Celeste was that she'd had the same romantic partner for the entirety of her career.

"We need to change direction."

It would be difficult, but Asha agreed. "I'll start over. Go back to the brief and review all the formulas. Instead of tweaking and adjusting ratios, I can begin clean."

"That is not what I mean."

Asha folded her hands in her lap and squeezed her fingers together to keep from shaking her leg again. "I can do this. I'll need a little more time, but I know Esme will like the next version."

"It is not my way to, as you Americans say, beat around the bush." Celeste switched to English. "Let me be direct. This was a big task for you. The pressure when you are not experienced can take its toll. It's obvious that this should have been under the advisement of a master perfumer. You did your best, but you failed."

Asha straightened her spine. It wasn't true. She had honed her natural ability with thousands of hours of work. She had competed against seasoned perfumers, and Guerlain had chosen her pitch. "It was my interpretation that won us the account."

Celeste waved her hand as if to dismiss the effort. "It isn't enough to *get* it; you must deliver. This miss is a direct reflection upon me and our company. We can't afford another disappointment. I was able to convince Esme to consider a shift in their release date and give us time to fix this."

That's all she wanted. "Thank you."

"You misunderstand," Celeste said. "Simon will take over. With his experience he can build something fast."

"No." Asha stood. Palms flat on the lacquered black conference table. "This is my fragrance."

"You work for IFF," Celeste said. "There is nothing here that is yours. It belongs to the company."

"I've spent close to a year on this." If she was no longer the perfumer, it would be known. Everywhere. The perfume industry in Paris was small, and success was very much built through reputation. She was on the cusp of becoming a name. "Give me one more chance."

Celeste shook her head. "You're a good chemist. But your nose."

"Is fine," Asha lied. "I'm going back to the lab. I have an idea of how to tweak it." She would power through it. Find a way. She wasn't going to give up. She had to figure this out. It was chemistry. Science would not fail her.

"That won't be necessary," Celeste said. "Simon will take over."

Simon Bardet was methodical, but he wasn't an artist. He would take her ideas and water them down to create a serviceable scent. In his hands it would be the most obvious interpretation of Gauguin's Tahiti. "Esme wants nuance. Give me a few weeks. I think I know how to—"

Celeste cut her off. "We are out of time to take such a risk. Give your notes and everything you have up until now to Simon."

"And what am I supposed to do?"

Celeste was quiet.

"Honestly, Celeste. Let me try." Asha moved to leave the room.

"No," Celeste said. "You should take time off."

"What?" That wasn't in her plans. Her grandmother Leela always said, *Doing nothing never solved a problem.* The mere idea of stopping just before the finish made her stomach hurt.

Celeste went to Asha. "You worked through the winter holidays and have spent all your time in the lab these past six months. Take a month, two months. You have accrued enough to have a proper getaway."

"I don't need a holiday. If you're determined to give this to Simon, I can work on another pitch." She could sketch out scent profiles, components.

"I am directing you to take a break," Celeste said. "This is not optional."

Asha couldn't comprehend what was happening. Even on vacation, she spent time taking notes of the smells around her, deconstructing different aromatics from food to flowers. She wasn't someone who could sit in a lounge chair and listen to the waves crash. Asha had a planner with a running list of tasks, and when one was crossed off another was added. Maybe she could go to Tahiti and immerse herself and get new ideas, then come back in a week and convince Celeste to give Guerlain back to her.

"We can sort out what's next for you when you return."

Celeste's words defeated her, and Asha watched the woman leave the conference room. She'd failed. Her career would go backward. Likely to the routine lab work that she'd grown out of. She could no longer control her shaking leg; then her body began to shiver from stress. She'd held it together these past few months through sheer will, and now things were breaking down.

Worse, she no longer knew who she was. The foundation from which she'd built her whole life no longer existed. All because she'd lost her sense of smell.

CHAPTER TWO

Thirty-two was too young for an existential crisis. Asha gripped the steering wheel of the car, paralyzed by indecision. Of all the places to be stuck, it shouldn't be in the rental car garage at San Francisco International Airport. Her colleagues at IFF called her the *décideuse*. Asha never second-guessed herself, yet here she sat in a silver Toyota Camry, frozen with indecision.

She could blame it on jet lag, the lack of sleep the past few days, or even her empty stomach because the only thing her body could handle were cups of calming tea. Her hands squeezed the pleather steering wheel. All she needed to do was type the directions into the GPS and put the car in drive. The only question was which address. The hard one, the medium one, or the easy one. As if she were Gujarati Goldilocks.

Asha let go of the wheel. It should be the toughest one first. She might not know who she was anymore, but she wasn't going to be a weak person who couldn't face her problems. Her finger paused at the third digit of the zip code.

Asha rolled her neck. With the forced time off, she could have gone anywhere—maybe Japan or Korea, to understand Asian markets as a way of staying current in her industry. Instead, she was so defeated and out of sorts, she'd landed here, a little over fifty miles from where she'd grown up. The idea of coming back as a failure made her want to roll down the window and vomit. Lucky for her, there was nothing in her stomach.

It wasn't so much the loss of her sense of smell but that she would likely lose her career. That wasn't something her mother would accept. But without her nose, her options were limited. She had never explored anything else. It was always and only this. And it wasn't just her family's expectations. Asha couldn't bear to see the pride in her grandmother's eyes fade if Asha couldn't fulfill the only request Leela had ever made.

One day you will make a scent for me. My very own perfume. It was an often-repeated refrain from Asha's childhood, especially when she and Leela were in the garden. And because she loved her grandmother more than anyone else in her family, Asha wanted to give her this one wish.

Resigned, she entered the rest of the zip code but changed the last two digits. *Merde.* She was taking the medium option. She couldn't justify easy and wasn't ready to face her mother, so she would split the difference. Without giving herself time to question or rethink, Asha shifted the car into gear and drove toward the highway leading north to Napa Valley.

It was the place of her birth and where she'd discovered her superpower, which had given her the chance to pursue a path that was different from everyone else in her ambitious extended family. They were hoteliers. Her father, Sanjay Patel, the grandson of the first Indian American hotel owner in America, still ran the original property, Goldfield. His best friend, Kirit Desai, had built an empire with more than 250 hotels in their portfolio. Millie, Kirit uncle's daughter and Asha's best friend, worked at Desai Hotel Group, along with her older brother, Neel. And while Asha didn't work in the family business, she was expected to be as successful, if not more so.

It was one reason she only came to California for major occasions and rarely stayed more than a few days. To date, she didn't have much to show for all the work she'd done. In her industry, success wasn't tangible and came not in the form of profit margins but in awards and recognition. She had yet to earn any. Guerlain was her first opportunity.

Her life was in Paris. Not among the rows of green-and-red vines that dotted the hills and slopes that fueled the economy of this place. Yet this was where she'd chosen to come thanks to Celeste's banishment. Staying in France hadn't been an option. It was too humiliating. Her friends and colleagues would have had too many questions, and Asha had no answers.

She had never relied on her family. She'd left too young. But right now, for reasons she couldn't fully understand, she wanted to be with them. It was why she hadn't let them know she was coming—to delay their disappointed reactions. She'd failed, and in her family, that wasn't something that was readily accepted.

Asha turned off Highway 80 and onto Route 29 toward Napa. The landscape changed dramatically as she drove deeper into the valley. The flatness of the land changed to rolling hills, and Asha felt her lungs open to the clear air. Deeper in, the vineyards came into view, planted with precision, the leaves budding in early spring. In the coming months, they would bloom, grow varietals of grapes, thanks to the rich soil tilled by generations of vintners. Then the tourists would arrive by car and bus to partake in their wine. She'd always loved this time of year, just before full bloom.

When Asha was four, in excitement, she would try to pinch off the first buds on plants in Sonanum, her grandmother's massive garden on the grounds of Goldfield. Leela would pull Asha away and onto her lap and explain that plants and trees needed time to regenerate. That with sun and water, they would flourish. Life happened in the waiting. Not at the beginning or end, but in the middle, during growth, as long as the soil was fertile and you gave the roots the right amount of water.

Asha pulled into the driveway of the small cottage, relieved at the sight of Leela's dark-blue BMW sports coupe Z4 parked under the shade of the valley oak trees that lined the drive. For all her sternness,

Leela loved fast cars and collected speeding tickets as a point of pride, much to her son's dismay.

As Asha stepped out of the rental, the heels of her black LK Bennett pumps made it difficult to steady herself on the gravel path. It was a quaint cottage with endless space on all sides. The house was the color of a cloudless sky, white clapboard framed the windows, and the roof had a metal weather vane that wobbled in the soft breeze. Planters full of colorful peonies and azaleas lined the steps up to the porch, where more flowers posed sweetly in hanging pots and window boxes.

Asha removed the black belted jacket she'd worn over her sleeveless gray shift dress and let the air cool her. She used the rose-shaped brass knocker on the weathered white door to announce her presence. Anticipation and emotion roiled inside her. She was too old to sit in Leela's lap, but all Asha wanted was to be folded into her grandmother's strong arms. She would even welcome the tough love that awaited her, as Leela wouldn't tolerate defeat. Asha would be expected to have solutions, a next step, a way to fix her situation.

She had nothing.

Her only plan was to not blurt it all out. She would test the waters, pretend she was here for a holiday and then, when the time was right, let her family know what had happened. For a few seconds, she closed her eyes and brought up the memory of her grandmother's scent. Sweet honeysuckle with a touch of camphor. Whenever she had time to experiment on Leela's perfume, the honeysuckle was the halo she strived for, an immediate explosion of fresh citrus and sweetness with the first sniff.

After knocking again, Asha went to the windows to peek in. The car was in the drive, though that didn't mean someone was home. She would wait in the back. The patio was large, and it overlooked a field that merged into the hills beyond. Maybe with the sun on her face, her mind could switch off long enough for a quick nap.

Or she could wander to the small garden Leela had shown her over one of their video chats. It wasn't to the scale of Sonanum, but

Asha remembered how vibrant it was, the plants and flowers blending with the greenery around the house. The French preferred symmetrical lines, precise hedges, and simple colors in their well-planned gardens. More architectural than natural. Leela, who never forgave colonizers, did whatever was the opposite of Western notions.

Asha unlatched the white gate and let herself in. Her heels clicked against the stone path that led to the patio. It was then she heard music coming from a speaker nearby. Lata Mangeshkar, her grandmother's favorite singer, crooned in Hindi. Asha lowered her sunglasses. The lounge chairs were occupied by two bodies who appeared to be sunbathing.

Topless.

CHAPTER THREE

"Poppy!"

Asha hadn't heard her nickname used in a long time, and it brought a smile to her lips. Her parents tried to force everyone to call her Asha, but much to their dismay her grandmother and Millie's family still referred to her by the endearment. Leela lifted her large black sunglasses and rested them on her silver hair, which was pulled back in a small bun. "This is a surprise. A lovely one."

"Who died?" Mimi, Leela's best friend and Millie's paternal grand-mother, sat up.

"No one," Asha said.

"Are you pregnant?" Mimi asked.

Asha's jaw dropped. "No. I'm here for a visit."

Where Leela was grounded and practical, Mimi was jumpy and reactive. And if there was drama, Mimi was the attentive bystander, while Leela walked away.

"That's not like you. Something bad happened." Mimi pointed a finger at Leela. "I told you this morning the energy felt off and my horoscope was all about loss."

Leela shook her head. "Ignore her. What it said was, an item you lost will come back to you, and in your case, it was your reading glasses you wedged into a book as a placeholder. It already came true.

Come, join us, Poppy." She patted the arm of the empty lounge chair next to her.

Asha couldn't look at them in this state. The quick glimpse was enough to know that Leela wore a long red silk skirt and Mimi wore boy-short bikini bottoms. The rest was exposed to the rays even though they both had different shades of natural brown skin. Asha stood with her back to them, facing the fields. "Do you want to put on your tops first?"

"Why?" Mimi said. "I'm proud of my mangoes. They don't look a day over seventy."

"She thinks she's aging backwards because she watched that Brad Pitt movie a long time ago," Leela said.

"I wish, but it's because I stay moisturized." Asha turned back around to see that Mimi held up a small glass bottle. "And hydrated."

"Spiked seltzer doesn't count." Leela reached over to turn down the volume on the speaker. "Sit down, Poppy. You're blocking the sun hovering like that."

Asha joined them on the empty lounge chair nearby and looked out onto the small garden and the hills beyond. Even in early spring, the landscape was lush. As leaves and fruit came in, the fields would take on the vibrant colors of the grapes.

"Oh, don't be such a prude looking everywhere but at us, Poppy," Leela said. "You live in France."

"You're my grandmothers!"

"And we are also women." Leela handed her a cup of hot cha. "I taught you better."

Asha nodded. It was Leela and Mimi who had raised Millie, Neel, and Asha while their parents worked long days, seven days a week. And Leela and Mimi were staunchly prowoman, even as they bowed to the norms they'd lived through for eighty years of their lives.

Leela refilled her mug from the ceramic teapot. Asha lowered her nose toward the steaming liquid in her hand to smell the sweet, spicy tea. For two years, she'd safely avoided the COVID virus until it found her eight months ago. She had handled the mild symptoms, thanks to vaccines and boosters, relatively well. But her sense of smell had never recovered. As soon as she'd realized it wasn't naturally going to come back, she'd started investigating any and all options, including working with a therapist to try to revive her abilities. But it was slow going. A few months into it, she'd started to get little whiffs of strong odors, but about two months ago, Asha had plateaued.

Then the therapist had told her that it seemed like she'd recovered as much as she ever would and therapy would no longer be helpful. That was when Asha had decided to fake it, lean on the science and scent memory to keep her career.

From the tea, Asha could detect faint notes of ginger but nothing beyond. She sipped, thankful that her taste wasn't as similarly affected. The spice burned as it slid down her throat and into her empty stomach. This was different from the blend she'd made for her flight from a mild black tea she'd picked up at her favorite tea shop in Paris, to which she'd added a few dried herbs, including a bit of orange peel. Leela's cha was made with milk and a homemade masala. She knew from memory that Mimi's recipe had mint and cardamon. Leela preferred cloves and black pepper.

"Is this a regular thing, sitting like this in the backyard?" Asha wanted to ask if they were wearing any SPF, and then she spotted a bottle of sunscreen on the small table between Mimi and Leela's chairs.

"When we're not busy," Mimi said. "Our doctor recommends plenty of vitamin D."

"They do sell it in pill form. Besides, aren't you worried about someone . . ." Asha cleared her throat. "Uh, seeing you like this? Like my dad or a delivery person?" Asha hadn't known she was prudish until this moment.

"Sanjay knows better than to come here unannounced," Leela said.

Asha believed that. Her father spent most of his time at the hotel anyway. Goldfield was the love of his life, above his mother, his wife, and his only child.

"And we know our delivery people," Mimi said. "They wouldn't care. They'd drop off the package and go back to their truck."

And likely try to wash the image from their brain. Knowing their stubborn determination, Asha gave in. "It really is a nice afternoon." She slipped out of her pumps, leaned back in the lounge chair, and stretched her legs out with her ankles crossed.

"Slide out of that dress," Mimi said. "Pretend you're in the Riviera."

"Yeah. No." That was one step too far.

They sat in silence, her two grandmothers with sunglasses over their eyes. Asha closed hers. Maybe now that she was here, she could rest. The jitters seemed milder as she tried to distance herself from the stress she'd been carrying. It was done. Likely permanently. She could feel Mimi's gaze, and Asha looked over only to have her turn away and take a sip from a water bottle.

Mimi likely wanted to ask a hundred questions, but Asha was Leela's, and Mimi would wait for her friend to do the pushing and prying. Mimi would take the lead on Millie and Neel.

Asha would see Neel, of course. Likely run into him a few times when she eventually went to see Millie in San Francisco. It would be fine. It always was. She and Neel would make small talk, then part ways. Childhood friends, high school sweethearts, and adult acquaintances. It worked for them. This time wouldn't be any different, even though she planned to stay for the full four weeks of her holiday.

She would deal. It wasn't as if she still had a crush, and whatever love they'd shared Asha had outgrown during their time apart. He had never been her type anyway, and attraction without substance wasn't sustainable.

She closed her eyes and slowed her breathing in the hope that sleep would take her for a few hours so her mind could focus on what came next. Leela wouldn't push, would wait until Asha was ready to talk. Right now, Asha let the silence comfort her. Ten minutes later, sleep eluded her, and she sat up to have another sip of tea, now lukewarm.

"How are you two?" she asked.

Leela lowered her sunglasses. Her dark-brown eyes saw into Asha's soul. "We've had a quiet winter. Things will be busier soon. The April calendar is already full."

"The Nanis of Napa are a hot ticket." Mimi gave a rundown of the various philanthropic events they were organizing. The moniker came from an article about a local group of women, all grandmothers from diverse backgrounds, who helped Napa and Sonoma's underserved and uncentered. It was Mimi's brainchild and in the past five years had grown to a group of over a dozen women. Asha had heard all about their adventures during weekly video chats. From kayaking along the river—with water bags filled with wine—to bringing over a male revue from San Francisco for a fundraiser.

"What are your plans for the day?"

"This for now," Mimi said. "Then we'll see how things unfold."

Asha shook her head in wonder—the idea of not knowing what she'd be doing hour to hour made her twitchy. "Oh, I brought you presents." Asha stood, rummaged through her large black tote, and handed over a sample box of scents. On each visit, she brought back vials of scents she'd been working on—some her own experiments, others from projects she'd assisted. This batch didn't have much in the way of anything new, as her focus had been Guerlain, so she'd brought them samples of fragrances already on the market.

Leela tugged off the glass decanter from one bottle and stroked the cool, scented tip below her palm, aired it out a little, and then brought her wrist to her nose. "It's familiar." Leela would recognize the repetition. "Not your work."

Asha bit the inside of her cheek. "No." She wouldn't lie to her grandmother and knew that with Leela, the less said the better.

"This smells the same as what you sent me last year for Diwali." Mimi rubbed her wrists together. "Not that I'm complaining. It was a male magnet. I've had several dates that ended at breakfast thanks to your magical nose."

Asha didn't want to know about that. "It also works for daily wear, to charity lunches and your Nanis of Napa meetings."

Mimi stood and shook her water bottle. "I'm out. Going to get us refreshments. It's getting hot out here."

"Thank you," Asha called after Mimi.

"She's not bringing back water." Leela rose from her chair.

"Oh." Asha knew Mimi drank socially, but today she seemed extra motivated. "Is she okay? Should we stage an intervention?"

Leela wrapped her white blouse around her and tied a large knot at her waist. "It's the anniversary of her husband's death."

"I didn't know."

"You didn't remember," Leela clarified.

"Right . . . Is there a dinner tonight?"

"No, shraddha is in September this year," Leela said. "We'll honor all our dead ancestors during that time. Today is the actual date in the Western calendar. You've been gone too long and have forgotten to keep up with our traditions."

Asha nodded, felt the reprimand keenly. She remembered the grandmothers conducting school-type lessons when Millie, Neel, and she were younger. Every summer until their freshman year of high school was spent learning about their culture, their religion, and all the customs of their family. She didn't know how much Neel or Millie retained, but for Asha, it was mainly scattered memories that she recalled through smells.

"Mahesh dada died before I was born," Asha said, a little defensive.

"Yes, Neel was almost a year old." Leela wiped off dried leaves and stems that had blown onto the small patio dining table. "He had a heart attack and didn't make it to the hospital in time."

Asha refolded the small blankets that were lying on the backs of the chairs around the table. They were askew, and adjusting them in precise lines made her feel better. "She must miss him."

"He was a romantic, always showering Mimi with gifts and grand gestures."

"What about my dada?" Her grandfather was killed by a drunk driver when Asha was twelve. Leela had refused to move in with her son, and that's when Mimi and Leela became roommates. "Was he romantic too?"

"He was a practical man," Leela said.

To this day, she'd never heard her grandmother refer to her grandfather by his first name. It was one piece of cultural history Asha remembered mainly because she would ask why Leela never named her husband, while Asha's mom freely referred to her dad as Sanjay. Leela had told her it was a sign of respect. Asha would push back that dada had called Leela by her first name—did that mean he didn't respect her? Leela would tell Asha that some traditions evolve with each generation and that Asha would never have to abide by some of the old norms. But for Leela, they were hardwired.

"Dada was always busy." Asha couldn't remember much about him beyond that.

"Work sustained him. Once he took over Goldfield from his father, the hotel became everything."

Like father, like son. "He didn't bring you flowers every day?"

Leela smiled wide, her entire face blooming with happiness. "He didn't have to. He gave me Sonanum."

"It's cocktail o'clock." Mimi came out on the porch holding a tray with three martini glasses.

"Put a shirt on," Leela said. "Gravity is no longer your friend, even if you believe your breasts are ten years younger than your actual age."

Mimi put the tray on the large round dining table on one side of the deck before grabbing her wrap from the lounge chair and tying it around her tall, lean frame. She looked like she belonged back in the fifties with her dyed black hair tied back in a bright-blue silk bandana. For as long as Asha could remember, Mimi never wanted to grow older. Age was not allowed to be mentioned in birthday celebrations. None of them knew the actual year of Mimi's birth. Only December 10.

"Here." She handed them each a chilled glass. "Dirty martinis to celebrate your homecoming."

They clinked glasses and Asha took a sip. Ice-cold vodka hit the back of her throat like a punch. Her stomach protested, and she put her glass down on the table.

"We should drive to Yountville for dinner," Mimi said. "There's a brick-oven pizza place, and I have a craving. I can ring up the Nanis and see who's free."

"I'd like that." It sounded tame enough that Asha could manage to get through it. She remembered them as a boisterous group that made their presence known wherever they went. The Nanis lived their lives out loud and made no apologies for their adventures. And if they embarrassed their children or had to be bailed out of trouble, all the better. She could hide within their midst and go unnoticed.

"You and I will go," Leela said to Mimi. "Poppy needs to settle in at home."

Asha closed her eyes and nodded. "I should unpack."

"Oh pish," Mimi said. "That can wait. Poppy hasn't been home in ages, and the Nanis will all want to hear about her Parisian life, especially the salacious bits."

"Unfortunately, most of it is boring."

"What happened to Micha?" Mimi sipped her drink. "The Viking. We've been watching that series. Violent, but the men are very burly."

"That ended over a year ago." For the same reason none of her relationships lasted more than six months—Asha's work was her sole focus. Everything else was only if there was time.

"She can join us another time," Leela said. "If she's here for a quick visit, she needs to see her parents."

"Actually, I plan to stay for a while."

Leela raised her brows.

"Vacation." Asha couldn't quite meet Leela's eyes, so she took another regretful sip of her vodka before handing it to Mimi.

"Oh good." Mimi took Asha's unfinished drink and poured it into her empty glass. "We'll have to teach you how to enjoy a good martini before it goes warm."

Asha gave Mimi a side hug. "Next time, don't make them all vodka, and add more olives."

Mimi defended her recipe. "There's a whisper of vermouth in there."

"I've never appreciated a cocktail in the same way as you," Asha said.

"I know this is wine country," Mimi said, "but God bless vodka, and gin, and tequila, and—"

"Go." Leela hugged Asha. "Her list is long."

She clung to her grandmother for a few long seconds. If she were younger, she could lay her head on Leela's lap and sleep. Grown women didn't do that. Leela's arms were strong, but the bones felt fragile, the skin paperlike. Asha stepped back. They used to be similar in height, but now, Leela was a few inches shorter and leaner. Her silver hair was soft as it brushed the side of Asha's face, and the faded eyebrows were penciled in to stand out on her brown face. It had been over three years since she'd seen anyone from her family, and her grandmothers looked older. Leela was still sturdy and managed her deepening wrinkles with a rigorous skin routine, but age showed. Asha felt keenly aware of Leela's mortality. She waved the painful thought away.

Asha said her goodbyes and went through the gate toward her car. She'd left without revealing anything. It wasn't the right time, she rationalized. And she needed to have solutions at the ready. Her grandmother never indulged self-pity, and Asha knew she had to stay steady and have a plan. In the very back of her mind, she'd had a tiny speck of hope that as soon as she was wrapped in Leela's arms her nose would work again. It was Leela who'd been the first to notice Asha's super smell, or as it was medically called, hyperosmia.

They'd been in Sonanum, and Asha, at the precocious age of five, had peppered Leela with dozens of questions until her grandmother put her near the sages and asked her to spot the differences. Asha sniffed each plant and streamed a running commentary: pineapple, wood, lilac, mint, fruit punch. Leela started paying attention to her, and Asha continued to make her grandmother proud by listing off subtle differences with her limited vocabulary.

As time went on, Leela had nurtured Asha's abilities, taught her how to concentrate and have patience. To wait for heady top notes to settle, then gently go deeper to identify the subtleties. Leela didn't coddle, was always honest. Her philosophy was love first, but truth next.

Thanks to a master's in chemistry, Asha could focus more on lab work, understand scents at the molecular level. The mere thought depressed her, and exhaustion brought tears to her eyes. It would be hard to not be involved in the art, the creation. Understanding components was foundational work, but what Asha loved was how it came together to invoke memories and feelings and gave the wearer a sense of self.

Pressure sat like an anvil on her chest. Every day she wasn't in the lab, she was backtracking. Simon was likely strutting around and offering quips about Asha bungling Guerlain. There would be others who would see her absence as an opportunity. Celeste had likely written her off altogether.

Across the driveway, she saw the distant hills as the sun lowered in the cloudless sky. For a few minutes she steadied herself before unlocking the rental car. The hard choice was now unavoidable. She had to face her mother.

CHAPTER FOUR

Asha stepped out of the car. The paved driveway held her steady. The yellow house with white window frames loomed over her. Its exterior was meant to impress, with its wide span and two stories, windows in various sizes and shapes highlighted. Tiny solar lights lit a path toward the front steps. The lawn was lush and evenly trimmed, the hedges in symmetry to one another. To the left, tall cypress trees lined one side of the drive, and through them she could see the vineyard fields owned by local vintners.

It wasn't home. She'd never lived in it, only stayed in the guest room on infrequent visits. Her parents had moved here from the small house next to Goldfield a decade ago. This one catered to her mother's aspirations for elegance and austerity. The back of the house was as impressive, with large french doors along the whole of it to look out into the hills and fields and a swing on one end that Sapna used to read magazines. Asha wondered if she'd ever seen her mom without *Vogue* or *Vanity Fair* tucked in her large leather tote.

Asha carried her luggage up the short front steps. She'd packed for a month and wondered how she would stomach staying here for that long. At least she was too out of sorts to be nervous. Her parents would be surprised—not only that she was there but that she planned to stay for so long. She *had* thought of calling after she'd booked her flight, but she hadn't had the energy to deal with fifty questions from her mom. If she mentioned work problems, her mother would push her to stay in Paris and resolve the unfixable. Asha wasn't sure how to explain what had happened. She knew that getting sick, losing her sense of smell, wasn't her fault. But she'd been raised to overcome, not give up. That's what was expected.

Asha rubbed her tired eyes. As soon as everyone found out, she'd see their disappointment. The mere thought of it made her chest tight; breathing became slightly tough. She'd spent her life making her mom and Leela proud. Her grandmother wanted Asha to create a commemorative scent based on her life, and her mother wanted to live Asha's life vicariously. This was their collective dream that Asha carried out.

She took a deep breath, rolled back her shoulders, and rang the bell. It was early evening, and the hall light was on in the house. She waited. Her parents could still be at Goldfield. Growing up in a hotel family, she knew they never closed. It could be a small blessing if no one was here. She could escape to the guest room and pray for rest.

The last time she'd seen Sapna was in San Francisco at Millie's parents' anniversary party three years ago. They did talk once a week, but the conversations were always about Asha's work and life in Paris. Her mom wanted to know everything about the day-to-day, from the markets to the cafés Asha went to with friends. Asha got into the habit of sending a picture of the day with a small caption via SMS to appease her. She did it because she knew it brought her mother joy, but also, and selfishly, because it was a way to get her to leave Asha alone.

She'd realized long ago that her mom wasn't interested in how Asha was feeling or doing, only the what and where. It helped Asha to compartmentalize the relationship, and she no longer wished for a deeper connection. She had that with Leela, and it was enough.

After the second time ringing the bell, Asha decided to use the spare key Leela had given her and let herself inside. The entry hall was cool even though she didn't hear the hum of the air-conditioning.

Temperatures in the valley had a wide range in the spring, and it had been a warm day. She dropped the keys in a teal glass bowl on the long console table and slipped out of her pumps. The cool tile felt nice on the soles of her bare feet.

She'd make herself some tea first before taking her two large suitcases and carry-on up to the guest room. Asha took out the small tin and a box of mesh tea bags she carried in her tote. The house was quiet and empty. And large. The living area alone was twice the size of her little one-bedroom apartment in Paris. Add in the dining room, the open-plan kitchen, and the wide french doors and it could fit all four apartments in her small two-story building.

Sapna had sent her clippings of the *Dwell* magazine feature on their home's decor, which was white, with different tones of teal for pops of color. Over the mantel was a large Yrjö Edelmann print, *Detection of blue vibration*. It was something Sapna had picked up when she and Asha spent a long weekend in Stockholm eight years ago.

As she heated up the electric kettle, Asha opened the tin. She expected to be hit by the sweet blend of Assam mixed with orange peel. Instead, the smell was faint and only accessible by putting her nose close to the container.

"Poppy!"

Asha jumped, and half the tea went flying over the large marble kitchen island. Her heart raced at the unexpected voice, and she put her hand on her chest to calm the panic. "Neel? Why would you sneak up on me like that?"

"I called your name from ten feet away."

Instead of looking at him, she wiped up the loose tea with her hands and looked around for the trash bin.

"It's the cabinet under the sink," Neel said.

Hands full, Asha looked at him until he walked over and pulled out the drawer.

"Thank you." She washed her hands, then found mugs after checking two different cabinets. "Tea?"

"No, thanks." Neel stood on the other side of the island. "I'm not in the mood for mildly flavored hot water."

"Still have the taste buds of a twelve-year-old boy, I see."

He laughed. "It's good to see you, Mademoiselle Poppy."

She hated when he called her that. He wasn't teasing or joking. There was a bite in his intonation of the French word. Because he still resented her for leaving. He'd wanted her to stay. "You don't seem surprised to see me."

Neel grinned. "Mimi sent out a text to the Desai-Patel group chat announcing your visit. Your mom replied that she was worried. Mimi clarified that you're on vacation and planned to stay awhile. My mother wants to know when you're going to go see her. And Millie is pissed you didn't let her know and plans on ignoring you until you reach out."

She noted that her father wasn't mentioned. Which wasn't a surprise. Sanjay Patel had checked out of his daughter's life a long time ago, and she knew he didn't care about her comings and goings.

"Why are you here?"

Not that it was unusual. Millie, Neel, and Asha were in and out of each other's homes at will. They considered both sets of parents and grandparents as immediate family even though there was no blood relationship between the Desais and Patels. Growing up, she and Neel had done everything together, from racing bikes to being each other's first kiss. First everything. Asha cleared her head. The jet lag was making her mind wonder about things she'd long put behind her. She didn't mean to make the question come out harsh. "I meant, what are you doing here? Don't you live in San Francisco?"

"Nice save," he said. "I'm crashing for a while, doing some work."

"At Goldfield?"

"In a way," Neel said.

He was still handsome. His light-brown skin had a touch of sun, likely because Neel preferred outside to inside. Thick black hair curled in short waves around his clean-shaven face. He'd grown out of his gangly teenager stage a long time ago, but in this warm glow of the kitchen he barely resembled the young boy she'd grown up with.

"If you're finished checking me out, the kettle's done."

That jarred her out of her thoughts, and Asha rolled her eyes. "You wish."

"Still struggling with the quick comeback," Neel said.

"*Tais-toi,*" Asha mumbled as she poured hot water into a clear glass mug.

"Cursing at me in French?"

"It's not a curse." She filled a bag with loose tea and tied it before steeping it in her mug.

Neel raised his brow.

"Fine, I told you to shut up."

"I'm telling."

Asha laughed, and some of her exhaustion eased. "You never could keep a secret."

"I don't know about that," he said. "Kept a pretty big one in high school."

He was referring to their relationship, and she was taken aback because they'd never mentioned it in all the years she'd been in Paris. "Not from Millie."

"Because we're both afraid of her."

Asha laughed again and waited for her tea to steep, and she sensed a whiff of sandalwood and musk along with leather. Her eyes watered and she blinked to clear them. She used to be able to smell Neel. Not in the "oh, he hasn't showered today" way, but when he was nearby or about to enter a room. His skin had a warm scent with woodsy notes. When he came to the valley from San Francisco, he carried with him the scent of salt from the sea. Among the vineyards, his scent changed to something earthy and sweet. Now she could only recall his smell from memory. It broke her heart to know that she might never be able to know him in that way again.

"Hey, are you okay?"

The vibrations of his deep voice made her skin tingle. Her heart skipped a beat as she waved off his concern. This was the Neel she'd always known. He could tease and care at the same time. Asha nodded to reassure him even though she was far from all right.

"The Desai-Patel group chat is very active?"

"Always," Neel said. "It's why I rarely have my phone with me. Even with all the notifications off, I know there's a constant stream of messages. Everyone shares everything at all times. My dad, your dad, and I are the lurkers. Then Mimi will demand our participation by using our names in all caps."

"That sounds nice." She'd never been added, as it started after she'd already moved to Paris. She had her own with friends and colleagues in Paris. And they mostly used it to answer quick questions, plan outings, and confirm meetup times and locations.

He nodded. "Your mom said she'd message you after her board meeting."

"I'm going to crash soon. I don't even know how long I've been awake," Asha said. "I'm tired, and the time zone change is tough. I'll see her in the morning."

Neel pointed to the almost empty mug of tea. "Hope that's decaffeinated."

"Nope." Asha finished it, then placed the mug in the dishwasher. "I needed a little fix before unpacking."

"Because you can't sleep unless everything is crossed off your to-do list," Neel said.

"It's less stressful that way," she said. "Oh wait, your entire life is free of stress."

He looked at his watch. "Well, that lasted longer than I thought—a whole ten minutes without you taking a jab at me."

"I was simply stating a fact."

"Because you know so much about me?"

She kept quiet. She only knew what she'd heard in passing conversations, but she couldn't imagine Neel having so much as a bad day.

"Nice to see you again, Poppy." He winked and left the kitchen.

Asha could hear him grumble about weight and knew he was lugging her bags upstairs with him. She didn't feel the need to offer him help. It was better to keep distance between them, especially when it seemed like they were going to be living in the same house while she was in Napa. She placed her hand on her belly and didn't know if the flutters were from excitement or fear.

CHAPTER FIVE

Asha was up well before dawn, unsure about the time. After staring at the ceiling for a while, her body had finally overruled her overactive brain, and she'd been able to sleep for a few hours. She'd come out on the back porch and sat on the top of the short steps that led to the yard. Wrapped in a blanket, she watched the sky brighten as the light changed from deep purple to cotton candy pink. Growing up, she'd loved this time of the day before anyone else was awake. It was time to herself, where she could watch the earth wake in the quiet of dawn.

Her rested nose would take in smells without concentrating on deciphering anything. The mornings weren't time for training, only for being. In France, she still rose early to spend half an hour sitting by her small apartment window.

This wasn't a familiar spot, and she couldn't pick up much beyond pungent dirt and wet grass. At Goldfield, where she'd lived until her teenage years, the morning smells were a mix of dryer machine steam and cleaning supplies as housekeeping started their day. In high school, her parents had moved them to the cottage where Mimi and Leela now lived. Those mornings were lush with silver lupine and the English rosebushes her mother loved. She would revel in the combined scented air without reaching for tones and layers. Whenever a bout of homesickness hit, Asha would buy the flowers she'd grown up with to assuage her heart.

There was a chill in the air, and Asha sighed. It was over. Unscented life was her new reality. Once she accepted it, she could move forward, make plans. Find new routines. In Paris, she'd perfected her day, which started with morning exercise, coffee from the same café, work, walk home, and takeout. Each day was the same, and there was comfort in the structure of knowing what came next.

She'd become accustomed to Paris. Not for what tourists saw as postcard prettiness. The idea of Paris was far more glamorous than reality. Tourist areas gave the impression of a life full of café culture, strolling along the Seine, women with red umbrellas walking along the streets of Montmartre. Living there, Asha knew the grittiness, the growing division and othering, especially toward immigrants. Paris was the manifestation of the French ego. It was a harsh place to live at times. She'd learned early on that she'd needed to find her little corner to live among overt ethnocentrisms. Regardless of how fluent her abilities, her French would always be accented.

Luckily, she'd found a small community. Living in the same area for close to a decade made her familiar to her neighbors. Her friends were mostly foreign like herself, and they'd meet for dinners and drinks or take the TGV to other parts of France to get out of the city for the weekend. There was a commonality, as they had met in school and worked in the same field. At times, competition arose when they went after the same opportunities, which made it difficult to share anything about professional problems or weaknesses without fear of being outmaneuvered. That's why Lisle and Edson only knew that she'd left for a long-overdue holiday. Lisle would likely hear something from Celeste, but Edson worked at Givaudan and would only know what Lisle shared.

"Asha."

Her body tensed as she stood and forced a soft smile. "Mom." Dread sat heavy in her belly at the idea of breaking the news to her mother.

"I came home early from the board meeting," Sapna said. "You were already in bed."

"I was tired from the travel." They didn't hug. Not in welcome or goodbye. It wasn't their thing. Hers had never been a demonstrative family. Hugging the grandmothers didn't become routine until Millie threw her arms around the ba whenever she would come and go. She suspected that Leela and Mimi didn't want Neel and Asha to feel unloved, so hugging became a regular way of life between the five of them.

"I hope you got some rest?" Sapna went back to the kitchen. "Did something happen? I spent the night worried about your spontaneous visit. This isn't like you."

Asha followed. "Can we save the twenty questions for later? I'm still adjusting to the time zone." She regretted the sharpness in her voice, but Asha felt enough stress already and didn't want to take on her mom's.

Her mother went quiet, which meant that her feelings were hurt, and Asha would be responsible for fixing things between them. It was their only dynamic. Nine thousand miles away, it didn't feel so laborious as it did when in the same room. Asha folded the blanket and left it on the bench by the french doors that led to the porch. "Is the hotel busy?" Small talk to break the tension was the easiest way to get her mom to reengage.

"We're working on a wedding," Sapna said. "The bride is a social media influencer, and everything must be perfect because it's great for publicity."

Asha sat on the white leather counter stool and watched her mom at the espresso machine. Tall and lean, Sapna moved through the kitchen with grace. Her mother loved telling everyone how she'd been a model before she'd given it up for marriage. Her father would add that it was for sari catalogs and not exactly the Paris runway. Sapna retaliated by hanging enlarged framed photos from her modeling days in the living room and her father's home office.

"*Un café noisette ou un café crème?*"

Asha winced at her mother's use of French, not because of the forced pronunciation of each word but that Sapna always tried. It was another way she knew how much her mom wanted her life.

"With milk." She noticed the slight annoyance in Sapna's eyes when she replied in English. It was petty of Asha, but she couldn't stop herself. Their relationship had always been something of a mystery to her. At times, they could chat congenially, especially if it was something Sapna was interested in and Asha wanted to share. Other times, it was a burden to merely take her mother's call.

It wasn't that her mom was a bad mother. Growing up, Sapna had supported Asha's quest to become a perfumer. She was the one who had organized all the extra tutoring to prepare Asha for a life in Paris. Her mom had researched the best schools and found ways to fund her education. She appreciated her mother's efforts but often wondered what it would have been like to have something more between them than just Asha's career. In a way, her mom didn't know Asha. Not on any meaningful terms. And she didn't really know Sapna. She knew of her mom's past and her wants but didn't know her as a woman in her own right.

Until now, Asha hadn't thought much about it.

"Can your work spare you while you're here?" Sapna placed a cup of hot coffee in front of Asha.

Asha went to the fridge to get milk. "I didn't take my leave last August." She should say the rest of it, but she wasn't quite ready for Sapna's full-court press to get Asha's career back on track.

"And you chose to come here?"

Asha heard the bitterness in Sapna's voice. It was for the place. Her mother had made a life here, but Asha knew she wasn't happy about it. For her mother, the glamour of being married to a hotelier with an esteemed legacy had worn off as the reality of a restricted life set in. It was no secret Sapna would rather be traveling to London or Milan, shopping, and sipping champagne.

"I haven't been back in a while, so I thought it would be nice." It stung that she'd been away for close to three years and no one had missed her enough to ask her to come for a visit. And now that she was here, there was barely a welcome. Even Leela and Mimi had shooed her away. Neel hadn't bothered to stay long enough to have a cup of tea. They had their lives, and Asha felt like she'd crashed in like an interloper.

"If you'd mentioned your plans when we talked last week, Leela and I could have come to visit you." Sapna sat at the small kitchen table. "We could have gone to Saint-Tropez or Côte d'Azur."

"Aren't you busy with the influencer wedding?"

Sapna sipped her coffee. Silence.

This time, Asha stayed quiet as well. There wasn't any small talk to be had. The weather was nice, the coffee tasted like coffee, and the house looked the same as it had during her last visit. She looked out the doors to her left.

"How is the Guerlain perfume coming along?"

Asha winced. In her excitement, she had shared her win on the high-profile project. She knew her mom would be proud and wanted to show her that she was well on her way to becoming a master perfumer. Unfortunately, since she got the account, it was the only topic of conversation they had, as Sapna constantly peppered her with questions about what she was using, how her trials were going, and how close she was to the finish. "It's coming along. I also brought you a few samples of what's going to market soon."

"I can't wait," Sapna said. She loved branded perfumes and getting sneak peeks of the latest scents from known luxury names like Hermès, Chanel, and Dior. "I have lunch next week with a few women who serve with me on the Visit Napa board. They'll get a kick out of the secret new scents. They always try to guess, and of course I would never tell them."

Because Asha would never disclose the brands or scents. They were highly guarded and not something to be talked about prelaunch.

"How about, while you're here, we go to San Francisco? We could make a weekend of it." Sapna added a teaspoon of sugar to her mug. "I'm sure you'll want to see Millie."

"I also need to see Jaya auntie," Asha said.

At the mention of Millie's mom, Sapna scrunched her nose. "I'm sure she's too busy. She's always talking about how much work it is to run the brand team at DHG, as if everyone else has it easy."

The two had to be in each other's lives since they'd married best friends. Their families were blended because the kids were also close. But Jaya and Sapna were too different to ever be anything more than civil. The Desai Hotel Group was a huge conglomerate with a presence in the United States, Canada, and most recently, South America. Jaya auntie never failed to remind Sapna of the vastness of their hotel empire. And Sapna always responded with the history and legacy of Goldfield being the first Indian American–owned hotel in the country.

"Are you going to Goldfield today?" Asha asked.

"No," Sapna said. "I have other appointments. Marta oversees events now, and my focus is marketing and public relations." Sapna perused the latest issue of *Vogue* as she sipped her coffee. "I was looking at last year's fragrance awards, and Coty had more than IFF. If they don't promote you after the Guerlain perfume, you should think about switching."

Asha steadied her shaking leg as she sat on the counter stool. This was the perfect time to put it all out in the open. Which would likely turn into a hundred questions and a listing of everything Asha had tried to regain her sense of smell. Then her mom would force solutions like specialists. The worst would come when her mother accepted there wasn't much left to do. The disappointment would hit hard, and Asha would have to bear it alongside her own fear and uncertainty about the future.

She should have already figured out her next steps. If not this, then three to seven other options. But she was stuck. Nothing stood out. Asha had only wanted to do this one thing. She didn't even know which of her skills could translate into something different—more importantly, to a career that would be as satisfying as the one she had.

"I'm taking a break from work, Mom. I don't want to think about something that's far into the future."

"But getting closer with each project," Sapna said.

She bit the inside of her cheek. "I'm going to change and go for a walk. If you need anything done, leave me a list and I'll be happy to help."

"I thought you were on vacation."

"Yes," Asha said. "From the lab, from perfume talk. It doesn't mean I can't go to the grocery store or pick up dry cleaning."

"Maybe Leela and Mimi need your help." Sapna rinsed their mugs and put them in the dishwasher. "I'm sure you'd prefer to spend your time with them anyway."

With that her mother walked out of the kitchen, picked up her tote from the hall, and left through the front door.

Guilt and irritation warred within her. Just once, she'd like to have a good interaction with her mom. Asha knew she was partly to blame but couldn't stop herself from poking at Sapna. There would be four weeks of this dance.

And it was only her first full day.

CHAPTER SIX

An hour or so later, freshly showered, Asha was back in the kitchen. Her mom had left for work and she'd sent off her word-of-the-day text to Millie—something they'd been doing for fifteen years—and added a few more messages to let her friend know that she'd come see her once the jet lag wore off. Millie had responded with multiple violin emojis, which meant her friend was still mad that Asha hadn't let her know about the visit. Asha knew she would have to make it up to Millie. Her friend could hold a grudge but would always come around.

Dressed in gray jeans and a white T-shirt, she eyed her tin of tea. There wasn't much left thanks to Neel sneaking up on her. Then she realized that at least this gave her something to do. She'd find supplies to make another blend. Just the mere idea of it relaxed her. It was in the early days at the Sorbonne when she'd first started creating her own tea blends. She'd been lonely, surrounded by new friends in a place where more than language was foreign.

Her messages with Millie had become less frequent during that time, and her heart was still sore from not having any contact with Neel. She couldn't complain. Perfumery was what she'd wanted to do, and Paris was where she had to be if she was going to do it well. But she'd missed home, and tea stepped in. She'd never acquired a taste for cha, but Leela would have three cups a day. One in the morning, then in the late afternoon, and the last one after dinner. Instead of the milky, spicy brew, Asha opted to create a blend that reminded her of Leela. It took a few months, and supplies that she'd saved up to afford, until she got close.

From there, it became a hobby of sorts. The touch of the woody texture, the coarseness of a dried berry, the silkiness of a flower petal . . . all eased the pressure of studying hard, worrying about internships, applying to the top perfume school, and waiting for acceptance. She could add hot water, at the right temperature, and watch the blend morph into something completely different. And while she used her nose, it was taste she relied on to assess the potency and perfection of the blend.

After getting her planner from the guest room, Asha sat at the kitchen counter, pen in hand. She flipped it open to the daily page and winced at the usual tasks her past self had written, believing she'd still be in Paris and working. With shoulders rolled back, she crossed out what would have been, then added squiggly lines on top to indicate that they weren't complete, simply erased.

She proceeded to the column of tasks, did the same for things like renewing her commuter travel card, and moved on to the blank lines.

Find a local tea supplier.

Source herbs.

She paused with her pen against her chin and stared into the blank space in front of her as her brain began to fixate on tasks. Asha left the counter and started opening cupboards and cabinets until she found a box. Not loose cha but a box of English breakfast tea bags. She brought it to the marble countertop. The tea wouldn't be fresh or whole, but likely overprocessed and, based on the approaching expiration date, almost stale. Asha looked through the french doors to her left. There were likely to be herbs out there. Leela would have made sure some were planted at the house.

Eager to explore, she found her mom's slippers with the embellished pink crystal straps by the door, slid into them, and let herself outside.

Down the three steps of the back porch, Asha eyed the garden off to the side. It was mainly roses, irises, and peonies, which were Mimi's favorite flower. They weren't in bloom but well tended and ready for spring. She wandered to the side of the house as her nose picked up something different.

Around the corner was a lush herb garden in a patch that spanned half the house. Her shoulders loosened at the sight. Leela's doing. Her mother paid people to take care of the exterior and interior of the house, and Asha couldn't imagine Sapna kneeling with a spade in hand and a large hat on her head. As she inched closer, she saw that the plants were in sections with stones creating space between them. A few were in large planter pots, but most were in the ground.

It was small compared to the scale of the herb area in Sonanum, which spanned half an acre. Asha remembered their overpowering smells occasionally made her nauseated when she used to spend time there. It was Leela who had taught her to control her hyperosmia and breathe softly to allow her brain to pick apart the notes. Once she could sort them, Asha would wander that space to test herself, to improve her ability.

She stroked the leaves of mint, chamomile, lemon balm, and milk thistle. She also recognized nettles, lavender, and dandelion. It was an abundance of herbs, along with the traditional thyme, rosemary, and basil. She dropped to her knees, not caring about dirt on her pants, and leaned her face into the mint. It was the strongest in scent, and she could inhale the familiar sweetness. It calmed her even though she knew her partial smell was tied to memory. Still, she was glad her nose wasn't completely gone. Asha stroked the rough stalk of milk thistle, its pink bloom still intact. Leela always potted it because it was invasive and could take over a garden.

Memories of time with her grandmother in Sonanum enveloped Asha. The herbs there were for use in the Goldfield kitchen, along with an acre of vegetables. Asha would help Leela gather them in her yellow-and-white wicker basket. She would present the bounty proudly to the chef, who would give her a chocolate-frosted cupcake in return.

Leela would give the chef ideas for their uses. Sage had an earthy flavor and worked well with squash and pumpkin. Adding dried marjoram to salad dressing gave it an understated sweetness. Never overboil nettles; they must only be blanched in hot water. Cooking had never been an interest for Asha, then or now, but Leela's tips for gardening and the uses of its abundance stayed with her.

She plucked lemon balm, chamomile, and mint leaves. It was an herbaceous palmful when she held it up to her nose, but the mint was the only one she could really decipher. No matter. With her free hand she wiped the dirt from her pants and carried the herbs back to the kitchen. She found a clear glass bowl, added water, and then the herbs to clean them off. While they soaked, Asha filled the electric kettle to heat water.

She had enough ingredients to experiment. Like what she did when she was stuck on a formula. The thought of her lab made her pause. Nine hours ahead, her colleagues were likely done for the day. Perhaps Simon was still there trying to undo the mess she'd made of Guerlain. Her shoulders tensed, and she rolled them to force them down and away from her ears.

Asha patted a few leaves dry. Once the kettle clicked off, she found a pair of scissors and the silver gurney used to strain cha. She opened the box of Twinings English breakfast and cut open a tea bag to pour the dried tea into the mesh bowl, then added lemon balm leaves, a bit of chamomile, and mint. She poured hot water through the strainer into the wide mug, then settled the handle of the gurney on the mug to leave the concoction to steep.

Her nose close to the cup, she could get a hint of citrus.

"Are you taking a naas?"

Asha jumped at Neel's voice.

CHAPTER SEVEN

"Stop sneaking up on me."

Asha's heart raced, and she placed a palm over her chest to steady herself. Neel wasn't threatening, and he never loomed. It was because she'd been so deep in her thoughts, she'd forgotten that she was now in a house where people came and went, not in the solitary quiet of her Paris apartment.

"I wasn't sneaking, you weren't paying attention. Stop being so jumpy. What are you doing?" He went to the cabinet and pulled out a coffee mug.

"Tea." Asha took the strainer, dunked it twice, then removed it to the sink.

"That looks like the water that comes off the patio when I power wash it." Neel peeked into the cup and sniffed. "Smells like it too."

She gently shoved him away. "You don't have to drink it."

"Neither do you." He pointed to the espresso maker.

She wrinkled her nose as she brought the cup closer to her mouth and blew to cool the tea. Neel was dressed in his usual faded jeans and white T-shirt layered with an unbuttoned flannel. She'd forgotten he was at least half a foot taller than her in bare feet. *It was because he drank three glasses of milk every day when he was a boy.* That had been the running line in their family, because Neel towered over everyone, except Mimi, who was the second tallest.

His black hair was combed back and wet, likely from a recent shower. She knew when it dried the short ends would go every which way, and he wouldn't bother. The idea of him using gel to control the messiness made her smile. If it weren't for Leela instilling daily use of sunscreen into the grandchildren, Neel wouldn't even bother with lotion. He'd always been cute, but now he was handsome. There were slight lines now around his wide, dark eyes. His brows were thick but not bushy. His jaw, square but not sharp. He was very different from the men she'd dated in Paris. They were polished, ambitious, and driven. Neel probably didn't even own more than one suit.

"You about done eyeing me up?" He leaned against the counter, ankles crossed, and sipped his coffee.

"I'm silently thanking Sai Baba you got over your goatee phase," Asha said.

Neel rubbed his chin. "Leela made me. I was going full beard, and she said I was too attractive to hide my face. Hard to argue with that."

She sipped her tea and couldn't hide the disgust on her face from the taste. It was bitter and unbalanced. The ratio of mint to chamomile was way off. She stared into the mug and tried to recalculate how much of each herb she'd added or whether it was the stale tea bag that caused the acrid taste.

"Here." Neel placed a cup next to her.

She quickly took a sip of coffee to get the bitterness off her tongue, relieved that the flavor was mild and sweet. "You remembered." He'd added milk and sugar because she hated the acrid taste of black coffee.

"It's been a while since I've seen you." Neel shrugged. "But I've known you our whole lives. Tell me something: Is it illegal to wear color in France? Like do you get kicked out or get a fashion violation if you, I don't know, wear light denim instead of dark jeans or—gasp!—a red T-shirt?"

"It's a good thing you didn't go into stand-up comedy; you would starve." Asha *preferred* a clean palette of gray, black, and white. Color was for flowers, art, and jewelry. A neutral wardrobe was functional and efficient.

"I'll leave the creativity to you."

"Are you hungry?" she asked.

He raised his brow. "Do you cook now?"

"Ha ha. I was hoping you would." For the first time in days, she was starving. It wasn't as if she couldn't fend for herself. There was likely bread for toast, and that would be enough. But Neel was an incredible cook. He'd learned from Mimi, who had tried to teach all three of them, but Neel was the only one who enjoyed it.

"Fine," he said. "But don't expect snails."

"It's like you've never been to France," she said. "Oh wait, you haven't."

"There are so many better places to go," he said.

It still stung that he'd never visited her. Not when she'd severely missed him, and home, the first few years at the Sorbonne. Nor had he visited anytime in the last decade. They'd been so close once. Everything had changed when she'd said goodbye the day before flying to Paris as a seventeen-year-old. There had been no phone calls or even texts between them. She'd been heartbroken, and then she forced herself to get over it. When she first came back for visits, Asha would practice cool indifference and have an air of snobbery about her to show him how great her life was in Paris. It wasn't a lie or the truth—something in between. From then on, it became a habit to be cordial but distant around him, and he would do the same. They'd mutually created a false air of friendship for the sake of their families, and both actively avoided being alone together.

Yet she didn't want to revert to that right now. For one, it was impractical because they were staying in the same house, and two, she was hungry and missed his cooking.

"My body clock is on dinner time," she said. "In case you're looking for suggestions."

"I'm making an omelet. Not the Julia Child version, so don't even ask. With all respect to the queen of French cooking, mine is better." He took out eggs and cilantro from the fridge and laid them on the counter before grabbing a cutting board. "No special orders or custom requests." He pointed the tip of his knife toward her.

The way his voice deepened when he tried to be stern made her smile. When they'd been together, she would poke at him just to see if he could get worked up. His voice used to make her toes curl.

"For someone who complains about all things French, your chef temperament is right there alongside all the greats."

He grunted and dramatically chopped an onion.

"Are you dating anyone?" Asha bit the inside of her cheek. She couldn't believe the question slipped out. She'd never once asked him that in the fewer than dozen times she'd seen him since she'd moved to Paris. "You don't have to answer that. I was making conversation. It's none of my business." She concentrated on her nails to make sure there were no chips in her light-pink polish.

"Chill." Neel grabbed a tomato from the covered basket on the kitchen island. "And no. Nothing serious. You?"

She almost laughed. "It's been a while since I ended my last relationship." Micha had been nice enough and they were compatible, so much so that it wasn't really an emotional end, merely an agreement to return their focus to work. Her career was her priority, and she didn't make time for anything or anyone else.

"The Viking?"

"Checking up on me?" Asha gave him a smirk. She didn't want to overthink why it felt good that he might have taken an interest in her dating life.

"Mimi is like an oral historian for our family," he said. "She tells us things we don't even ask about."

"Mm-hmm." She finished her coffee, and though she wanted him to make her another cup, she kept quiet. "For your information, Micha is half Finnish, half French."

"Was he also friendly and fabulous?" He chopped the cilantro he'd laid out on a paper towel.

Asha swallowed a laugh. "Seriously, comedy is not your thing. Stop trying."

He winked at her. "There is no try. Only do."

She groaned, then stopped as she recognized the whiff of cumin toasting in the skillet. It was so slight that she edged closer to the stove and yearned to smell the nuttiness and pungency of the seeds as they hit the hot pan.

"Are you okay? If it's too much, we can open the windows."

She quickly moved back and took a seat at the counter. "I'm fine." Neel knew there was a downside to her abilities and that sometimes odors became so powerful, they made her uncomfortable or gave her a headache. She longed for that to happen again.

He served her a fluffy omelet with cumin, cilantro, onion, tomato, and cheese. *"Buon appetito."*

She exaggerated her frown. "You and I both took French for four years in high school. Don't pretend you don't know anything."

"I got all Bs."

"Only because I tutored you. Underachiever." She took a bite as long-buried memories embraced her. He had that cooking gene, in the same way Mimi did—the hath, as they said in Gujarati.

"Yeah," he said. "You and my parents always agreed on that one point."

Asha regretted the barb. It was a sore subject, because in a family of fast talkers, Neel spoke slowly and only when necessary. He was fine to stay on the sidelines and observe. His parents and sister ran at warp speed when it came to doing anything, but Neel strolled. Often, he'd been chided for being "less than," simply because he did things at his own pace. She remembered all the times she tried to get him to make a little effort on behalf of himself, but he would brush her off or simply ignore her suggestions. Neel was surrounded by people with drive, and Asha never knew if he'd developed any of his own. His life plan had been to eventually take over DHG. For some reason he never rose to the challenge, and she assumed he was at Goldfield because something had changed. "Are you staying here for DHG business?"

"Nope."

She waited. "Are you going to expand on that?"

"Nope."

Likely because she'd hurt his feelings. Asha watched as Neel ate standing up across from her. Still, she felt bad about her comment. "Just so you know, I've realized that getting good grades isn't everything."

He pointed his fork at her. "This coming from a person who waged a full-on campaign to get her history teacher to change the grade on her final paper from a B-plus to an A."

She shrugged. "All I did was ask for his reasoning."

He laughed. "By having the principal mediate a conversation."

"I wrote a whole other paper to show my grasp of the European Union."

"Because?"

She didn't meet his eyes and mumbled, "I didn't want to mess up my perfect GPA. Besides, my point was that it doesn't matter so much. You're smart, everyone knows that about you. You just don't try."

"Wow." Neel glanced around the kitchen. "Dad? Is that you? Show yourself."

"Funny." Asha savored the perfectly seasoned omelet. The cilantro added freshness and complemented the slightly tart tomatoes. "So, how's the job?"

"It's great." He sipped his coffee in between bites.

She was surprised at his wide grin.

"You're enjoying working with your dad?"

"That didn't pan out," Neel said.

Of course it didn't. "You got fired."

"If it makes you feel better to think that, sure. You like being disappointed in me."

"That's not true," she said. "And you're being vague."

"Since when are you so interested in my life?"

"I'm making conversation. It works something like, one person talks, and the other—"

He threw a black-and-white gingham kitchen towel toward her. He had excellent aim, but she had good reflexes and caught it with her left hand.

"What did you do to lose your lofty title of VP of operations?" She resisted the urge to scrape her plate now that she'd eaten her entire portion.

"Hmm. First you check me out, then you ask if I'm single, and now you're being nosy. Your interest in me is going to make me think you've never gotten over—"

Asha threw the towel back at him. Her aim was off, and it landed two feet short. "Sometimes Millie talks about you. I listen out of courtesy."

"Uh-huh," Neel said. "She mentions me in your daily texts?"

"No. Besides, it was a while ago. Just tell me. Being mysterious doesn't work on your face."

He turned away from her. "I showed up to a big meeting in jeans."

She knew he'd sabotaged himself. "On purpose, I bet."

"I like to be comfortable." He cleared their empty plates and loaded them into the dishwasher before washing the pan in the sink.

"You *like* to get under your dad's skin."

"Just because Kirit Desai chooses to wear a suit and tie every day doesn't mean everyone else should."

"Did Millie get stuck in the middle?"

"That's my sister's favorite place to be," Neel said. "Anyway, it worked out for her. She's better at that gig than I was."

"That's because she's better than everyone at everything," Asha said.

"Don't get any ideas of you two joining forces against me while you're here. I'm stronger and smarter."

Asha snorted.

He looked up and mimed as if to throw the wet sponge. Asha didn't flinch. The sponge could have soaked her outfit if he threw it hard enough, but he would never do that. To anyone. The towel had been an old thing they did, something Asha had started when she got frustrated that she couldn't keep up with their verbal sparring.

"I have to head to Goldfield." Neel's voice interrupted her memories. "Do you need anything before I go?"

"I hope you don't lose this job," she said.

"Your dad likes me more than my dad." He wiped his hands on a towel, then hung it on the handle of the stove.

"Yeah, and he likes you more than me, that's for sure," she muttered.

"Want to come with me and say hi to him?"

His voice softened, and she didn't want his kindness when it came to her own dad problems. Asha shook her head. She and her dad could go for weeks without connecting, and usually only did when Leela or her mother forced them to chat over video. He hadn't been interested in Asha's life for as long as she could remember. It was the Goldfield and not much else. "He knows I'm here. He must have come in late and left early. I'll catch up with him at some point. Besides, I have a few errands to run."

"You already have a full list of things to do?" he said.

"Always." She didn't want to admit that there were only two things on her schedule.

Neel waved as he left the kitchen. "Suit yourself."

She stayed where she was and, when she heard the front door close behind him, flipped open her planner to the scribbles of things undone. Canceled. At loose ends, she wrote down what she had to do but was continuing to avoid—telling her mom and Leela. It was the hardest one. A part of her knew, once she said it out loud, that she could no longer pretend to be who she'd been. The truth would be exposed, and she had no idea what that meant for the rest of her life.

CHAPTER EIGHT

The soft din of voices woke Asha. Disoriented, she blinked and sat up. She was in her parents' house in the guest room decorated in various shades of green, from mint-colored walls to a forest-green reading chair. The wood floor was covered with a white shag rug; the bedding that she'd lain on top of had little green flowers on the white duvet. She rubbed her eyes and sighed. Even though she didn't technically live here, she felt as if she'd moved back in with her parents as she faced unemployment.

Asha rubbed her sternum with her thumb. She'd been unfair to Neel. She shouldn't have teased him when she wasn't in any better position, even though her failure was because of something beyond her control. She glanced at her watch and was shocked she'd taken a three-hour nap. She had been tired. And bored. Not used to being so idle, she'd read through three magazines. She learned some tips on contouring and practiced with her makeup, which turned her face into a splotchy mess that she'd immediately washed off. She tried watching TV, but nothing caught her attention enough to keep her mind from obsessing on all the wrong things. Sleep had been her only option.

She groaned and slid out of bed. The room was dark, and she flicked on the lamp on the bedside table. After splashing water on her face and brushing her teeth, Asha headed downstairs.

"Poppy, how was your nap?" Mimi hugged her. "I came up to check on you and you were out. Curled up on your side, just like when you were a toddler."

"Sleeping during the day won't help you adjust to the time," Leela said.

Asha looked around at the busy kitchen as the three women prepared dinner. Her mother had changed into yoga pants and a light silk tank with an apron to cover her as she mixed dough on the counter.

"Come. I'll reheat cha for you. I saved you a cup in the kettle." Leela ushered her to the round white dining table they used for casual meals.

"Thank you." She wanted water but waited for the milky tea. Unaccustomed to naps, it always took her a while to clear the fog before she could process information. Millie was a morning person, and when they'd spent summers together, she would chatter away and want to do everything when all Asha wanted to do was sit by herself in the quiet and ease her way into the day.

The kitchen buzzed with activity. Mimi, in a long multicolored caftan, stirred a pot on the stove. A faint aroma of garlic permeated the air, but it wasn't strong enough to bother Asha. Leela placed a warm cup of cha in front of her granddaughter, then went back to the counter by the sink to finish chopping cabbage.

"What are you making?" Asha sipped the strong, spicy sweet tea and welcomed the much-needed jolt of caffeine.

"We're having a family meal to welcome you home," Mimi called out.

"Or as we say, our weekly Friday dinner," Leela said.

"It can be two things." Mimi pointed the tip of her wooden stirring spoon at Leela.

"Is it just the four of us for dinner?" Asha wondered if Neel would be there. She realized that she hoped so—she wanted to see him again.

"Your father will be home," Sapna said.

Asha nodded. There wasn't much to say, really. She had yet to see him. Not that she'd expected Sanjay to pause his life or make an effort when he'd never done so in the past, but it would have been nice to get at least a text welcoming her home. It wasn't their way. He'd never made it to her cross-country running meets in high school, though he had shown up for her graduation. Likely because Leela had made him be there.

"What about Neel?" Asha asked.

"He comes and goes," Mimi said. "I put dinner time in the group chat—we'll see if he shows up. If not, I'll leave a plate for him."

The three women moved around the kitchen in a knowing way, like they'd done this week after week for years. They joked, instructed, and gossiped. Like family. It had been this way since she'd been young, except back then she and Millie had assignments. Asha would shell peas and Millie would wash the rice. They would bump into each other in passing. Asha and Millie would listen to the ba and their mothers gossiping or sharing stories from the past. There was none of that now. Asha had been away for so long that she couldn't see herself among them. Even her grandmother had brought her a cup of tea as if she were a guest. She could barely remember the basics of the recipes she'd watched them make.

"Hello, family."

Her father walked into the room, and the kitchen became more animated. Sanjay Patel was a man whose presence was large and notable. He was affable, gregarious, and naturally charming. He patted Asha on the shoulder by way of acknowledging her presence.

"Asha. It is nice to see you."

She nodded. "Dad."

He was a tall man with a runner's build. His thick black hair was styled as immaculately as he was—like one of the heroes of the black-and-white Bollywood movies Asha and Millie had watched with Mimi growing up. Her impression of Sanjay had largely been formed by others, as he hadn't been as involved in her life as Kirit uncle was with Neel and Millie's. She rarely spoke to him while in Paris, and they only chatted if he happened to be near Sapna and she handed him the phone.

"I understand you're here for a long vacation," Sanjay said. "It's good. Your grandmothers are happy they'll be able to spend so much time with you."

But not her parents. She swallowed the comment along with her tea. "How is Goldfield?"

"We're recovering." He sat in a chair across from her and crossed one knee over the other and checked his phone. "The pandemic was tough, but we are survivors."

"Your father has it handled," Leela said.

"I would never let anything impact the legacy my grandfather built." Sanjay had removed the jacket and tie and appeared more casual than she remembered.

"I survived too." It was a petty comment, and she hated that it still bothered her that Sanjay cared more about Goldfield than his own daughter. When Asha couldn't travel and things were shut down, Mimi and Leela had sent her care packages. When she'd caught the virus, her mom had called or texted every day with tips on how to take care of herself. All her dad had done was make a short video call to say he was glad she'd come through with minimal damage.

Life-altering, career-ending damage.

"What's new with you?" Sanjay asked.

"I don't know how to answer that since we haven't talked in months," Asha said.

"And why would we? I know that I rank below my mother, Mimi, and your mother." He gave her a smile and a wink to soften the barb.

That's what happens when you check out of your daughter's life once she starts high school. "They stay in touch."

He looked up with a raised brow. "While you and I prioritize our work above all. We have that in common."

"Mom told me about the celebrity wedding." Going back to hotel talk was safer territory.

"It's going to help us, especially with the publicity," Sapna said.

Her mother grabbed the patlo-velan to roll out the bhakri. Her long black hair was swept up in a french twist, and her beautiful face was adorned only by mascara and lip gloss.

"Goldfield is the best in the area. On its way to becoming the best in the world," Sanjay said. "It's the perfect place for a destination wedding."

"If we do this right," Sapna added. "With the publicity and referrals we can be booked out for five years on weddings, corporate retreats, and other events. Her fiancé is a tech executive, so there's a lot of opportunity."

"Sounds great."

"And your mother will tell you, she made it all happen," Sanjay said.

There was no pride or support in her father's tone, and Asha could sense the tension as her mother went silent and focused on making bhakri.

Sapna slapped the dough ball hard enough for Asha to hear it hit the wooden patlo. Then she expertly rolled the dough out into a perfect small circle, continuing to flick it with her wrist as she grew the circumference until it achieved the perfect shape, the size of a small Frisbee.

"That's great, Mom. You should take credit for your hard work." It was something Asha was learning as part of her own career. She didn't want her dad to diminish her mom's contribution.

"The hotel itself is a sought-after venue," Sanjay said. "My grandfather had a small dream to run a motel as a way to support his family. My father elevated Goldfield into a hotel. Now it is a prized destination in and of itself, not merely a place to stay while in the area."

"That's where Mom and her marketing skills come in," Asha said. "If no one knows about it, they can't choose it."

"A perfumer that knows about business," Sanjay said. "Impressive."

She didn't hear it as a compliment. "There is art and science, but it's a multibillion-dollar industry. I do more than just play around with essences and oils."

Sanjay looked up from his phone. "You've always been smart."

She narrowed her eyes. She heard sincerity in his voice but couldn't quite believe it.

"I have an idea," Sanjay said. "Since you're here for more than a weekend, come by Goldfield. I'll give you a tour. You haven't seen the updates I've made since your last visit."

"I'm sure she doesn't have time for that," Sapna added.

I have nothing but. "It would be nice to see Sonanum." She hadn't visited the garden in ages.

"Then you better come quick," Sanjay said.

"She'll get there in her own time." Leela cleared up the counter.

Asha noticed a look pass between her grandmother and father and knew she was missing something. She glanced at her mom, who continued to roll out the bhakri.

"Come to think of it, since you're here," Sanjay said, "I can put you to work. We're busy and short staffed. And you're like me—we can't sit around and read magazines all day."

Asha hated the undercurrent between her parents. It was never overt. If they argued or fought it out, it would be more bearable than barbs and swipes. Her dad would do it with a smile, as if to play it off like it wasn't a sharp insult. Her mom would either shut down with hurt feelings or push back, which would then escalate until Sapna left the room, and then her father would shrug as if to imply that she was oversensitive.

"Don't be ridiculous, Sanjay." Sapna handed the plate of flat, precise circles to Mimi, who would cook the bhakri on the tava. "She's taking a rest. You can't ask her to work."

"It's her legacy. I have no other children. At least none that I know of."

The joke was in poor taste, and Sapna grabbed a towel and aggressively wiped the wooden velan she'd used to roll the dough. "Her career is in Paris. She's on her way to being one of the best perfumers in the world."

Not anymore.

"And Goldfield is one of the top hotels in the country, not just Napa Valley." Sanjay put away his phone.

"We agreed," Sapna said. "It's our burden, not hers."

"My family's business isn't some weight around our necks," Sanjay said. "My grandfather paved the way not just for us but for Indian American hotel owners everywhere."

"That doesn't mean Asha has to sacrifice her gift, her talent, to deal with paperwork and cater to other people."

"This isn't about her." Sanjay pointed. "This is about you."

Asha looked from one to the other. This was different. Her mother had raised her voice, and her father had lost his veneer of congeniality. She was surprised that neither Mimi nor Leela intervened.

Asha had believed for a long time that whatever love her parents may have had for one another had long faded. There was never open animosity, and most of the time they tolerated one another. She didn't want to be the rope in their current tug-of-war as they argued. The pressure became too much.

"I lost my sense of smell."

She'd said it. Out loud. With a raised voice. Heat rose in Asha's face, and her skin burned as she stared at her mother's shocked expression. All movement stopped. She swallowed, her throat dry, and she didn't know what else to say.

It was Mimi who handed Asha a glass of water, then placed a comforting hand on her shoulder.

"When?" Leela asked.

"A few months ago. When I had COVID. I lost it and it just never came back."

"This can't be true," Sapna said. "Did you talk to your doctor?"

"Several." Asha drank half the glass.

"What did they say?"

She heard the panic in her mother's voice. It was the same sort Asha had felt when the doctors first explained there wasn't much they could do.

"The specialists agree that it's come back as much as it's going to. My progress has plateaued."

"This isn't permanent," Sapna said. "It can't be."

Except it was.

"Enough. The food is ready, and, Poppy, we will figure this out," Leela said. "For now, we're going to finish cooking and have dinner together as family."

Sapna shook her head. "No. This isn't something that can wait." She wiped her hands on her apron and located her phone. "We'll find doctors in San Francisco, specialists."

Leela went to her daughter-in-law and placed her hand over Sapna's. "Tomorrow. We can wait until then."

Sapna pulled away. "No. This is too critical to take lightly. It's going to impact her career, her aspirations. Everything she's ever wanted. How is she going to become the best perfumer in the business without her nose?"

The roar between Asha's ears grew and her face heated. This was what she'd wanted to avoid. The panic and desperation at not being able to do the one thing her mother wanted. Asha pushed back from the table. She couldn't stay and listen to her mother try to fix her. She left the kitchen and went upstairs to the guest room.

It wasn't until she was on the bed with her arms wrapped around her knees that Asha realized she'd reverted to her teenage self. Her parents would argue. She would try to defuse it; she'd bear the brunt and then escape to her room. Asha closed her eyes and mentally kicked herself for not having learned anything from the past.

CHAPTER NINE

She'd been kidnapped. After a restless night spent in the mental vortex of self-pity, what-ifs, and tough talk, Asha had sat on the back porch steps and nursed a cup of coffee. The house was quiet, and she was dreading having to face her mom today. She'd been rehearsing the conversation in her head when Mimi and Leela came through the house and ushered her off the porch and toward their car. They'd shoved her into the Prius with Mimi behind the wheel. She'd tried to object, protest, but it wasn't until they were en route that there was enough of a break in their chatter for Asha to be heard.

"Where are we going?" She tried to recognize the road, but without GPS it all looked similar, and she couldn't get her bearings.

"You'll see." Mimi adjusted the seat belt around the zipper of her pink-and-white sweatshirt with a large rhinestone peacock on the back.

"Have a little patience, Poppy." Leela turned to look at Asha. "Just know that this is for your own good."

"That sounds ominous."

"Oh, beta," Mimi said. "Where is your adventurous spirit?"

Asha stared out through the window. She'd never had one. She and Millie were the same that way. They only jumped when they knew the depth and temperature and had assessed all risks. "It skipped a generation."

"That's true," Mimi said. "Your mother would be off gallivanting all over the world if she could."

Asha caught Leela giving Mimi a look from the passenger seat.

"Not that there is anything wrong with that," Mimi added.

"Poppy, how are you feeling this morning?" Leela said. "I hope you didn't go to bed hungry."

She still had leftover embarrassment for the way she'd behaved. "I came down later. Thank you for leaving me a plate on the stove, Mimi. If it was for Neel, I ate it anyway."

"I left two covered dishes, so he must have eaten his."

"I hope you got some rest." Leela smoothed down her paisley-printed maxi dress.

Asha bit the inside of her cheek. "I'm sorry for the way I behaved. I shouldn't have blurted it out like that."

"I enjoyed it." Mimi gave her a wink through the rearview mirror.

"Don't encourage it," Leela said. "You're out of sorts, Poppy, and now we know why. That's what we will concentrate our energy on. Don't be put off by your mother's reaction. It was a surprise to her."

"Right," Asha muttered. "Because all I am to her is a super nose with a glamorous life in Paris."

Leela turned to look at Asha. "Would it make you feel better to stomp your feet and stick out your tongue?"

Asha shook her head, ashamed of her glib retort. Even when Asha was a kid, Leela called out what she considered childish behavior. If she and Millie got into a fight, Asha had to be the one to resolve it. *You're older.* She'd never been allowed to throw tantrums. Leela's philosophy was that anger didn't resolve anything. Calm and composed. That was how one led a grounded life.

Asha closed her eyes as they drove along the twisty single-lane roads dotted with wineries, each with a different type of building to show off their brand. Neel had taught her how to drive on these roads, but nothing looked familiar. She'd aced the written test for her license but barely passed the driving portion. Even then she'd known her life was going to be in Paris, and she wouldn't need to have a car there. Still, Neel and Leela had encouraged her, with Leela stressing the importance of independence and self-sufficiency. And whenever it was time to renew her license, she would do it during one of her infrequent visits, so everything was kept up to date.

With her head back against the seat, Asha accepted the uncertainty of where she was being whisked away to. And she was still tired and jet lagged. She must have dozed off again because when she opened her eyes, the car was parked on a dirt road, the windows were down, and she could see the tall row of Italian cypress trees through the windshield. Asha rolled her tight shoulders and stepped out of the Prius.

Sonanum.

The ba must have already been in the garden that lay on the other side of the trees. For the first time since Asha got sick, she could breathe. Deeply. For a minute, she stood there simply taking full breaths as air moved deep into her belly. It was clean and dry. Her chest loosened, and the constant weight she carried on her shoulders eased a bit. For now, it was enough to stand with her ballet flats steady on the gravelly earth. The warm breeze cooled her skin as it floated through her gray silk T-shirt. She turned her face up to the bright morning sun.

In the distance, she heard the murmur of conversation between Mimi and Leela and went toward it. At the edge of the trees, the path narrowed as clay-colored sandstone led her toward Sonanum. For a few minutes she stood to admire the vastness. She couldn't see the whole of it but knew it from memory. To her right, Mimi and Leela moved through the vines of the rose garden. It was her mom's favorite. In a few months they would be at full bloom with palm-size flowers in reds, yellows, pinks, and white.

The roses led to a cluster of trees. Sonanum also held a pond surrounded by a smattering of rustic benches. It also sported a few hedges and her grandmother's topiary garden, which was an homage to children's book characters. Asha grinned. In middle school, she'd once snipped the trunk off the elephant while helping Leela. It took ages to grow back, and Babar never looked the same again.

Next to it, on the far quadrant, were wildflowers as far as the eye could see. It was the chaotic part of the garden. When she narrowed her eyes, she could see the tips of the red lupine, blues that were likely cornflowers, and the white-and-yellow daisies. There were large swaths of color interspersed with green. The path cut among the field so visitors could stroll through without stomping the plants. Asha and Neel had their prom photo shoot there. She remembered how Neel fidgeted with his navy silk tie that matched Asha's strapless dress. She wondered if he still had the photos somewhere.

"Poppy, come." Leela took her by the hand and led her to the left.

They walked toward the herb garden and saw the tilled land where the vegetables would soon be planted. Tomatoes, eggplant, different types of methi, squash, peppers, and so many other items that would provide the restaurant at Goldfield an abundance of options.

The herb garden took up half an acre and was her grandmother's labor of love. Nearing the area, Asha could pick up a gentle aroma of thyme or maybe rosemary. It was difficult to decipher, but she didn't push herself to figure it out. The perennial herbs were starting to come back, and annuals had already been planted. Right now, the garden was still in the early stages of growth, but Asha knew it would be mature in a few weeks.

"Did you let her know about the plan?" Mimi flanked Asha from one side.

"You've been with me all morning; did you hear me say anything to her?" Leela stood on Asha's other side.

"Tell me what?"

"Wait," Mimi said. "I need to go get my hat from the car. My head is baking."

"Get it after," Leela said.

"What plan?" Asha looked at Leela.

"It's genius." Mimi put her hands on the top of her head to protect her scalp.

"I know you're struggling with your nose." Leela took Asha's hand. "It may seem hopeless, and even though you've tried a lot of things, nothing has worked."

Mimi jumped in before Leela could finish. "We're going to get your sense of smell back."

The two of them stared at her. Mimi in excitement. Leela in determination. Asha's shoulders tensed. It would be an exercise in futility, and she didn't want to give anyone false hope. She'd tried it all, and nothing had worked. Her grandmother wouldn't accept anything less than acquiescence, though—she wouldn't be satisfied until every corner was explored. Asha shrugged. She'd been looking to figure out a way to fill her days anyway. Why not?

CHAPTER TEN

Most of Asha's childhood memories came from stories told *to* her. Especially the origin story of her hyperosmia. Another was how she became a superhero. Asha had been eight when she had taken her mother's Kashmiri shawl and wrapped it around her neck like it was a cape. She and Millie had spent hours on what her superhero name should be. Smell Girl didn't work. Neither did Flower Power. Then Neel called her Super Nose and it stuck. She and her sidekick, Millie the Marvelous, investigated crimes of odor. They'd ask Mimi to hide a spoiled piece of fruit or a dirty sock somewhere and then try to locate the stink. Sometimes they'd get distracted and move on, until Leela mentioned a stink and they'd quickly find it before they got in trouble.

The recollections that were strongest, though, the memories that were her own, were from Sonanum. She would be in this garden with Leela, and her grandmother would ask her to describe whatever was held against Asha's nose. Later, Leela would tie a bandanna over her eyes and teach her how to do the same without sight. If there was one place Asha associated with her childhood, it was this piece of land where everything was pretty, always—thanks to a lot of hard maintenance.

Once again, Asha was plunged into darkness. Instead of a blindfold, Mimi had slipped one of her furry sleep masks on her.

"What's this?" Mimi said.

Asha could feel a coarse leaf or stem of some sort against her upper lip and leaned away. "Thyme? Rosemary?"

The sigh was heavy as Mimi moved whatever it was away.

"Clear your mind," Leela said. "Try not to force it."

"Kind of hard with Mimi shoving things so close she might as well stuff my nose like a turkey."

"Hey, that's not a bad idea." Mimi held a clump of something fuzzy. "What if we got a baster and shoved things up your nostril. Like a jumper cable to kick it back into gear."

Asha lifted the mask to see a bunch of lavender stems in Mimi's hand. "Absolutely not."

Leela slid the mask back over Asha's eyes. "Mimi, drop those since Poppy saw what you were holding and try a bit from that plant over there."

The sun was strong, and the top of her head was hot. She wished for a hat of her own, though Mimi seemed to have forgotten to get hers from the car. At least the ba had brought water bottles. Asha recognized a waft of sweetness, and hope bloomed in her chest. "Mint."

"Type?"

Asha concentrated. Nothing. She knew from memory that Sonanum had a dozen different types of mint, from chocolate to pineapple. Her favorite was the water mint with its lavender flowers and dark-green leaves. She shook her head.

"Stop trying to stump her," Mimi said. "Poppy has to walk before she can run."

"You and your nonsensical clichés," Leela argued. "She's not a beginner."

Asha removed her mask.

"Put that back on," Mimi said.

Asha did as she was told and resigned herself to darkness. They meant well, she muttered quietly. It was better to go along if it made them feel better about her predicament. Both her hands were taken, one by each grandmother.

"Walk with us." Mimi pulled her.

"This way." Leela tugged her in the opposite direction.

"No, this way to start."

Asha stood her ground, glad she was strong enough to become immovable. "Where are you taking me?"

"We're going to the basics," Mimi said. "Flowers, where you'll be able to tell what you're smelling. Once you get your confidence back, your nose will follow."

"That's like asking her to recite multiplication tables," Leela said. "She knows them. What she needs is to remember there is more to aroma then just the top note."

They went back and forth tossing out analogies and examples to suit their agenda. Asha stood her ground, if only literally, while they forced their help on her. She knew it wasn't psychological, at least not according to her therapist. A few minutes later, Mimi won that round and Asha was led to the roses, where she was only able to identify their singular sweet scent. Then Leela led her to the sages. There, Asha got nothing.

An hour later, she was hot, sweaty, and dehydrated. Figurative nails were pounding against the sides of her forehead. The mere thought of the rosemary shoved within an inch of her nostrils caused a wave of nausea.

"What's all this, then?"

She had never been so relieved to hear Neel's voice. Asha pulled off the eye mask and silently pleaded with him to save her.

"Neel beta." Mimi pounced on him. "Go get us more water from the hotel. We're out and still have work to do."

"I'll go with him." Asha clutched at the lifeline.

"Why don't we all go?" Neel said as he ushered the grandmothers. "I brought my truck down. We can hop in there, and I'll have someone come bring your car up to the parking area."

Asha rushed ahead of them toward the big black pickup. It was an electric Ford F-150 that was large and intimidating. In high school, Neel had a beat-up Toyota Camry with a comfy back seat where they used to spend hours talking about life, dreams, and a future that had already been mapped out for them both.

"I'm not getting up in that monster," Leela said. "The two of you go ahead; we'll bring Mimi's car."

"But I like it when Neel picks me up and puts me in it," Mimi said. "Makes me feel like a delicate flower."

"Give me the keys." Leela went to the driver's side of the Prius. "I'll drive your fragile highness up to Goldfield."

Asha used the side handle to hoist herself into the passenger side as Neel waited for the ba to climb into Mimi's car before getting into the cab of the truck. "Okay?"

She shook her head. "They mean well. At least that's what I keep telling myself."

"I saw the car when I got to the hotel, and it was still there a few hours later so I came down to check on them," Neel said. "When Leela is at Sonanum, she loses track of time. And it's a warm day."

For all his lack of ambition, Neel had always been a caretaker and protector. Once when they were on their way to Asha's prom, Neel had seen a puppy on the side of the road and pulled over to rescue it. They'd spent the first hour of the dance at the vet making sure the tiny fur ball was all right. He'd eventually kept Westley, who went on to live a full and fun life with his person until six years ago.

"What was going on down there?"

"They have this grand plan to help me get my sense of smell back."

"Did you lose it somewhere in the garden?" He smiled and wiggled his brows.

"Wait, are you serious? You mean the Desai-Patel group chat didn't blow up over my confession last night?"

He ignored her. "What happened?"

She shrugged. "Side effect from a mild case of COVID."

He stared straight ahead. "I didn't know you were sick."

"It wasn't a big deal," she said.

"Clearly not since you've lost the thing that makes you uniquely you."

Tears rose in her throat, because he understood in a way that no one else did. She was untethered without her sense and didn't know who to be without it.

"Maybe instead of Super Nose, you could be Subpar Nose." He did the *burmph bhump* drumbeat on the steering wheel to punctuate his comment.

Asha couldn't help it. She laughed, then groaned at his poor attempt at a joke. It felt good, and her worries eased a bit. "That's terrible."

"I'm practicing for my comedy tour," he said.

She shook her head. "Like I said, you're going to starve."

"Mimi will feed me." Neel waited for Leela to spin her car around before he followed them up the dirt road.

"It's nice that you watch out for them," Asha said. "My dad probably doesn't notice."

"Everyone in the family keeps tabs on the location of their cell phones," Neel said. "And they're both very active in the group chat, so the rule is that if either one goes silent for more than six hours, one of us tracks them down."

"Meaning you," she said.

"I'm the one with the loosest schedule."

"In other words, you have a lot of free time on your hands."

She saw his hand clench the steering wheel. "Did I say that?"

"No. I'm sorry. I'm hot and cranky." Asha closed her eyes. "Ignore me."

"If only I could."

CHAPTER ELEVEN

As they drove away from Sonanum, the hotel loomed large in front of them. Goldfield had changed a lot since its start as the twenty-room budget motel her great-grandfather had bought shortly after Prohibition was repealed. The wineries were coming back in business again, and based on the stories Asha's grandfather shared, he couldn't buy it outright because of the restrictive laws for minorities and land ownership. Instead, her great-grandfather worked for the owner, who ultimately willed it to him, which was how the Goldfield had become her family's hotel legitimately. Though Ambalal Patel was the first Indian person to own a hotel in America, now over 40 percent of hotels were owned by Gujarati Americans. Her dada had helped many learn the ropes, and they in turn made it easier for others. The community grew and eventually became so large that they now had their own association where her great-grandfather was an honorary lifetime member.

For his part, her father wanted Goldfield to be an impressive example of legacy and status. To Sanjay Patel, it was a symbol of how Gujaratis didn't just survive as immigrants but how their perseverance enabled future generations to thrive as Americans. The original motel came with a large swath of land that allowed for expansion in the number of rooms and the additions of an upscale restaurant, an on-site spa, and an event space for weddings and conferences.

Closer, Asha saw Goldfield as a first-time guest might. Three attached buildings made up the resort. The one in the front was the oldest and had been restored several times to ensure that the white stone facade and the black roof reflected the luxury that awaited inside. A renovation took place in the late nineties when her father used a DHG architect to transform the Mexican design to California modern that was a mix of rustic, natural, and eclectic. Visually, it had a palatial aesthetic that was just understated enough to appeal to those with a lot of money who liked to pretend they were down to earth by surrounding themselves in simplicity.

Large columns lined the open walkway on three sides around the building. The second floor of the two-story main building had wide private patios accessible from the rooms. The two additions built as part of the renovation sat behind and to either side of the main house. They were in black and white, sleek with large floor-to-ceiling windows for each hotel room. In between the two and behind the original house was an open space that was lush and elegant, reserved for quaint but exclusive parties. Instead of the main parking lot, Neel pulled the truck to the side of the building in a hidden area reserved for staff parking.

"I didn't realize today was dress-like-an-adult day for you." Asha noticed his white shirt, slacks, and navy tie, already loosened.

"I had meetings this morning." Neel hopped out of the truck. "Want me to spin around so you can get the full effect?"

She rolled her eyes at his grin. "That joke is officially dead. You killed it with repetition."

He came around to Asha's side. "Here, Princess Poppy, let me get the door."

She didn't move. Instead, she closed her eyes and leaned her face in her palms. "If I get out, they'll kidnap me again."

Just then Leela came around to the driver's side. "Poppy, we think the supply room or laundry room would be a good place to spend the afternoon. The soaps, cleaning products, and linen will all work as triggers."

She sat up and took a deep breath. It was unavoidable, so she should just get on with it, even if her head felt as if it were in a vise grip that couldn't stop squeezing.

"Why don't you and Mimi have lunch in the restaurant," Neel called out to the ba. "Take a bit of a break. Don't forget to hydrate. I'll bring Poppy to you in a little while."

"Very well." Leela left them and trailed Mimi through the side door to the hotel.

"I owe you," Asha said. "You can name your price if you drive me far, far away."

"Here." Neel grabbed a bottle of water from the back seat. "Drink this. You'll feel better once your headache goes away."

She took a sip. "How did you know?"

He smiled. "You have this vein." He tapped the side of her forehead. "It pops out when your head hurts after concentrating for too long. I remember it from when you studied too much and made your brain hurt."

Her insides fluttered, happy that Neel had noticed that about her. It was what had led to her crush—he would see little things and then help her fix them. If she had a fight with one of her parents, he lent her a shoulder without her having to ask. It was like he had this instinct when it came to Asha. When they'd been together, these small acts were grand romantic gestures for her. She pressed into her vein, placed her finger over where his had been. It was warm, and she could feel the blood pump through.

"It's an angry shade of blue," he said. "I don't think even the French make skin creams good enough to hide that sucker."

He had to go and ruin it. She opened the door and shoved him with it. "Your compliments need work, just like your jokes. By the way, there is a very expensive eye cream in my makeup bag. It's in our shared bathroom. Use it regularly and the wrinkles around your eyes will magically disappear."

"I like the gravitas of my aging face." He rubbed his chin.

"Does Millie give you a word a day too?"

"Right. Because I only know small words."

"That's not what I meant," she said.

"Let's go eat. I'm hungry, and you can pay since you got a fancy job and I work in the back room."

"Stop making me feel bad," she said. "It's just that nobody our age uses 'gravitas' as part of casual conversations."

"You're still paying." He tugged her out of the truck.

"Fine." She followed him. "But don't order anything fancy."

"You're in luck; I'm craving fish and chips." Neel walked beside her.

"That sounds a bit casual for Sultana."

"The chef's trying out simple fare with an upscale touch to bring in a local crowd. Your mom's been doing soft promotions around it. There's been an uptick, so it seems to be working." He held the door, waited until Asha walked through.

The cool air eased a bit of her aggravation as they walked down the narrow hall of back offices. Through open doors she could see cubicles with signs for the audit and finance teams and the revenue management and marketing teams. The far corner was for the executive office of the owner and general manager, Sanjay Patel.

"He has a meeting in Calistoga." Neel pointed to her father's office. "Won't be back until tomorrow."

"I'm not trying to avoid him." She didn't glance through the open door.

"Just like I don't avoid my dad."

"It's different," Asha said. "Yours wants to be involved in your life. Mine has zero interest in me or anything I do."

"I guess it's easier when you have a continent and an ocean between you." He went ahead of her. His long legs ambled, and it was easy to keep pace.

Asha couldn't tell from his tone if he was needling her for being far away or making a factual statement. "Where's your office? In the boiler room?"

"Look at you trying to do comedy."

They walked through a nondescript door to the lobby and front desk area. The white-and-gray marble floor was pristine, and Asha felt bad for bringing in the garden dirt stuck to the bottoms of her shoes. The lobby had a warm, welcoming vibe with sand-colored sofas and red-cushioned chairs organized into quaint seating areas. From the high ceiling hung round circles of gray metal lighting fixtures.

"Something sweet." Asha sniffed the air and glanced around for diffusers.

"Cookies?" he suggested.

She faced him. Hands on hips. "Concentrate," she said. "What else?"

He stepped closer and crossed his arms. "I'm not Super Nose's sidekick."

Asha softened her face. "It's an itch in my brain that I can't scratch. Like I know what it is, but I can't quite figure it out. Help me, please?" She touched his forearm. "Is it a floral, tropical, or sugary?"

Neel turned his nose up. "Fruit. Like a pear."

"What else?"

"Sea? Not the fishy sea, but you know when you get out and when you're dry, the salt that's on your skin. It's kind of like that."

"Thank you." Ever since she started getting small whiffs of top notes or the halo of a strong odor, her mind would reflexively try to dissect the layers underneath. Like an opera singer who lost her range and could hear the note but not hit it. It was frustrating to know that there was depth in the aroma that was no longer accessible to her.

"It's hard for you."

Neel said it so simply that she wanted to hug him, have him hold her and tell her everything would be fine. Instead, she nodded. "It's there and not there at the same time."

"Your brain wants to understand."

"Exactly." She chewed on her cheek, then blurted out her biggest fear. "The doctors say it's likely permanent and I don't know what I'm going to do."

He faced her, hands in his pockets, as they stood in the lobby. "One thing I know about you, Poppy, is that you will always find a way. Nose or not."

"But I am Super Nose." She cleared her throat to make light of her circumstance.

He gave her a small smile. "Maybe this is an opportunity to figure out what else you can be. The smell is your origin story; write the sequel."

"Your metaphors need work."

"See?" Neel said. "You're already on your way to being Super Bossy, Super Annoying, Super Know-It-All."

She laughed and moved past him. "Let's go eat. If you make it so we don't have to sit with the ba, I'll treat you to dessert *and* fish and chips. But I'm not paying for the wine."

"I prefer beer."

CHAPTER TWELVE

Asha took Leela's advice and tilted the spout of the metal watering can over the boxes attached to the porch railing. There were azaleas, salvias, and miniature roses, along with petunias and geraniums. Each year, Leela chose a color scheme for each house, from the cottage to Millie's parents' house in San Francisco. This season seemed to be yellow, white, and a touch of purple. It was a gray morning, but she knew the clouds would lift and the dry heat and full sun would nourish their leaves and stems. She missed this simple act of communing with plants. Her apartment was too small, and she wasn't there enough to grow anything, so she settled for fresh-cut bouquets on weekends.

"There you are." Her mom stepped out on the porch, dressed for the office in a white fitted suit jacket over a coral dress. "Thank you for doing that. I'm getting a late start. I was up until midnight doing research."

"You don't have to do that, Mom. I've done it all."

"I don't understand why you're so passive about this." She held out a mug for Asha. "Aren't you worried about what's at stake?"

"I want to relax," she redirected the conversation. "I've been working nonstop."

"I did read something about nose fatigue." Sapna moved a few cushions and sat on the porch swing.

She wanted to tell her mom that this was more than that. "Thank you for the cha."

"Your father needs a thermos to take to work," Sapna said.

"But you prefer coffee." Asha savored the cardamom her mom preferred over the ginger Leela used.

"It's too much of a hassle to make multiple things," Sapna said. "What are you planning to do today?"

"I have to meet Leela and Mimi at the cottage." She wasn't looking forward to whatever they were going to do to her. The past two days had been nonstop with their various remedies.

Sapna handed Asha a piece of paper. "These are some specialists in San Francisco. Call them and see if they have any appointments this week. I can make time in my schedule to go with you."

The urgency in her mother's voice made her shoulders stiffen, and Asha had to roll them to ease the pain. "I've seen some of the best in Paris."

"Maybe they missed something."

"Can you just stop," Asha said.

"I'm trying to make you feel better."

She saw the hurt on her mother's face and sat down next to her. "I know."

"I don't know what it's like for you or how to relate," Sapna said. "But I see that you're upset about it, and I don't want you to hide under the covers and ignore it. I can help you like I did when you were little. I still have the contact information for that expert who helped you hone your smelling skills."

Asha rubbed the tension in her chest. "I know you're worried, but you have other things to focus on, like the wedding. Besides, Leela and Mimi are on the case."

Sapna stood. "Of course. She knows what's best for you since Leela raised you."

Asha wondered what that meant. "She knows me."

Sapna took Asha's mug and headed inside. "And I don't. I understand. I need to do what I do best and head to the hotel. I have calls to get some travel bloggers from San Francisco to come for comp stays."

Asha sighed, stayed on the swing, and watched the flower petals flutter in the breeze. They had no direction, merely swayed with the wind. She only knew what it was like to be pressed from all sides. From the time she'd set out to become a perfumer, there had been nothing else but that goal for her mom and Leela. Together, each pushed her to do more to secure her future. They'd put in so much effort on her behalf.

Her mom, especially, as she worked long hours and still made time to help Asha memorize the periodic table and edit her college essays. She appreciated it, and also wished they hadn't done so much. Then maybe she wouldn't feel this overwhelming guilt right now. Even though it wasn't her fault, she'd been responsible for both her mother's and Leela's dreams for her, and now she wouldn't be able to fulfill them.

Asha unfolded the piece of paper her mother had handed her. There were three names. An ENT, a neurological specialist for olfactory nerves, and an acupuncturist. Her mother had left nothing to chance. It couldn't hurt to call at least one of them for a fourth—or was it fifth?—opinion. If only to make her mom's efforts on her behalf worth it.

CHAPTER THIRTEEN

She'd gotten a next-day appointment with the San Francisco otolaryngologist due to a cancellation. Dr. Varma was pleasant and methodical. She'd done her own examination and went through a thorough timeline from the time Asha lost her sense of smell to the progress she had made to date. As expected, the doctor offered the same assessment as Asha's ENT in France. For an hour, Asha had wandered around near the medical center, then sat on a bench with an iced tea to stare into space. The inevitability of it all was obvious to everyone. Except her family.

Instead of heading back to Napa Valley, she stopped by to see Millie. The executive offices of Kirit uncle's Desai Hotel Group were on the eighteenth floor of a building in the Financial District. A little over sixteen years ago, DHG had opened its first office on half the fourteenth floor and eventually grew to take over the rest of the fourteenth and the four floors above it in their entirety. There was a hum to the way people moved around Asha as she stepped off the elevator. A glance here and there but no one paused, and Asha greeted the receptionist, who gave directions to Millie's office at the far end of the hall.

Asha was glad to be away from what Mimi called Operation Incense for its double meaning. All day yesterday, wherever she went, someone had tried to get her to take a whiff, then asked her for a list of scents she'd picked up. This morning, before anyone could whisk her off, she'd made her escape.

Asha walked through the wide hallway, passing offices on one side and conference rooms on the other. The walls were standard beige with framed watercolors of DHG hotels from around the country. It wasn't that different from her Crystal Park business offices in Paris. Profit was the driver there just as it was here, and everyone worked for market share. Even in the lab, it was less and less about experimentation and creativity and more about demographics, segmentation, and the whims of a target audience with disposable income. The sheen of glamour, the aesthetics, the celebrity campaign drove the luxury fragrance market more than nuance and artistry.

At the door, Asha paused. Millie was behind her large executive desk, stacked with folders on one end, two side-by-side monitors on the other, and a laptop in the middle. She was on the phone when she spotted Asha and held her finger up. Classic Millie. She'd aged into her face—that's what Leela would say. Millie had an old soul and wore it on her expressive face. Her high cheekbones, full lips, and sharp eyebrows had been a part of her since she'd hit puberty. Sometimes, she'd be confused for being Neel's older sister even though she was two years younger.

So much time had passed since they'd been in the same room. Their daily texts were the only connection and the thing that allowed them to maintain the facade of friendship. As teenagers, knowing they were separated by a two-hour drive, they moaned about the distance so much that one or the other grandmother would drive them to each other every Friday and the other would do the same on Sunday. They'd cram a week's worth of happenings into two days and dread the five-day separation.

Summers were the best. Neel, Millie, Asha, and the grandmothers would spend it all at the cottage for three months. That's what family had meant for her. It was a temporary bubble that popped once Asha left for university. She and Millie had made pinkie promises to never stop being besties and to always stay in touch. And they did, for a few years. Until they both learned that adult life was so much more complicated. The list of to-dos never ended, and things that used to be so important fell off their agenda altogether.

Every time Asha had come for a visit, it hurt to leave until it became easier to make the trip annually instead of every three months. Their careers took off, and they had less time to share or offer each other support. With less and less contact, the idea of catching up became overwhelming. The distance grew. And while Millie would still be her best friend forever, it was the ones she shared proximity with, her colleagues and friends from her graduate program, that she knew better now.

She looked at the beautiful woman behind the sleek walnut desk. Her hair was plaited and rolled up in a fancy knot at the nape. Her sleeveless sheath dress was cherry red, her shoes five-inch tan leather pumps. Her friend had changed so much. As a child, Millie was never put together. Her grandmother would spend long mornings taming the giant head of frizzy hair that could only be brushed out and braided. By the evening, the hair tie would cling to a small tress with the rest having made their escape around her face and down her back.

"Since when are you one for surprises?"

Millie's thick, raspy voice interrupted Asha's trip to the past. "I thought I'd try something new."

Millie raised her right eyebrow, the same way Neel did.

"I owed it to our sismance to see you as soon as possible."

Millie laughed. "Nice use of your daily word."

Asha lowered herself in a quick curtsy to acknowledge the accomplishment. "I thought we could have lunch."

Millie came out from behind her desk and made her way to the seating area, where there was a long sofa in yellow with two red throw pillows and a coffee table that matched the large desk. Somewhere along the way, they'd stopped hugging hello and goodbye, and Asha couldn't remember why. The distance was still present even though it was barely a few physical feet.

Two tall armchairs sat on either side of the couch, a setup designed for power and positioning. The person in the chair would tower over the sofa occupant, and Asha imagined Millie used that to her advantage often.

"I haven't taken a nonworking lunch in, well, I honestly can't remember."

It was sad that Asha could say the same. She took a seat on the sofa instead of the chair across from Millie, taking ownership of their estrangement. After all, it was Asha who'd left.

"These flowers are beautiful." Asha pointed to the vase in the middle of the coffee table. "Yellow Asiatic lilies, pink roses, and lavender daisy poms."

"At least you won't be nauseated by all the smells," Millie said.

Asha lowered her head. "You heard."

Millie waved the phone she had in her hand. "The Desai-Patel group chat is going strong. Everyone has been drafted into Operation Incense. And I know you didn't come all this way just for me. How did your specialist appointment go?"

Asha groaned. "They put all that in a text?"

"The thread is forty messages long—thirty of them are just Mimi sending GIFs and memes of people sniffing. It's very disturbing. I could kill Neel for showing her how to do that. So?"

Asha scrunched her face. "Nothing new. No magical cure."

"Damn," Millie said. "We were taking bets, and Leela was really hoping for a surgical treatment."

"She wants me to go under?"

"Only because then there would be an actual cause," Millie said. "And it would lead to a speedy cure."

Then they could send her back to Paris. "You can let them know they're out of luck."

"Step two is for me to take you to the smelliest places in the city."

"We're not doing that!"

Millie put down her phone. "I don't have time anyway."

"I'm not in the chat, so we can pretend you never mentioned it," Asha said.

"Nope," Millie said. "I just got back into Mimi's good graces after ignoring her requests to bring another sourdough starter. I swear she kills them on purpose just to get me to go see her. I'm not taking the heat. I'll just say you didn't want to go."

"Or don't say anything."

The phone buzzed and Millie checked it. "Now the ba are going back and forth with each other about whether to make khichdi with lilva or with potatoes for dinner. They have their own texts but sometimes just type into whatever is on top." Millie closed out the app. "The dads stay quiet. They don't want to be a part of it but can't leave the chat because last time mine did, Mimi gave him a three-hour lecture on how the family that texts together, stays together."

Put that way, Asha felt cast aside. Yes, she lived in another country, but she was family. "Guess I should be relieved they're at least worried about me."

"Since you finally showed up." Millie crossed one leg over the other. "Why did you fly into SFO and skip coming to see me first?"

Asha hung her head. "I'm sorry." Millie would have been the easy option, but too much time had passed. "I was exhausted, and I wanted to settle in and unpack before coming to see you."

"Mm-hmm."

"But I'm here now."

"Poppy, I have a meeting with the carpet supplier in twenty minutes, then an hour with finance, and back-to-back until six tonight," Millie said.

"Fine," Asha said. "Be mad. I deserve it. And I'm sorry. I should have at least called you when I landed."

"Apology accepted," Millie said.

That was the best part about her friend. While Millie could hold a grudge, if the apology was sincere, she forgave, moved on, and never brought it up again. But if she didn't receive a satisfactory *I'm sorry*, she could hold it over your head forever.

"I didn't mean to interrupt your day," Asha said. "I wanted a little time away from all the ways they're trying to fix me."

Millie grinned. "The pic of you blindfolded and sniffing clear bowls is your profile picture in my contacts."

She reached for Millie's phone. "They're taking photos? Let me see."

Millie held her arm out of reach. "You'll just delete them, and I need them for posterity. That pink fur sleep mask really works on you."

Asha sat down and crossed her arms. "It *is* comfortable. I took a nap with it on yesterday." She looked over at her friend. "I miss you."

Millie patted Asha's knee. "We text each other every morning." She rose and opened a wooden door in the bookshelf. It was a hidden refrigerator, and Millie pulled out two bottles of Perrier.

"We share our arcane word of the day in the morning and then send a check mark if we managed to work it into a conversation." Most days neither reported back. They'd invented the game while studying for their PSATs and SATs, long distance, and eventually it was just their thing. And because international calling was expensive, it had been a way to stay in touch.

"We have busy lives. There's no shame in that." Millie handed her one of the sparkling waters and sat.

Asha glanced at Millie, who stared back. They both sipped their water, then put the bottles down. Slowly each smiled. "Quick Catch!" They said it at the same time.

Millie set the timer on her phone. "It used to be one minute for each day that we were apart, but we don't have that kind of time so one minute for each year. Ready. Go." Millie started the timer.

Asha started. "Best vacation."

"Get real." Millie rolled her eyes. "I haven't taken more than two days off in years."

"That's not okay."

"Hey, follow the rules," Millie said. "No judging. No lectures. Most expensive purchase."

Asha tapped her finger on her chin. "La Mer."

"That's cheating, you live in the land of La Mer."

Asha cleared her throat to remind Millie of the rules. "Worst romantic decision."

"Slept with my favorite physical therapist and had to find a new one." Millie shook her head. "I still miss Arno. Not for the sex, but he really was great in the way he adjusted the stiff parts of my hips. Worst work mistake."

Asha picked up the bottle and played with the label. "Getting pulled off my first high-profile account because I couldn't get the formula right."

Millie reached over and shut off the timer. "We took the long way around but finally the truth."

Asha rolled her shoulders to ease the tension that seemed to have taken permanent root at the base of her neck. "Someone else, my professional nemesis, replaced me. I won't get another chance. Not with my busted sense. I might get demoted to lab tech. Or fired."

"Well, that's bullshit." Millie picked up her bottle. "You have one setback and you're ready to give up? Isn't this what we wanted? We love our jobs. We need to work. The days are exciting, and now that I'm in executive leadership, I savor the rush of telling people what to do."

Asha laughed. "That seems right. I never got to order many people around, but I do miss doing that to Neel when we were younger."

"That's okay, I make up for it on your behalf." Millie went back to the built-in and opened another door next to the fridge and grabbed a box of peanut M&M's. "He always says no and then winds up doing whatever we ask. Though he's been tough ever since he grew taller than me. We have an agreement now. He gets to reject five of my requests a month."

"How generous of you."

"Chocolate, *mon amie*?"

It felt good to hear Millie use the endearment. *"Oui."* Asha held out her palm.

Millie shook out a few for Asha and some for herself.

"What do you do in this executive role?" Asha asked.

"Vice president of operations," Millie said. "Just a few years away from CEO and president."

Neel's old role. Millie knew her father wanted her brother to eventually head up the company but was too stubborn to accept it as a given. It didn't surprise Asha that she was still determined to get to the top. She didn't know how Neel dealt with Millie's aspirations. He loved his sister and would do anything for her. She now wondered if he'd purposely tanked his job to make way for Millie.

"Your forty-year plan is still on track?" It was something they'd done in their very first planners at the age of ten.

"CEO of DHG by the time I'm fifty," Millie said. "To show my dad that daughters can run conglomerates just as well as sons."

A lump rose in Asha's throat. "I was supposed to be the best perfumer in France."

"To make your mom and Leela proud," Millie added.

Asha furrowed her brow. "What?"

"We had to write down our why, remember? It wasn't just about the goal, because knowing the reason would keep us motivated." Millie took another sip from her bottle. "And trust me, my dad is getting it. I'm twice as good as Neel was when he was in this role for a hot minute."

"Your brother is okay with all of this?"

"Better than that. He helped me." Millie munched on an M&M. "By being completely incapable of doing the job."

Asha couldn't imagine him in this office, back-to-back meetings, and inside all day. The shirt and tie he'd worn a few days ago had been completely out of character. When they played hotel as children, Millie and Asha took turns being general manager and Neel always chose maintenance or concierge. Or did they assign that to him?

"Millie." A person in red skinny jeans and a printed black-and-white shirt popped their head into the office. "Five-minute warning for your call."

"Thanks, Josh."

Millie went to her desk. "You're welcome to hang out here until I'm done for the day. We can grab dinner after, unless you need to head back."

"I'll wander and then come back. I'm not ready to face what's waiting for me just yet." Asha watched as Millie turned on her laptop and dialed into the virtual call.

She didn't want to sit around and watch her friend work. She'd spent a lot of time near the Ferry Building whenever they came to San Francisco to visit Millie's family. It would be nice to see how much had stayed the same. It was a warm day, and she strolled over to the small park where the three of them used to play as children as Mimi stood guard. Her memories were fuzzy because it was well before planners and goals. Asha watched a small child climb on a polygonal set of monkey bars. All the kid cared about was how to go from one rung to another without falling. She envied the freedom of not worrying about the future or unfulfilled promises.

If only to live that way as an adult, which was an impossible task. Even on the playground toy, Asha would worry about tearing a shoulder or twisting her knee. She closed her eyes and wished for a few minutes of weightlessness, just enough to have her shoulders release all that she held on them.

Unfortunately, there was no respite. At least not today.

CHAPTER FOURTEEN

The restaurant was full and lively, but because Millie was a regular, they had no trouble getting a table near the front windows. Her friend was a creature of habit and had mapped out her geographical footprint between the office and her Mission Hill condo with all her routine stops.

"It's stuffy." Millie situated herself in a dark-brown leather chair on one side of the table with her back to the dark paneled walls. "But the food and the staff make up for this old New England library vibe."

"I'm not picky."

Millie laughed. "You're the worst, especially when it comes to food. Nothing can touch. You eat one thing at a time, which makes Neel's eye twitch, and when you really want to tick him off, you pick instead of taking a full bite."

"Fair." Asha pushed herself toward the table. "I'm better, though. I don't mind if things touch, and sometimes I put hollandaise on *top* of my poached egg."

"Whoa," Millie said. "Who are you and what have you done with Poppy Patel?"

They laughed, caught up on gossip about mutual friends, and each ordered a drink—a Kir Royal for Asha, while Millie ordered a dirty martini, extra chilled, extra dirty.

"You are definitely your grandmother's." Asha made a face as the waiter left with their order. "I drank one of Mimi's, and I swear it burned off a layer of skin on my esophagus."

"She's the one that taught me how to drink them," Millie said. "My dad hates that she imbibes, as he puts it, but I give Mimi a break—she was a late bloomer and never touched alcohol until after my dada died."

"I think it was the same for Leela ba."

Millie nodded. "It's like they didn't have to be traditional wives anymore. Widowhood meant grandmas gone wild."

"Literally." Asha told Millie about the topless incident.

"I would have snapped a pic for blackmail purposes."

"Tu es horrible," Asha said.

"The French language sounds like everyone talks with a bunch of marbles in their mouths and slurs their words."

It was true, French pronunciation was extremely difficult. As was Gujarati, which their family expected them to speak—and made sure all of them were fluent from birth. A phonetic language, there were some sounds only native speakers could make, which made certain things, like the word for "faucet," *nuruh*, impossible to pronounce by non-Gujarati speakers.

"What's good here?" Asha scanned the menu.

"The cod with porcini risotto is very popular, but this is my regular place so I can't have you embarrass me by picking out the mushrooms one by one." Millie closed the leather menu and set it aside. "I'm having the chicken under a brick with mashed potatoes. We can share the clams with pancetta and white wine broth."

"I'm glad Neel isn't here. He'd torture you by asking our server to explain every dish just to annoy you."

"I don't let him have a menu and always order for him whenever we eat out," Millie said. "We fight less that way."

"I bet he really likes that." With only two years separating them, the siblings were so close that they knew the exact buttons to push.

"He hacks into my calendar and blocks out a day with fake meetings to get back at me," Millie said. "Then makes me go to Big Sur or Muir Woods with him to do nothing. I'm not even allowed to hike. Just sit and listen to the wind or some nonsense."

They put in their order and Asha sipped her drink. Music played softly in the background, but she didn't know who or what it was, just noise added onto the clanging plates and the boisterous conversations around them. "I could stay for the weekend. We could take in some live shows or go to Sausalito."

"What's the goal?" Millie said. "If you want to relax, we can go to a yoga class and then have massages. If you want to reminisce about all the places we used to go, we can drive around. If you're avoiding the ba trying to help you, then you're out of luck, because I'm on their side."

"Seriously?" Asha waited until the server finished placing their appetizer down.

"Since when do you procrastinate?" Millie said.

Asha chewed on a clam. The salt, citrus, and slight bitterness from the wine hit her tongue all at once, and it felt so good to taste something so sharp and flavorful. "The old me didn't, ever. The one without her nose, I don't know."

"I don't like this waffling version." Millie dipped a wedge of bread in the clam sauce. "Let's fix it."

When the server brought out their entrées, she ordered another drink to ease the hopelessness about her future. "It can't be fixed. Most experts agree, including the doctor this morning."

Millie snorted. "So that's it, then?"

Asha shrugged.

"We don't give up so easily," Millie said. "Have you forgotten the rules we wrote down about how to live our lives? Number three was exhausting all possibilities before calling it quits."

"There was also one on not wasting energy on an exercise in futility," Asha said.

"Did the doctors all say zero chance?" Millie said.

"No, not definitively, but—"

"Then there's still hope," Millie said. "My dad, yours, all the uncles, they all told me there was no way I would be voted in as the first woman chair of the AAHOA board. Two years ago, I was. And the youngest too. If it's within your control, keep fighting for it."

Asha nodded. "You're right." Maybe she'd given up too easily. It hadn't even been a full year. She'd told Dr. Varma this morning that it wasn't all gone, but she'd been acting as if it were. "Enough about me; what's going on with you?"

"I'm busy and I love it," Millie said. "Right now, I'm trying to figure out a signature something to tie all the DHG properties together. An umbrella item, one that says 'this is a DHG hotel' and doesn't violate any of the franchise agreements."

Asha sipped her cocktail. "I can send you a lot of research on scent and brand loyalty."

"Oh, I'm loaded up, but the fragrance ship has sailed," Millie said. "We would be followers in that space, and some of our luxury brands have signature scents tied to Four Seasons and Ritz-Carlton, so I can't go that route. Candles, atomizers, and everything in between is a no-go. I want something, though; there is so much revenue opportunity. We'll do something different and unique. Relevant. Something that has connotations of *welcome* and *be our guest*."

"Why not just play *Beauty and the Beast* music in every lobby?"

"I hate you."

Asha ate a sliver of the buttery, flaky cod. It was simple, mild in flavors, and still delicious. "Do you have something in the works?"

Millie dug into her chicken. "I've commissioned research on options."

"That's great."

"Back to you," Millie said. "If there's still a chance, keep working at it."

Asha toyed with the stem of her glass. "It's not like I haven't tried."

"By yourself in a land far, far away. I'm saying stop avoiding Operation Incense," Millie said. "Embrace it. Let everyone help you. Leela is the one that saw it first; your mom nurtured it and put you on a path. They want to help you get back all that you've worked towards. Also, I'm having a slice of chocolate cake for dessert and I'm not sharing, so if you want something, get your own."

"I remember a berry tart on the menu."

Once they finished off their meal—amid nonstop chatter—they placed their orders and spent the rest of the evening laughing and reminiscing. It felt good to have Millie boss her around again. Asha needed someone else's perspective. She was tired of moping and napping. She had let Celeste and the demotion get in her head. It was time to snap out of it, make a list, and focus on the task at hand. Home was the place where she'd found her superpower. It could be that she could revive herself. Use the next three and a half weeks to prove the experts wrong. No one had said this was permanent. They'd all implied it, but there were examples of exceptions to the statistical likelihood of never regaining one's sense of smell.

Millie had reminded Asha of who she'd been, and it was time to roll up her sleeves and do what she always did: figure it out.

CHAPTER FIFTEEN

Asha hadn't thought being at the second winery after riding an e-bike for ten miles was how this day would go. After spending the night at Millie's in San Francisco, she'd come back to her parents' house and told Leela and Mimi to do their best. She would be a willing participant. What she hadn't counted on was that the ba had spent the previous day brainstorming with the Nanis of Napa, which led to today's adventure. Designed to give her nose a rest, while stimulating her muscles with physical activity.

That was how she found herself on a motorized bike-and-wine tour with the Nanis. Asha was told to ride hers manually, while others made use of their motors. And she was not allowed to so much as sniff the air. Today's group was smaller than usual, with only eight of them along for the activity, but they'd enfolded Asha as one of theirs. Luckily, she hadn't fit into any of Mimi's collection of velour tracksuits, which seemed to be the required uniform for this outing. They made quite the picture wheeling around the narrow roads in a sea of colors. Everyone laughed, teased one another, told tall tales, one-upped each other, and showed Asha what it meant to simply enjoy the experience.

She'd learned that they weren't all retired, as she'd previously assumed. They were a diverse group too, not just race but class, backgrounds, and points of view. The things they shared were a dedication to philanthropy and a commitment to live their best lives.

Once the group reached the last winery for the day, all of them congregated around outdoor tables and settled in once again. The bikes were with their exhausted guide off to one side.

"I smuggled some snacks." Ming Na, a former ER doctor who'd retired to the area with her husband a few years ago, unzipped her fanny pack and took out several small baggies and placed them on the wooden picnic table. "Cheez-Its, Trader Joe's chocolate-covered almonds, Goldfish, and gummy bears."

"Goldfish are the only kind of fish I eat." Mimi popped one in her mouth as she took a seat.

Both Mimi and Leela adhered to a vegetarian diet. Leela also avoided eggs, while Mimi loved baked goods too much to be that strict.

"They go well with white." Dominique raised her glass.

Asha took a small sip of wine. Her heart rate was still recovering after Bonnie, a former professional golfer, had popped a wheelie on her e-bike as they entered the winery, trying to scare the young woman from the tour company who led their group.

Once they'd settled and put in their orders with the vineyard staff member assigned to them, the nonstop chatter continued. They'd spread out among three tables, and Asha hoped that the Nanis stayed contained enough so as not to bother the other guests.

As their wine flights arrived, they yelled across to each other and passed around glasses based on who liked which wine, without giving the tasting guide a chance to run through the different characteristics of each of the six glasses. After a few minutes, the winery team left the group, realizing these women were not there for a lesson but simply to drink.

"I like this cabernet." Mimi pointed to the last glass in the tasting flight. "We should order a bottle."

"Uh, that's not a good idea," Sarah, the tour guide, said. "We'll need to head back to Yountville in thirty minutes."

"This is our last stop, isn't it?" Mimi patted the young brunette's arm. "We can take just a wee bit more time."

"What winery is this again?" Bonnie swirled the last sip from her glass of red.

"Saddleback." Leela's face was slightly flushed.

"That reminds me," Yulie said. "We need to find a country-western bar with a mechanical bull. I'm doing this annual bucket list challenge, and since I'm eighty-four, might as well see how far I get."

"As a doctor, I wouldn't advise it," Ming Na said. "You just had a hip replacement."

"Two years ago." Yulie finished off her wine. "Besides, you were an ER internist, not an orthopedist."

Ming Na took off her straw hat and fanned her face. "General medicine means I know all things."

"Did we order a bottle?" Mimi leaned back in her chair and called out to Sarah, who paced nearby while chewing on a cuticle.

"We should go," Asha said. "She might have another tour after our group."

"She can leave us here. We'll make our way back." Bonnie pushed back and stood. "I'll go tip her and tell her we'll call a few rideshare cars. That other table of Nanis looks fully tucked into their wine and cheese boards."

Asha went after Bonnie. "We could buy a bottle and open it back at Mimi's house. The back deck is nice."

"They don't have the delicious fig jam, crostini, or even the basic fixings for a charcuterie board." Bonnie pulled out her wallet from her purse.

"I'm sorry," Asha told Sarah.

"Here." Bonnie handed two one-hundred-dollar bills to Sarah. "We release you of all liability. We signed the forms before we started."

"I need to take you back," Sarah said.

"Take the bikes." Bonnie pointed to them lined up in rows near the parking area. "My butt hurts too much to get back on one anyway."

Asha winced. "Sorry again. I'll make sure we get back to the shop and pick up our cars."

Sarah reluctantly agreed and went to the multiple tables to thank everyone before rushing off to load the e-bikes into her van.

"We need to give her a nice review," Leela said.

Yulie stood up. "I'll go order more bottles and cheese."

Asha took her seat, resigned to her fate of being their senior sitter. She'd have to figure out how to get all of them out of the winery before they ordered even more bottles. And take their car keys, though she didn't believe the Nanis would let anybody get into a car after drinking. The logistics of it all would require her to keep a clear head.

"Isn't this nice, Poppy?" Leela stroked Asha's loose hair, then brushed the thick curtain back over her shoulder. "At first, I wasn't convinced about this rest business. I didn't believe your mother until she sent a few articles. I still think we haven't tried enough of the smelling, but if this day helps relax you, then it might be for the best."

Asha took Leela's hand and held it in hers. "I haven't said this, but thank you. I know it's my problem, and I should have come here with a plan. It's nice to have the help. I've missed seeing you these past few years." More than she'd realized.

Leela waved her off. "You're working hard, using your talents. That's all that matters. We're here and then we're not. It's what we leave behind that stays. For you it will be the fragrance they will talk about and use decades from now. Something original that connects our past to our future."

Asha knew that was what her grandmother really wanted. A signature perfume, based on Leela's life. One that captured the richness of their Indian culture her grandmother had left behind and continued to nurture, as well as the family she built here. It would be Asha's greatest achievement. In high school, when she'd read about perfumers, the history of scent, and saw the way fragrances were inextricably linked to people, Asha planned to do that for Leela. She wanted her grandmother's perfume to be what White Diamonds was for Elizabeth Taylor. And also a way to honor Leela's life. It wasn't until Asha started at ISIPCA that she'd realized her industry wasn't glamorous behind the scenes. Perfumers were beholden to brands and briefs.

Still, Asha worked to create that signature scent. And if she made a name for herself in France, she could use her influence to work with a brand to make Leela's fragrance. It was daunting and perhaps naive, but as Millie said, Asha planned to exhaust all possibilities.

Having been raised by Leela, Asha knew that her grandmother had a love-hate relationship with America. It had been her home for sixty years of her life, ever since she came from Gujarat as a twenty-year-old bride. Asha had grown up listening to her grandmother's disdain for Westerners who used what Leela believed was rightfully Indian and exploited it for their gain. When Millie and Asha took yoga in high school, Leela would ask if their instructor was of Indian origin—if not, then what they were doing was merely glorified stretching, not the Vedic practice. If a non-desi celebrity wore a sari, her grandmother didn't see it as appreciation for another culture but as appropriation.

Leela had been born before the partition, and the British rule of her birth country was something her grandmother refused to let go. They couldn't pass by Starbucks without Leela being irritated by their chai and turmeric lattes. And Deepak Chopra was never to be mentioned in her presence. Leela believed that just as the British had looted India for hundreds of years, the same was being done here, but under the guise of false respect and interest. The lectures had waned in recent years, but no one doubted where Leela stood on such matters. Asha wanted to make up for Leela's pain. She wanted to capture her grandmother's identity in a bottle. A perfume shouldn't be solely for celebrities.

And Asha wanted to do this for her grandmother at scale, not a craft scent she could bottle and give Leela. She wanted for Leela to go into a Nordstrom and see her own signature perfume on display.

"Stop thinking so hard." Mimi nudged Asha with her shoulder. "This is a brain break. Drink your wine, enjoy the company, and don't smell anything."

"I'm going to use the facilities and ask for two bags of ice on the way back." Leela rose from the metal chair around the iron table where they sat.

"For water?" Asha truly hoped so.

"My knees." Leela left the group.

Asha gave Mimi a questioning look.

"She had them replaced a few years ago," Mimi said. "Isn't that a funny way to say it? She didn't exchange her old knees for a new pair. Or did she? Now I don't remember. Ming Na, do they actually replace the kneecap with another one?"

As the two went back and forth about the procedure, Asha watched her grandmother hobble into the winery. She hadn't known about the surgery, and no one had thought to mention it to her. "Was it because of an injury?"

"Just wear and tear," Mimi said. "Don't worry. She's strong. We all are. There is still a lot left for us to do in this life."

"I got two bottles." Yulie returned to the table and began to pour cabernet into their glasses. "And more food. Coating the stomach is very necessary." She looked at Asha. "For indigestion." Then winked, then cackled.

Asha gave in. How could she not? This was the joie de vivre that she never adapted to in Paris. Their approach to living in the now was inspiring even as it was uncomfortable. She took a deep swig of the wine and let the fruity flavor explode on her taste buds. She wanted to be as joyful. For one afternoon, Asha would truly rest her nose in a way she hadn't before.

CHAPTER SIXTEEN

Asha sneezed. Again. And once more. Hers often came in threes, but so far it had been ten rounds since she'd arrived at Sonanum a few hours ago. She'd been given orders to sit in the rose garden and open her nostrils. With a notebook in her hand, she needed to catalog the layers. She would have to concentrate to pick up the honey and spice from the petals, the earth and murkiness from the stamen. So far, all she'd done was write down the faint scent of a classic rose often found in generic candles.

She sneezed and missed footsteps coming toward her.

"Bless you," Neel said.

She wiped her irritated face with a small handkerchief Mimi had tucked into the sleeve of her black cardigan. It was a cool day, and the sky was heavy with clouds. "Tissue?"

"Tissue? I hardly know you."

She laughed and groaned at the old childhood joke.

Neel put both his arms up in victory. "Yes. Made you laugh."

"You are ridiculous. *Achoo.*" Asha sneezed into her elbow.

"Are you sick?"

She shook her head and caught her breath after the last round of sneezes. "Castor oil. The latest test is two drops in each nostril. It's awful. Now I can't smell or stop sneezing."

He crouched down and rubbed her back as a few more sneezes escaped. In a moment of respite, she took a sip of water and laid her hand on her stomach. "On the plus side, I'm going to have abs of steel. What do you want?"

"I came to check on you," he said. "Make sure you didn't get lost in the weeds."

"I'm fine." Her stuffy nose and hoarse throat made her sound like Eeyore. "I've been without a babysitter for a long time. I can handle anything."

Just when it couldn't get worse, a raindrop plopped on her nose. She looked up and was surprised as clouds burst open with a sudden shower. Neel grabbed Asha's hand and pulled her up, and they made a run for it toward her car. Luckily, she'd left it unlocked and they slid in.

Her hair was soaked, and she shook it out of the loose bun, further saturating her clothes. She wiped her face with her hands, then dried them on her damp yoga pants. For a few minutes, they sat in the quiet of the car and listened to the pitter-patter.

Asha glanced over and watched Neel wipe his face with the sleeve of his thick flannel. There was immediate déjà vu of all the times they'd spent in cars, just the two of them. Cocooned in the back seat, it was their space, away from the pressures of their meddling loved ones. It was in his car that she'd first told him she loved him. When he said it back, she vowed to keep his words permanently tattooed on her heart. It was special between them as they shifted from friends to more.

For an entire year, they kept their relationship a secret from everyone in the family except Millie, because that would have been unfair. She was part of their little trio, and even though she was younger, they never made her feel left out. Not that Millie would allow that. His sister had been indifferent about the shift in Neel and Asha's friendship, though she would poke at Neel by loudly telling Asha, in his presence, that Asha could do better.

As for their parents and the ba, Neel and Asha weren't sure of their reaction. The two of them were young and had a lot of pressure to deliver on their planned futures. They wanted to have something that was just for them, without any interference. They did go to proms together, but that wouldn't strike their parents as unusual—they did everything together. Once Asha left and they'd broken up, there hadn't been any point in mentioning it to anyone. To this day, Asha didn't know if anyone in the family ever suspected that she and Neel had been together. She doubted it, as there wasn't really much to tell besides a high school romance that ended. They grew into adults separately.

Who they were now was a mix of this strange intimacy of strong childhood love and memories, with these large gaps in time that made them familiar strangers.

"Your mascara is running."

She flipped down the visor to look in the mirror. "It better not be. I spent too much money to make sure it's waterproof."

"Made you look," Neel said.

"Jerk." She snapped the visor back in place.

"At least you stopped sneezing." He adjusted the seat so he could stretch out his long legs.

"Do not fall asleep." Neel could close his eyes and slip into a nap at will. It was a talent he inherited from Mimi. The story went that when he was a baby, Mimi wasn't allowed to drive him around to lull him because they worried that his grandmother would also doze off behind the wheel.

"Join me." He held out his hand. "This is the best weather for resting the eyes."

"It's eleven in the morning." Asha was tempted to take his hand but didn't want to give in to the intimacy of it. "I bet you just woke up."

"If there was a rule about how many hours need to pass between sleep and nap, you would know." He closed his eyes and crossed his arms over his chest.

She turned away from him and stared through the windshield. It was coming down hard, and the brightness of the cypress trees was muted in the gray. She should start the car and drive them back to Goldfield. He must have walked down, since his truck was nowhere in sight. Yet she sat and listened to the rain pelt down on the roof of the sedan. Here, her worries seemed far away, and the car protected her from the outside. If she were a different type of person, she would start the car and drive off—not anywhere in particular, just away. And Neel would join her, wouldn't make her turn around or face her responsibilities. His only demand would be lunch.

But she was Leela's blood. There was no avoidance, especially not for the hard things.

Yesterday afternoon, she'd gone to an acupuncture session, not in San Francisco but in Sonoma, to balance her olfactory qi. As uncomfortable as it had been, she'd felt better for a little while, not that she'd magically recovered. While she appreciated these attempts, with every trial and failure was evidence that her loss was likely permanent.

Meanwhile, Neel dozed next to her as if he had no care in the world. She envied him. To be able to relax whenever and wherever was such a foreign concept. Asha had never questioned that her way was the right way, to always be doing, striving, moving. But as she sat in this car, surrounded by a downpour, she was the one with a racing mind, a heavy chest, and tight shoulders, while he slept.

Asha poked his shoulder. "It doesn't bother you to not have a career?"

He didn't open his eyes, but she noticed the corded muscles of his neck flex. "What makes you think I don't?"

"You're not at DHG, and from what I hear, you don't have an official role at Goldfield." Mimi had mentioned that he helped wherever he was needed.

He ignored her.

"How badly did you mess up?"

He opened one eye, then shrugged and closed it. "You always assume the worst about me. How's the air up there on your high horse?"

Asha ignored his comment, because soon she was going to be the one without a career of her own. "I'm just making conversation."

"More like picking a fight."

"Right, and you don't do that." If she annoyed him, Neel would shut down instead of taking the bait. With Millie, he would walk away. When it came to conflict, he never entered the fray, always stayed on the perimeter.

"If your nose itches, scratch it," Neel said. "Don't drag me into whatever is going on in your head. I haven't been your business for a very long time."

It was rare for him to snipe back but when he did, he knew just how to land the blow. "For your information," Asha said, "it was the rational thing to do. Long distance with the time zone differences would have been impossible to manage. It was you who decided that we were no longer friends. You couldn't even bother to come to my goodbye dinner or see me off at the airport." She'd never said so in all the years in between, but it still hurt her, how he'd just stopped being a part of her life. They'd been each other's safe place, and then he dropped her, never bothered to see if she had any scars.

Asha had been anxious when she left for college in France. She had never been on her own, and at seventeen, she was going to be in another country, far away from everyone she knew and loved. A month later, she turned eighteen alone, and while everyone called to wish her happiness, she was in a café by herself with a chocolate *gâteau* as she reached that milestone. Neel had missed the day entirely, and when Millie had called, she'd said Neel was asleep and couldn't come to the phone. "Guess sleeping is more important than anything else to you."

"It's the healthiest thing you can do for your body."

She wanted to throw something at his head. The indifference in his voice when she still carried the hurt from their breakup was too much to ignore. She found a tissue box in the little cubby in between the seats, took it out, and tossed it at his face.

He caught it with one hand as it ricocheted off his forehead. "You need this more than me, especially if you start sneezing again."

"Forget it." She shouldn't have even mentioned it. They'd become so good at being acquaintances this past decade and a half, it was better to leave it all alone. Besides, there was no such thing as closure for a high school sweetheart.

"What I want to know is why are you still sitting here with the engine off, talking about the past?" Neel asked. "Aren't you all about the future and five-year plans? Isn't your motto 'going backwards means you're not moving forward'?"

One of them. Not that she would give him the satisfaction and admit it. "I forgot my glasses. It would be too hard to drive in the rain."

"You're farsighted." He kept his eyes shut and tucked his chin in to get even more comfortable.

"You think you know everything," she muttered.

They sat in the silence, and when she could feel him doze off again, she poked him. "Did you get fired on purpose to help Millie?"

He rubbed his arm and sighed. "If my sister heard you say that, she'd kick you. Besides, I already told you I didn't want to wear a tie every day; it's not my style."

"But you wore a suit last week."

"That was for a one-off meeting," he said. "And why does it matter to you anyway?" Neel went back to his relaxed form.

"Because you're wasting your potential." She knew her behavior was childish, but she was out of sorts, and he was too passive. As usual, Neel was right—she wanted to pick a fight. If only to see if he cared about how they wound up being virtual strangers.

He sat up and sighed. "Is this because of your ego? Your record is intact. When we were together, I was still considered the eventual CEO of DHG. You're in the clear."

"What are you talking about?"

"You and Millie don't exactly whisper around me," he said. "About ten years ago, when you'd come over for Mimi's weeklong 'seven parties for seventy birthdays' celebrations, I heard you talking about your list of relationships and the various business titles and accomplishments of each man you dated."

Her jaw dropped. "We were dumb twentysomethings. We didn't know anything, and the only criteria we had were good looks and some sort of a career."

"So, you've dated men without jobs since then?" Neel asked.

She turned her body to face him. "This isn't about me. I'm trying to make you see that there is more to you than aimlessness."

"Wow."

"You can't throw your life away like this just because DHG isn't an option."

There was a flicker of something in his eyes. "Project much? This doesn't have anything to do with me. You can't control what's going on with you, so you're trying to fix me."

All the anger left her. Asha swallowed the words stuck in her throat. It was all true. And because Neel was safe, she could be the worst version of herself with him, secure in the knowledge that while they weren't as close as they once were, he would still put up with her.

She could see that she'd hurt him. The echoes of what he continuously heard from his father now came from her. "I'm sorry."

"Forget it."

She sneezed.

"Bless you." He handed her the tissue box still in his hand.

She took it and turned away from him to stare through the windshield. The rain hadn't let up, but the earlier coziness was replaced with sadness and pain. At Neel's expense. He didn't deserve it.

"Do you enjoy what you're doing now?" She said it gently to make peace.

He nodded. "Very much."

She liked that. He may not want the power or the suit, but he'd found something to do that he wanted to do. "I'm glad."

Asha started the engine. Neel sat up and reached over to lay his hand on top of hers before she shifted the car into gear.

He looked at her. She could see everything on his face—frustration, sadness, and pity. The last part she didn't want or need, but she stayed quiet, not up for another round with him taking the brunt of her anger.

He squeezed her hand. "I didn't come to see you off at the airport because I couldn't say goodbye. Do you understand?"

Her heart opened in a way she hadn't allowed since she'd shut down her feelings for him all those years ago.

"I just couldn't say goodbye," he whispered.

She nodded. He removed his hand and fastened his seat belt.

His words stayed between them even as Asha performed the basic function of driving them up to Goldfield. She stopped next to his truck, and without a word, Neel got out and closed the door behind him. She watched as he walked into the building. He didn't look back.

CHAPTER SEVENTEEN

Wood. Asha closed her eyes and focused. She was on the narrow path near the wide bed of blue sage on the upper slope of Sonanum. Leela was in the distance, bent over, likely pinching deadheads, plucking off dried leaves, and giving love to her precious plants. It was a cool morning, but the early-spring sun was already warm at the back of her neck.

She and Leela had developed a morning routine. They would meet at Sonanum. Leela would bring a thermos of cha, Asha would pick up something from the bakery, and they would spend a few hours gardening. Like when she was young, it was the two of them starting their day together. At least Leela didn't have to keep too close an eye on Asha anymore, who was now tall enough to be spotted over the two- to three-foot-high sages.

She relaxed and tried not to force it, merely stayed still. A slight breeze fluttered the leaves, and there it was again. Wood and more—musk, earth. She put her hand on her belly to keep calm, because in her excitement Asha didn't want to lose the layers she sensed. Focused, she kept her breath normal. Sweetness. She grinned. Four different scents that gave dimension to what was originally just herbaceous. It was brief, and had she not concentrated she would have missed it, but she hadn't imagined it. It had been real.

She wrapped her arms around herself and squeezed to mark this moment of happiness. Instead of running to Leela to share her progress, Asha kept it to herself. For the first time in months, she had hope. It could come back. All of it. Then she could go back to who she was.

Neel had been right. It was Asha who was aimless. The security of her job in Paris was merely coating. No one said it aloud, but everyone knew there was no such thing as a perfumer without a nose. She knelt on the path, surrounded on two sides by rows of sage. Elated, she ran her fingers over the leathery leaves and reveled in their hardiness.

Sage thrived in drought conditions, preferred to be left alone to bask in the sun. She was beginning to appreciate the plants she'd grown up around but had long forgotten in the businesses of life. With her hands in the earth, she patted around the roots and pruned stems to give them enough space to flourish.

Home.

The word caught her by surprise. Napa Valley was always a place that she was from. Paris was where she lived. Home had never been a sense of place or feeling. Sonanum was the closest to what home felt like for Asha. It wasn't a physical structure or a somewhere she lay her head at night. This was where she could simply be herself. To her parents, she was Asha, which meant hope. She was the future. To her grandparents and others in the wider family, she was Poppy, a childhood nickname that would always keep her in the past. Here in this garden, she didn't have to be either.

An hour later, she and Leela walked among the wildflower beds with Leela inspecting the condition of the area. Organized chaos was Leela's vision for this section, and Asha knew that in a few months when in full bloom, it would be spectacular. The hotel guests would wander through and take pictures. Little kids would hide and peek their heads out among the tall stems. Her chest loosened, and she could breathe more fully.

"You've been smiling all morning," Leela said.

Asha hugged her from the side. "It's a beautiful day and I love it here."

Leela patted her hand and moved away. "That's nice. I'm worried, beta. We've been working to get you back in shape for a week and a half. We've tried so many things. I just wish something was working. We're running out of time."

Heaviness rose in Asha's chest. "I have a few more weeks left before I have to go back." She was about to tell Leela about what had happened to her by the blue sage, but her grandmother cut her off.

"We don't have a few weeks." Leela removed her hat and played with the green silk ribbon. The strands of her gray hair lifted as they caught the wind. "I was confident that your sense would fully recover in a few days, a week at the most. Your mother and I have been through all the advice, spoken to experts."

"I didn't realize it was weighing so much on you." Asha knew that her career was important to Leela and her mom, but she hadn't wanted them to carry the stress on her behalf. "It's going to be okay. It may take more time, but I believe I'll get my abilities back. If I lose my job, I can—"

"You will not," Leela said. "No negative talk about that. You've worked too hard."

"I'm being pragmatic," Asha said. "And it's not like I can't do other things. I'm a chemist. I can work in essences and synthetics, break them down and deconstruct."

Leela patted Asha's cheek. "You're a perfumer. That is all you've ever wanted. We will keep trying."

"In the blue sage, I—"

"This is a lovely sight." Asha's father came toward them on the path.

He was dressed in his customary suit and tie, this one gray with a pink shirt. His hair was thick and brushed back with gel, face clean shaven. Like Asha, he rarely strayed from his schedule.

"Sanjay," Leela said. "We agreed to meet in your office."

"It's a lovely morning, Mom. I had a break, so I came for a stroll."

"Poppy." Leela touched her arm. "I need to talk to your father. We're done here for the day, so go up to the hotel or home."

"What's going on?" Asha didn't understand the tension between her grandmother and father. They'd always had a good relationship.

"We'll talk later. Go."

"Asha is not a child," Sanjay said. "Even though she plays with flowers and oils all day, she has a basic understanding of business."

"*She* is right here," Asha said. "And I'm a scientist and an artist. I don't 'play' with flowers."

"Now is not the time." Leela stepped forward. "Poppy, don't speak to your father like that. Sanjay, I will see you in your office."

Asha was taken aback that her grandmother had reprimanded her like a badly behaved child. She reined in her irritation and spoke calmly. "He's right, ba. I'm not a five-year-old that needs to be sent to her room so the grown-ups can talk. Tell me what is going on."

Both looked at her. Then she saw Leela's shoulders sag and her father shrug.

"I don't understand why this is an issue," Sanjay said. "It isn't as if Asha is going to mind. We are mowing down Sonanum."

It was the last thing she expected to hear. "I'm sorry. What?"

He turned around to survey the area. "My mother has finally agreed to give this land back to Goldfield. I've had long-standing plans to repurpose it."

Asha stared at his back and then beyond to the flowers that were just coming to bloom, the plants that were soaking up the sun for energy to grow. In the distance, the trees stood like centurions guarding it all. "This doesn't make sense." She looked at her grandmother. "What is he talking about?"

Leela clasped her hands together. "It is time, Poppy beta. This garden is too much for me to tend to regularly."

"So? It's not like you need to do it alone," Asha said. "Obviously, the size and scale of the garden means it hasn't been a one-person job for a long time. There's an irrigation system and a landscaping team to oversee the big work."

"At an expense," her father said.

Leela put a hand on Asha's arm. "Even with the help, this place has always been mine to care for, you know that. It's my vocation—apart from raising you, Sonanum has brought me joy and fulfillment. It's hard on me to know I can't make it out here every day."

"But you have been, with me. All week." Panic rose, and she tried to keep her voice tempered.

"For you. To help you." Leela took Asha's hands. "Once you've recovered, you'll go back to where you're meant to be. This will all be in the past."

Asha pulled her hands away and faced her father. In the distance, Goldfield glimmered in the sun. "No. I can't accept it. Won't. It's your doing. You want this back from her, from us."

He put his hands in his pockets. "Think what you like. This land is part of Goldfield."

"It was a gift from dada to ba," Asha said, then pointed at Leela. "You're taking it back."

"I offered it," Leela said.

Asha shook her head, shocked by what she heard. "I don't believe you. This is your happy place. You love it here. Did he pressure you?"

"I told you it is what I've decided," Leela said. "You may not like it, but it's done."

Her grandmother's tone meant there was no more discussion. Except Asha couldn't let it go. "This is sixty years of labor. It was your wedding gift from your husband." She pointed at her father. "From your dad. You can't destroy it."

Leela put her hand on Asha's shoulder. "Don't blame him. My son should have listened to me and waited in his office and not disclosed it so bluntly. However, it is settled. Sanjay, you and I will go have that meeting."

In shock, Asha stood as they walked away, then called out, "How long before the bulldozers arrive?"

"That's what your father and I are sorting out."

Sanjay led Leela toward the row of cypress trees.

Asha stared at their backs as they grew small in the distance. Stunned, she stayed rooted. Over to the right, she could see the blue sage in its glory. Butterflies and hummingbirds flitted near the blue-purple flowers. She closed her eyes at the memory of the layers she'd finally been able to identify. A bitter laugh rose in her throat. Just when she rediscovered her love for this place, it was going to be taken away.

It may have been her grandmother's decision, but she knew her father had somehow persuaded Leela, appealed to her generosity and gentle heart. Whatever Asha felt for her father, and usually it was indifference, now morphed into hate and resentment. She glanced at the looming hotel on the hilltop.

For Sanjay Patel, it was only Goldfield that mattered to the sacrifice of all, including his own mother's happiness. She would never forgive him for taking this away from Leela.

CHAPTER EIGHTEEN

An hour later, after walking the perimeter of the garden, Asha sat on the stone bench under the shade of an old weeping willow in the far corner of Sonanum that was designed for picnics, napping, or relaxing with a book. It was in a clearing, and when she was little, Mimi and Leela would send the three children up here to play so they could be seen but not in the way. The pond water before her was still as she considered the idea of this place being plowed through. Concrete didn't belong here. The soil was rich and fertile. It was cultivated for life to grow and thrive, not heads in beds.

Her empty stomach burned, not with hunger but anger. How much was enough for her father's ego to be satiated? This place was so full of happy memories of her childhood. She'd been free here, honed her superpower, basked in the security and contentment of friendships and the love of her grandmothers.

In middle school, Asha wanted ducks in this pond. She'd waged an all-out campaign against her resistant grandmother. She drew out a presentation on printer paper with visuals, then added a three-page research report cataloging all the reasons they should have ducks. Finally, she added a contract that made her responsible for their care. In a rare victory, Leela relented.

"Poppy?" Neel walked up to her.

She didn't look at him. "Do you remember when I asked you to get rid of the ducks?"

Neel sat next to her. "It took the whole summer," he said, "and I learned basic engineering skills for you. Leela was so mad at the wire fence I built to cage them in."

"We tried so many things."

Neel leaned back on his hands. "You'd signed a contract in colored pencil. There was no way Leela ba was letting you out of it."

She smiled. "I didn't know ducks were so mean and violent."

"Didn't come up at all in the research?"

Asha looked at him and scrunched her nose. "I only added what would serve my cause."

"Figures." He faced the water. "The three of us pooled all of our birthday money and savings to buy those scary black swan decoys."

"You thought Tilly would chase them away," Asha added.

"She preferred to nap near the water's edge instead," Neel said.

"She was a good dog."

"The best."

The chocolate Lab had been Neel's first dog. His dad had believed taking care of a puppy would teach him responsibility and commitment. For Neel to understand that he wasn't only a product of privilege provided by his parents but that he had an obligation to work in service to others. What Kirit uncle hadn't counted on was that caring for Tilly didn't require any sacrifice and was no burden. Neel was always at his best, Asha realized, when he was taking care of others.

Neel sat with her for a few minutes. "Leela told me to come find you."

"The group chat must be blowing up." It still gnawed at her that she wasn't included in it.

"Everyone is worried about you."

"And you drew the short straw." Asha clenched her jaw and pressed her lips together at the thought that all this would be lost. "Is this really happening?"

"I know it's hard to think about."

"When did Leela decide?"

"They started talking about it a few years ago." He cleared his throat. "Your dad wanted to expand Goldfield. A few boutique luxury cottages for guests who wanted privacy and anonymity. Leela told him this year would be the last spring. There's talk of breaking it down at the start of summer."

She stood and paced. "Why the summer? Can't he wait until fall?"

Neel shrugged his shoulders. "There's some financial pressure."

She turned to look at him. "More. That's all he wants. He won't be happy until Goldfield is all there is." Growth. Greed. Goldfield. Her father's drive was going to take away the place Asha hadn't known she loved so much until now. And she would lose it just like she'd lost everything else. "He wore her down."

"I'm not sure how it played out between them," Neel said. "But nobody pressures Leela ba into doing something she doesn't want."

Asha shrugged. "I got her to add ducks."

"And you were the one who learned the lesson." Neel sat up and clasped his hands. "I was the one who paid the price, by the way. Those suckers were stubborn and mean. I still hate them. Hate all ducks."

"Did anyone even think about telling me?" Asha said. "I talk to my mom, Leela, and Mimi weekly. Millie and I text. No one thought to mention it?"

"It was a business decision," Neel said.

She wanted to lash out, except this wasn't his fault and she'd already made that mistake with Neel. Asha clenched her fist. "And that doesn't have anything to do with me. You're looped in. Leela and my dad are talking right now. Everyone here knew. Except me." Anger turned to hurt. "I don't really have a place here, do I?"

"Poppy."

She faced the pond, her back to him, and crossed her arms as if to keep all the pain inside. She needed to let it go and accept it. Her life was in Paris; it was fine that she'd been left out of the day-to-day. Their lives had gone on here without her. "Why did it take three years? Why wasn't it all gutted back when he had the idea?"

Neel stood and joined her. "It was all set to go, and then the hotel sector took a big hit with the pandemic. You know how tough it was when travel stopped. Unoccupied rooms cost money each night they sit empty. Goldfield wasn't immune. There was no income, and your dad had to put it all on hold."

"If it wasn't for that," Asha said, "this wouldn't have even been here for me to see it again."

"I know it's a shock," Neel said.

"No one told me!" She whirled on him and banged his chest with her fists. "You knew how much I loved this place."

"When we were kids, Poppy." He grabbed her wrists and held her still. "And it wasn't like we talked or texted."

"I guess that makes it okay, then." Asha pulled out of his grasp and regretted her outburst. She was hurt and mad.

"That's not what I said."

The rational side of her knew it wasn't his fault. But she wasn't feeling generous. "Was this some kind of payback because I left?" She couldn't stop poking at him. Mainly because there was no one else who would put up with it.

"Stop putting words in my mouth." He said it sharply. Neel rarely raised his voice and only when he was furious. "You had a plan and you stuck with it. And this isn't about you and me."

She forced a few breaths to calm down, then hugged herself.

Neel ran his hands over his face. "How could you think I would intentionally hurt you like this? Honestly, I didn't think you'd care. It wasn't like you were ever coming back here except for flyby visits. And

114

whenever you were here, it was for a wedding or some special occasion, and you never came by this place."

"You're right." If Asha hadn't lost her sense of smell, would she have come back? Would the loss of the garden have mattered as much? "I took it for granted that Sonanum would always be here." Just like she thought her family would still consider her as part of them.

"Not everything lasts."

"You know what's funny?" she said. "A few hours ago, I was strolling through the sages, and I could smell again, more than I've been able to since I lost it."

He turned around. "It's back?"

She shook her head. "Not all of it, but I can feel myself recovering. I thought, if I spend more time here, keep up with the daily visits with Leela, that maybe in time I could be Super Nose again."

"Did you tell Leela?"

"I was going to before Dad came down and, well, I'm sure they filled you in on the rest."

He nodded. "Tell her."

"Would that change anything?" She sat on the bench and stretched her legs out in front of her. The black denim she was wearing was uncomfortable as the temperature rose. "They're still going to destroy this garden. For cottages."

"It could make a difference," he said. "I don't know if expansion is still in the works. This land itself is valuable."

She gave him a questioning look.

He shrugged. "He's had a few offers to buy this plot outright."

Asha shook her head. "He would never sell. It's part of Goldfield. Dada owned all of this. It's his legacy." It would be a shame on her father to make the hotel grounds smaller. His ego could never handle it.

"Recovery is tough," Neel said. "DHG divested a few hotels to stay right side up. Goldfield's operating costs are high."

She looked closely at him. "For someone who doesn't want to do the whole suit-and-tie thing, you seem to have a pretty good grasp of all of this."

Neel sat next to her, leaned in. "I grew up around this. I'm not dumb."

He was so close she could feel his breath as he spoke. "I never said you were."

"Right, just lazy, unambitious, and aimless."

She looked into his dark-brown eyes. Those words hurt him. They were his father's, and he carried them close. Asha put her hand on his chest. "I'm sorry if I ever made you feel that way. I've been the stupid one."

He cupped his hand over hers to hold it against him and gave a sly wink. "I won't tell Mimi you used a rude word."

The mood shifted. He was no longer the boy who'd once chased away ducks for her, and she didn't know who he'd become. But her heart recognized him. If she inched closer, she could kiss him and see who he was to her here in this moment.

It was Neel who leaned away and let go of her hand. "You ready to head back? Otherwise, they'll send a search party for both of us."

Asha cleared her throat, embarrassed by what she'd been about to do. She nodded as if to shake off the rejection. She and Neel had been over for a long time. As everyone had reminded her over and over again, her life was in Paris now.

CHAPTER NINETEEN

Tea was more tactile than the way a complex fragrance came together. With perfumes, the formulas were rigid, the ratio exact. There could be upward of a hundred ingredients, and precision mattered. Then there was a cost—using a more expensive natural ingredient meant the price had to be adjusted for the end customer.

Not that tea couldn't be as indulgent. The most expensive in the world had a price of over $1 million per kilogram, and its history dated back to the Ming Dynasty. That wasn't what she was going for in her parents' kitchen. The ingredients she'd picked up from a local supplier were simple. To create her own blends, she needed a good base of black and green.

After a morning alone in Sonanum, Asha was back in the kitchen playing with ingredients. It had become another ritual of sorts, from the garden to her tea. She'd bring back fresh herbs and flower petals, some to dry, others to use fresh. Then with her notebook at her side, she'd experiment. Now that her sense was more awake, her blends were richer, had more depth than a week ago.

Asha hadn't spoken to her grandmother since she'd learned about the plan to repurpose the garden. Being left out of major family decisions made her revert to her solitary life. She was still here, but it was best to keep everyone at arm's length. She reminded herself that she'd be going back to her life in France in a few weeks.

Leela hadn't reached out to Asha either. It had been three days, when she'd gotten used to seeing her grandmother every morning. Her mom would come and go, but they hadn't spent any time together except for a few comments about who would be where for dinner. The influencer wedding was coming up, and Sapna worked long hours to secure as much publicity as possible to highlight the hotel. As for her dad, Asha hadn't sought him out, preferred to keep her distance. There was no point in talking to him anyway—she'd never held any sway with her father. Millie was always working and rarely texted back. And Neel. They passed each other in the hallway, but besides a smile or a wave, they kept their distance too. It was best to stop being so open with him. He'd pulled away from her when she'd leaned in, which was the right thing to do. Everyone had a life, places to be.

Asha focused on the task in front of her. Bowls with Assam, cardamom pods, rose petals, and chips of cinnamon stick were gathered on the counter. She'd also picked fresh tulsi leaves from the herb garden in the backyard. The seeds had been brought over from Gujarat decades ago, and the original plants still thrived in Sonanum, here, at the cottage, and in San Francisco, where Neel's parents lived. The minty fragrance was strong, and the taste sharp and sweet.

Asha scanned notes from yesterday's experiment. She'd worked on a green tea with dried ginger—it needed something more, but her creative well had run dry on that one. Today, she'd wanted to make a fragrant masala blend.

"What's all this?" Sapna unwrapped her silk scarf and folded it before placing it on her Kate Spade handbag.

"Tea."

Her mother leaned down to sniff the rose petals. "It's always cha in this house. Your father, Leela, and Mimi prefer it over loose tea or bags."

"What about you?"

"Oh, you know me," Sapna said. "I can make do with Lipton." Her mother put others' wants and needs before hers to keep up with the archaic notion of a servile wife and daughter-in-law. It still irritated Asha, because it was always in the small domestic things that this showed up. In other areas of Sapna's life, she was vocal and willful. Her mother expressed opinions, led teams, and ran an entire department while sitting on the board of the local visitors' bureau and volunteering for community activities.

Asha didn't want to argue, so instead of pointing out the shiny espresso/latte maker on the counter by the sink her mother often used, she asked if Sapna wanted to try a blend.

"If you're doing an iced version, I'm happy to try. It's a warm day."

The composition would have to be adjusted, but Asha decided to go in that direction. There was something freeing about being able to change course on a whim. There was no brief here, no client to please. It was just her, and she could go where inspiration led.

"Are you doing okay? I know you were upset about Sonanum."

"It's been a few days."

"Leela checked in last night to see how you were. I told her you'd gone to bed early."

Asha added fourteen grams of Assam into a clean bowl. "Group chat?" It was convenient that she wasn't included in there so they could all talk about her instead of to her.

"No." Sapna donned an apron and started pulling ingredients out of the refrigerator, though Asha didn't know what she planned to make. "She called me to check on you."

"She could have reached out to me."

"She's worried that you are taking this too hard," her mother offered. "I told her that it was because you didn't know, but you'll come to terms with it."

"Will I?"

"There is no point in getting caught up in all the family drama," Sapna said.

Asha bit the inside of her cheek. Code for *Stay out of it*. "Is that why you never mentioned it in any of our calls?" She didn't want to sound petulant but couldn't stop herself from asking.

"It's about Goldfield. You know that the hotel will never be your problem."

"Because it's not my place." Even though it would be her legacy eventually, passed down from her father the way his father had turned it over to Sanjay.

"You have the talent and the tenacity to do more." Her mom expanded her arms out. "Live a bigger life."

Which was beginning to feel more like an obligation, an expectation.

"So tell me, what is the next trend in fragrances? I really hope it's a return of the classics. I adore Hermès Twilly—it reminds me of the floral surge in the nineties."

Asha picked and weighed cinnamon sticks that were in various shapes and sizes to see how much would work. "It's more about ingredients right now. Vegan, sustainable."

"I hope they don't sacrifice the halo."

Her mother had read just enough about Asha's industry to throw in jargon here and there. She liked the idea of perfumery, the romance of it. The books she'd given Asha over the years were about the aesthetics, tradition, and elitism. It wasn't until a few years ago that Asha had become more aware of the industry's impact on the environment. She wasn't in the mood to educate her mom about it, so she changed the subject. "Jaya auntie called. She wants to meet me in Calistoga, spend a weekend at a spa."

"I'm surprised." Sapna poured herself a glass of water from the filtered pitcher on the counter. "She's always talking about how busy she is with DHG. More like bragging disguised as complaints, even though they had to downsize and sell off quite a few hotels in their portfolio."

"We haven't spent much time together over the years. I called them when I was with Millie in San Francisco, to say hi," Asha said. "She wants to catch up."

"I'm sure you two will enjoy yourselves."

The hurt in her voice was evident. "You should come too," Asha offered. "And I'll see if Millie can spare some time away from her work and life."

"My schedule is packed right now," Sapna said. "If you do something after the wedding, I can make it. Unless you have to go back to work earlier."

Her shoulders stiffened. Most mothers would be glad to have their daughter spend an extended holiday with them; hers couldn't wait for Asha to go. "I'm in no hurry." She realized that was true. Over a week into her stay, Asha was finally decompressing, and the idea of going back to fight for her tenuous place at IFF wasn't so urgent in this moment.

"I'm glad IFF doesn't know about your nose issues." Sapna took out vegetables from the crisper and began chopping cucumbers on the counter near the sink. "You're in such a competitive arena, it could be risky to have them doubt your abilities. Are you seeing any progress?"

"A little." Asha tasted each different petal to see what would work.

Sapna stopped what she was doing and came over. "That is amazing news. Tell me everything. How much of it has come back? Can you pick up the layers in these ingredients?"

Asha sighed and stopped what she was working on. "It's a work in progress. Can we leave it alone?"

"But if you're recovering, we have to do more, take aggressive measures." Sapna grabbed her phone from her purse. "I need to text Leela and see what our next steps should be."

"Don't," Asha called out.

"This isn't something to take in stride, Asha. Your sense is returning. We must encourage it."

Asha closed her eyes and regretted saying anything. Her mother was already typing away, and all she wanted to do was finish the blend and see how it would work as an iced tea.

"Hello, family." Sanjay held his arms wide as he entered the kitchen. "My wife and my daughter cooking. This is a nice sight to see."

"You're home early." Sapna wiped her hands on a towel and poured her husband a glass of water. It was a tradition instilled in the women of the family by Leela and Mimi to their daughters-in-law. As much as her parents were Westernized, having been born in the United States, some rituals survived.

"How is this smell business going? Are you trying another remedy?"

The tea steeped in a long glass of filtered water. She'd done it loose and planned to strain it after it brewed in the room-temperature water. She glanced up at her father. He'd removed his suit jacket, then sat at the small table, phone in hand.

"Not exactly," Asha said.

Sapna had finished fixing a kachumber of diced tomatoes, red onion, cucumber, and cilantro. Asha knew it would be dressed in lemon, salt, and pepper right before being served with their meal.

"I had an idea today," Sanjay said. "You're spending your days doing nothing. But if you don't get your smell back, you'll need to find a different path, and I can help."

Asha stared at the glass of browning liquid. It had taken a week and a half for someone to mention what came next. But there would be no suggestion like taking a break or a gap year to figure it out.

"You could stay here. Move back."

Asha's eyes snapped to look at her dad. It was the first time she'd heard someone bring up the idea of her staying. It had never been an option, not since her mom and Leela had suggested Asha's career path as a perfumer in France. She'd been raised to leave home and had done it. The most foreign concept was that of staying.

At the same time, the idea that someone wanted her here made her happy. Except it was her father, which meant she needed to be cautious. This was unlike him. Sanjay never got involved in his daughter's life. There had to be an ulterior motive.

"Why would you even say that?" Sapna said. "She's not going to give up all she's worked for, her dream, her passion, just because she can't smell as well right now."

"Based on the hundreds of messages, the things you tried, what didn't work, it's all posted and discussed among you all," Sanjay said. "At some point, you stop and accept that this is what it is."

"I didn't realize you were so invested in my progress." Asha couldn't keep the sarcasm out of her voice.

Sanjay seemed surprised. "You are my daughter."

Asha almost laughed. "Biologically."

"I may not seem so." He waved his hand, searching for the right word. "So mixed up in all these things, but I do care about your future."

"Which is to become a master perfumer for one of the world's best fragrance companies," Sapna said. "We've come too far and it's so close. This is not about your work."

"We?" Sanjay glanced at his wife.

"Yes. Asha, Leela, and me. We. I was the one who researched summer programs. I paid for her chemistry tutors when you wouldn't. I've supported her at every step."

Asha didn't want this to turn into another argument with her in the middle. "I appreciate the thought, Dad."

"Don't even consider it," Sapna said.

"She hasn't heard my offer yet," Sanjay said. "You're here for a few more weeks, correct?"

Asha nodded but kept an eye on her mother.

"Instead of picking flowers and doing whatever this is"—he pointed to the glass—"work at the hotel. I'm shorthanded, we're busy. I can show you the beauty of Goldfield."

Her jaw dropped. Goldfield. He wanted her there when it had been something she'd been kept away from her whole life. Sanjay had left the raising of Asha to Leela and his wife, and in that, he'd made it so that the hotel, his legacy, her history, was never for his daughter. "I don't have any experience."

"That's an easy fix," Sanjay said. "You have the basics, a solid work ethic, an openness to learning, excellent organizational skills, and you finish whatever you start. Everything else is teachable."

Another surprise. She wasn't aware that her father knew her—not just what she did but who she was and how she navigated life. She couldn't believe she was considering it. "I *am* good at making a bed with hospital corners."

"Don't indulge him," Sapna said.

"Think about it." Sanjay held up both hands. "At the very least you could spend your valuable time doing something besides staring into a muddy glass of water."

Her tea had turned gray, likely too much Assam and too little rose. She would wait a few minutes before tasting.

"She would rather focus on all of the awards she'll win with all the perfumes she's going to create," Sapna said.

"So you can live vicariously," Sanjay said. "Her success is your success."

The color of the tea matched her mood.

"So what?" Sapna faced her husband. "Parents want their children to have a better life than their own."

Sanjay swept his arms around. "And this is such a bad way to live."

"What time is dinner?" Asha interrupted.

Her mother turned back to the stove. "Seven."

"I am well aware of your goals and dreams, Asha," Sanjay said. "I also know you're bored and restless. Think about it. I'll be in my office until we're ready to eat."

The air was thick with the aftermath of the words they'd exchanged. Her mother stirred the cauliflower and potato shaak that had been cooking in the pot. When Asha was a teenager, their bickering was just that—casual disagreements. But somewhere in between then and now, she'd gotten the sense that there was a deeper resentment that gave their fights a darker tone.

She grabbed two glasses and ice, then strained the tea. She handed her mom a glass. For all the issues between her and Sapna, there was still love, and she didn't want her mother to be sad.

Her mother sipped. Asha could see the grimace, but Sapna held her tongue and put the glass down. Asha took a taste, then grimaced too. "This is not good."

"You'll make it better," Sapna said.

This was yet another shock. Her mother had praised her for tea, not perfumes or anything related to her profession. They'd never been an openly affectionate family, but for some reason, Asha wanted to reach out and hug her mom to show her how much it meant. Instead, she nodded and smiled. "I have some ideas. The rose is too overpowering, needs more balance."

"I always associate rose with falooda or gulab sharbet," Sapna said. "Syrupy sweet and heavy."

Asha tapped her chin. "You're right. If I was doing a masala, rose could work with the heavy spices, but iced needs milder flavors."

"Sultana has a lot of dehydrated fruits stored in the pantry," Sapna said. "I can bring a few ingredients back."

"Or I can go forage for them," Asha said. "Thanks."

"For?"

"Just thanks."

Sapna waved her off and continued with her cooking. Asha made notes in her book. For once, her mother's presence didn't feel stressful. Yes, there was an unspoken agreement that Asha would return to Paris, but for now, it seemed as if there was a truce between them.

CHAPTER TWENTY

There were over nine hundred different types of sage in Sonanum. Her grandmother loved them, for both their fragrance and their versatility. They didn't simply live in the garden for their wild beauty like the other sections of Sonanum. This was a working garden, where Leela often cultivated different plants and used them in everything from soaps and creams to food. Because of the soil and weather in Napa Valley, these plants turned over year after year. Leela found ways to preserve them and replant what could be saved.

Having spent every morning here for the past two weeks, Asha appreciated that it was hard work to take on every season. Leela had finally joined her again this morning. As was their way, any issues between them were resolved without ever talking about them. It was assumed that time apart was for Asha to accept the way things were, and now it was the way things are.

The familiar pattern of her childhood was so ingrained that when Asha found Leela in the herbs, she said hello, knelt nearby, and helped with what needed to be done. This morning they were working around the recently planted Greek sage that would grow three feet tall. Leela wanted to ensure that there was enough spacing between the plants to allow for "elbow" room.

"This is exhausting," Asha called out to Leela, who was on the other side of the bush. "It's only been an hour, and my knees are already sore."

"Imagine if you were fifty years older." Leela stood and stretched her back with her hands supporting the lower part.

Asha nodded and sipped from her bottle of water. "I'm sure it's tiring and physically challenging, but are you sure this needs to go away?" Asha took in the vista. It was one of the most beautiful spots on earth, and standing in the middle of it made her feel more connected to not just this land but her roots. She'd spent so much of her life away that she'd forgotten what it meant to be from somewhere.

"This was always my hobby," Leela said. "I've had my hands in this soil from the time it was a patch of dirt. I love the process of it, to nurture these plants, watch them grow. This work has fulfilled and sustained me. I never felt like I was a foreigner when I stood here."

"It is your legacy."

Leela shook her head. "No. That is what your grandfather and father want for themselves. A building, land. I don't want that for me."

"But you built this. It's your life's work."

"Being a wife to a good man, raising your father, raising you, is my life's work." Leela sipped from her own water bottle. "This was only a way for me to contribute when I arrived here as a young twenty-year-old bride. The vegetables fed us during the slow periods, the flowers brought joy and beauty into our lives while we worked long days and many nights. Before you were born, we used to charge for tours to add income. Even when you were young, Sonanum served Goldfield. It wasn't simply a place of pleasure as you know it. It was my contribution to our ability to survive."

"You make it sound so fleeting," Asha said. "When I used to sit on your lap while you told me about these plants and flowers, I could hear the love in your voice for all of this."

"Well, of course," Leela said. "I was a farmer's daughter. We had a very large khetar in Nadiad, the village of my birth. We lived off it. Land provides us food and shows us the way of life. Gardening teaches us to tend, nurture, prune, till, cross-pollinate. Some plants cycle through one season, others thrive year over year, in the same soil. I was passing on those lessons. Because of this, you are now a resilient woman. The scent of this garden gave you your gift. I am thankful for it, and once you regain your nose, Sonanum will have served its purpose."

Asha always saw this place for its memories, its grandeur and beauty. Leela's perspective was in the usefulness of Sonanum. Function, not just form.

Asha worked up the courage to ask the question she'd never known the answer to. "It was here that you told me over and over again of the signature perfume I would make for you one day. Is that why you wanted me to create a scent? Did you always plan to let go of Sonanum?"

Leela turned her face to the sun with a hand on her head to keep her hat steady. "Oh, I did ask that of you, didn't I. It was so long ago, I hardly remember."

Asha had never forgotten. It was, to this day, something she wanted to do for Leela.

"Oh, Poppy. That came from my ego. It's as strong as Sanjay's, and yours. It would be lovely, though. Only you would be able to capture my eighty years on this earth in a pretty crystal bottle." Leela clapped her hands. "I used to dream about that when I was raising your father. We lived simply, but one time, your dada brought me a bottle, a real one, not a knockoff, of Chanel No. 5. I would only dab a little on, for very special occasions, and think of how this woman likely made so many others feel happy and glamorous and worldly. I suppose I must have passed those dreams on to you."

"It's something I tinkered with here and there, whenever I had time," Asha said.

Leela reached over and took Asha's hands in hers. "Of course, you *would* be so industrious. Imagine me captured in a perfume. One that speaks to the struggles of making a life in a country at a time when no one knew what we were. Our names were foreign, our skin different colors. There were so many times when we had to explain the difference between Indian American and American Indian. Then many would simplify it with insults in the form of a question—dot or feather? Many never saw us beyond our struggles."

Asha heard the pain in her grandmother's voice. Leela was the only one in the family who explicitly spoke about her experiences. When Asha was a child, she would be embarrassed that her grandmother harped on what she'd assumed were slights to let go, but it was more. Leela carried the pain of them in the core of her being. She never asked her son or granddaughter to bear the weight of her experiences, simply shared them to show what drove her to be who she was.

Base notes of birch tar and quinoline for smoke and leather. Cinnamon and pepper at the heart. Bergamot at the top. It was the first time her mind saw the components of her grandmother's fragrance so clearly. She would write it down as soon as she got to her phone. It may not be right, but it was a start.

Asha was beginning to understand her grandmother, not from a child's perspective but through adult eyes. Leela was a woman in her own right, with her own experiences. She carried scars alongside her joy. She could grasp why Leela fought so hard to preserve the culture she saw being forgotten with each generation. Asha's mom and dad cooked Gujarati food, but also Mexican, and Italian. Asha spoke Gujarati with an American accent. These things that didn't seem as important to her mattered to her grandmother. It wasn't about legacy; it was about preservation.

It was a different sort of pressure now. Not based on her grandmother's unspoken wishes but what Asha silently vowed to make happen. "I will find a way to honor you, the whole of you."

Leela patted Asha's cheek and smiled. "I can see the determination back in your eyes. My Poppy."

Asha nodded. "And I'm sorry. I should have paid more attention to all your lessons when we were kids. I'll try harder to remember how to celebrate which Hindu holiday. I'll even learn how to make proper Gujarati dal from Mimi."

Leela stepped back to tend to the plants. "I know that I could never compete with the way the world influences you children. I just want you to try. Not for me, but for you. It's important to know not only where you're going but where you came from. My parents. Me. Dada. Your parents. Buildings are not legacy; history and memories are."

She nodded. The idea of Leela not being here, with her forever, wasn't something Asha was ready to consider. "And I'm going to find a way to preserve your presence."

"I'm glad to see you've made peace." She looked in the direction of footsteps to see Sanjay approach them. He was dressed in a navy suit and tie with a sky-blue shirt.

"Here to give us a hand?" Asha asked.

Sanjay looked at his manicured nails. "Another time. Mom, where is your hat?"

"On the ground," Leela said. "My head was sweaty."

"Your scalp will burn."

"I know when I need a hat and when I don't." Leela turned away from her son and knelt to continue her work.

Asha noted the exasperation before her father's face changed back to neutral. "How's the nose coming?"

Her father wasn't a man to poke around. Asha knew he had an agenda. He'd given her time to think about his proposition, and now he wanted her answer. She shrugged. The slight stiffening in his shoulders was the only indication of his annoyance. "Not at a hundred percent yet."

"Your afternoons are free, correct?" He turned his back to face Goldfield. "You're usually wrapped up here by ten or eleven."

"I didn't think you noticed." Asha knelt to clear up the dirt around the base of the plant and give it some room. "Besides, I work on my teas in the afternoon."

"To pass the time," he said. "I need some help at the front desk."

"Why are you pressing the issue?" Until recently he'd never asked her for help with anything to do with the hotel.

Sanjay surveyed a plant and touched its leaves. "Growing up, you were always your mother's and grandmother's. You and I never spent much time together. Maybe this can be our opportunity."

"Are you dying?"

Asha heard Leela's snort.

He waved her off. "Is that the level of motivation you need to be around me?"

She felt guilty. "Of course not. I didn't mean it like that."

"A few hours in the afternoon to cover lunch and shift change between noon and four," Sanjay said. "That's all."

It was the least she could do, but it would mean taking time away from her blends. Her notebook was half-full of recipes and trials. "I don't have any experience. It might be better to get someone more seasoned."

"I need the help."

There was an openness about him in that request. He was sincere.

"I know your opinion of me is, well, what it is," Sanjay continued. "This is a small request. While you're here."

"It's always about the hotel for you," Asha added.

"Yes."

She hadn't expected that simple declaration to pierce her heart.

"It's your choice," he continued. "If you agree, I'll have someone train you tomorrow afternoon."

"I'm going to San Francisco to spend the weekend with Millie," she said.

"Monday, then." He nodded and left them.

Asha looked over at her grandmother.

"You have some time left of your vacation," Leela said. "It's only a few hours a day."

"You're on his side?"

"Poppy, there are no sides when it comes to family."

Her grandmother unknotted a few tangled branches.

Asha glanced at Goldfield. There was something in the way her father had sought her out that felt different. Yes, he likely needed a warm body, but he'd asked her, not somebody else. There had to be an agenda of some sort. If she took him up on his request, she could figure out what he really wanted from her.

CHAPTER
TWENTY-ONE

No matter the time or day, the one consistent thing about heading into San Francisco was traffic. For an hour she'd meandered the curves, the steep grades, until she hit the slow-moving stream of cars in Napa proper. Asha wasn't the best of drivers—she hadn't had much practice because she'd left within two years of getting her license and never had a car in Paris. Driving didn't come naturally to her, and she flinched and tried not to overcorrect when she perceived another vehicle passing too close to hers.

She didn't mind so much right now because she was looking forward to time with Millie for a few days, away from the emotional roil of family dynamics. That was the thing about disconnection. She'd spent her life without both feet in a single place. In Paris, her friends knew the adult version of Asha, but they only had passing knowledge of her life growing up in this area. She hadn't really been embedded in either of those spaces. That suited her. It was enough to focus on the work and keep everyone at arm's length.

This visit, because of its length, helped her see a different side to people, learning who they were now, not frozen in time a decade ago. She'd let her relationships with her family lapse, perhaps not intentionally but by way of prioritizing other things. She didn't know them, and in turn, they didn't know Asha. Not at thirty-two. Weekly conversations with her mom and grandmother couldn't make up for the time in between. Daily texts with Millie didn't cover anything more than a perfunctory check-in.

Then there was Neel. She had yet to sort him out. So much of who he had been was still a part of him. The nurturer, the way he ambled through life, the peacemaker. But there was a bite to him now. He pushed back against her attempts to characterize him. Even when they crossed paths, he kept her at a distance. His heart wasn't as open to her as it once had been. She had to wrestle with that, accept it.

Asha took the exit for Interstate 80 toward San Francisco. It was then she programmed her GPS. The streets narrowed as she drove through the Financial District. The tall buildings all around her gave her comfort, the restriction she needed as opposed to the open vineyards of Napa Valley. She found a parking garage nearby and walked a few blocks to the DHG offices. The smell from the bay a few blocks west was stronger than when she'd been here a little while ago, and she hugged the familiarity close to her.

Asha couldn't see it but knew the Ferry Building was close, standing wide along the edge of the water. She remembered the scents of this place. The briny sea, the grease from restaurant cooking, the bitter aroma from coffee shops, all mixed with a hint of sewage, made this place a part of her history.

That was before Asha had her life mapped out. Or had it been mapped out *for* her? Ever since her father had mentioned the word *choice*, she couldn't stop thinking about whether she'd decided to be a perfumer or was pressed into it. She remembered the nudging, the books, the tutors. Was the time spent in Sonanum her training ground?

She'd been exposed to little else. And while she enjoyed her career, she'd spent the last twenty-four hours wondering. Alone in the elevator up to the eighteenth floor, Asha chewed on the inside of her cheek. It shouldn't matter that maybe the idea of becoming a perfumer hadn't been hers. She didn't regret the effort or her achievements to date. She was good at what she did. Then should she even care? She knocked on Millie's open office door.

"I'm still wrapping up a few things. Can you hang?" Millie didn't look up from her computer screen.

Asha sat on the sofa. "I'll keep myself busy."

"You can always watch me work," Millie said. "See how a successful woman does it all."

"I didn't realize you were an exhibitionist." Asha grabbed the current issue of *Lodging* magazine. Her eyes glossed over at the overwhelming amount of information, so she perused the pictures.

Millie's office looked as if it could be featured in one of the articles. The fabric-covered chairs and sofa were bright yellow. Fresh flowers adorned the small round glass table in one corner. The large walnut desk where Millie worked was along the wide windows. As the sun was setting, Asha could see the Ferry Building and the Bay Bridge in the distance. "I like what you've done with the place."

"No, you don't."

"Yeah," Asha said. "It's too cold and masculine."

Millie went over to the cabinet and grabbed two crystal glasses, then poured amber liquid from a decanter.

"Did I just walk into a scene from one of Mimi's soap operas?"

Millie handed her a glass, then clinked hers against it. "Are you implying that I'm Victor Newman? If so, I'll take it. He was badass."

Asha sipped. The Scotch was smooth, and even though she knew nothing about the quality, Millie would only serve the best. "I was thinking Edward Quartermaine."

"He was never as controlling as Victor," Millie said. "We're celebrating my win today. You are now looking at the senior vice president of operations. I'm that much closer to COO and then ultimately CEO."

Asha clinked her glass again. "Congratulations. You're doing it."

"Soon you will too, now that you're getting the sniffer back."

"Group?" Asha's FOMO about the chat was strong, but her pride was stronger, and she would not ask to be added. It had become important to her that she be invited.

"Your mom started a separate group chat without the dads about how Sanjay uncle is pressuring you to work at Goldfield for the rest of your stay and is trying to get people on her side to make sure you know it's a bad idea."

Asha said nothing as she took another sip.

"My mom, of course, is saying that it would be good for you to have a backup plan and that the hotel business is technically in your blood." Millie put her glass down and crossed her hands in her lap. Her orange sleeveless sheath was elegant and showed off Millie's long, athletic legs.

"What do you think?"

Millie shrugged. "I poke at them for the entertainment as they go back and forth. But . . ."

Asha waited. Millie liked the dramatic pause, and Asha knew rushing her would only delay whatever stunner she wanted to drop.

"Neel, out of nowhere, is on our mom's side. My brother, who rarely carries his phone with him and only lurks in the group chat, actually added an opinion."

Asha hadn't realized how invested she was in hearing Neel's comments. She clutched the glass and waited, not wanting to seem too eager.

"He says, and I quote, 'It wouldn't hurt for Poppy to spend a little more time at Goldfield.'" Millie slapped the arm of the chair. "What could that mean?"

"He's making peace between the moms." Asha didn't want to read too much into his comment.

"Or . . ."

"Don't." Asha held up her hand to stop Millie from going there.

She said it anyway. "Maybe he wants to spend more time with you."

"No," Asha protested. "Anyway, it's not like I'll be working with him. He's in the back offices, and I would be at the front desk. Our paths wouldn't even cross."

Millie snorted. "You'd be in the same building."

"Don't make this a thing," Asha said. "What are we doing tonight?"

"Changing the subject won't change Neel's intentions," Millie said.

"He has none when it comes to me." Asha waved her off. "Things between us ended before we went off to college. Neither one of us has been pining away."

"Interesting phrasing. Do you have any feelings towards him?"

"Stop trying to imply something where there's nothing."

"But you've seen each other more than a few hours recently," Millie said. "Technically live together. Has he accidentally run into you in the hallway wearing a towel like he used to when you came for visits? Gross as that is, it worked on you in high school when he would casually walk through the hallway during one of our sleepovers."

Asha threw the magazine at Millie. "And Mimi would yell at him to put a shirt on."

Millie laughed. "I miss those days."

Asha nodded. There was comfort, history, and love between her and Millie that she'd never felt with her Paris friends or anyone else in her life. "I'm sorry. I should have made more of an effort to stay in touch."

They sat quietly for a few minutes before Millie said, "It wasn't all you. Yeah, you left, but we all went on with our lives. You did come back for the big things like my high school and college graduations. I came for yours."

"Then it all faded."

"But nothing disappeared," Millie said. "We can—wait, how do I keep the metaphor going? We can brighten it up? Give it more color?"

Asha shook her head. "Don't even try. But I get what you mean. So, what should I do? Give a few hours to Goldfield? It'll only get my dad's hopes up. It's not like I would eventually take over. In two weeks, I have to go back to my job. Nose or no nose, my life is there."

"If that's what you want," Millie said. "But it's not like IFF doesn't have offices and labs here in California."

Asha was taken aback. "What are you saying?"

Millie shrugged. "If you love Paris, totally fine. But if you want to be closer to home, you have that choice. Look, as someone with a Stanford MBA, figure out not just what you want but how much you're willing to invest. Each decision is about what you gain versus what you lose."

"I know that. I have two master's degrees by the way." Their one-upmanship was a game they played, never with malice or envy but to support each other's success.

"And I'm the one ordering a new tag." Millie tapped the gold metal lapel pin on her upper-right chest with her name, title, and the DHG logo.

"I need to do a value equation," Asha said.

Millie stood. "Let's go to my place, put on yoga pants, and I'll help you." She went to the small closet by the door of her office and grabbed her jacket and purse. "You drove here?"

Asha rose and jiggled her car keys.

"Go get Chinese and meet me at my apartment. Szechuan. Chili chicken. Extra spicy. I'll text you the name and address of my favorite place."

Asha gave Millie's shoulder a little nudge and quoted Mimi. "The youngest one is always the bossiest one."

"In that case, leave your suitcase in the car. I'll open my closet for you so you can wear color this weekend. I'm not walking around with the black-and-white pantomime."

"Isn't that the name of your ex-boyfriend?"

"No, it's the title of your biography that I plan to write one day," Millie said.

"Wow, taking over DHG and writing my life story. Is there anything you can't do?"

Millie grinned. "Not a damn thing."

Asha exaggeratedly rolled her eyes then. They both burst into laughter. She hadn't felt this light, this content, in a long time. The pressures, the loss of her sense—she was able to push it away. This weekend, she wanted to simply be on vacation. She planned to convince Millie to postpone the career analysis for a few days so they could spend time together as friends. She needed forty-eight hours of respite before she had to deal with all the rest.

CHAPTER
TWENTY-TWO

The sun streamed through the sheer curtains, but Asha wasn't ready to open her eyes quite yet. Last night, she and Millie had a grown-up version of their childhood sleepovers. Granted, there were no parents in the house, and Neel hadn't popped in to try to annoy them, but they'd watched movies, laughed, ate more than their stomachs could handle, and finished off two bottles of a crisp sauvignon blanc from Millie's stash.

The bed was comfortable, and the pillows were the best part. She snuggled into it, curled up on her side as she assessed her hangover. The Chinese food and the ice cream must have canceled out the tannins, because apart from grogginess, she was fine. She smiled into the pillow. It had been fun. She'd been missing that these past few years. Dinners out with colleagues, a few weekend trips to Amalfi and Athens with friends she'd made in Paris, didn't hit in the same way as spending an evening with someone who had gotten you in trouble and then sat next to you in time-out for solidarity.

"Do you need a kiss to wake up, Princess Poppy?"

Her eyes flipped open at the sound of Neel's voice, and she sat up. "What are you doing here?"

"You keep asking me that, you're going to give me a complex."

"Then stop showing up wherever I am." She pulled the comforter over herself even though she was in a borrowed San Francisco 49ers tank top.

"I could say the same." He stood with his back against the red-and-gold dresser with a T-shirt in his hand. It was then she noticed that he was wearing nothing but a pair of loose boxer shorts. His chest was sculpted, not in a gym body type way, but his arms and shoulders were toned, his belly flat, though no lines and ridges of definition. He had a smattering of hair but was not hirsute, a vocabulary word from one of Millie's text messages.

"I'm getting used to the way you keep checking me out." He grinned.

She threw a pillow at him. It fell short of reaching him and landed at the foot of the bed.

Neel picked it up. "I taught you to throw better than that. Want a do-over?"

"What are you, five?"

"If I was, I would have crawled into bed with you when I came in last night."

She remembered how the three of them shared a bed when they were very little and their families vacationed together.

"Don't you have your own place?"

"No, he doesn't." Millie came in and poked him in the side with her elbow. "He's a vagrant who mooches off his little sister."

"For your information"—Neel tugged the end of Millie's long ponytail—"I have three homes. This one, Sanjay uncle's, and the ba cottage. Being the only boy makes me everyone's favorite."

"Ugh," Millie said. "At least you're unpopular with women, being homeless and all. He hasn't had a date in over a year."

"That you know of." Neel rubbed his T-shirt over Millie's face, then left them and headed into the guest bathroom.

"Is he staying here? Did I sleep in his bed?" Asha heard the shower and didn't want to think about Neel under the hot spray. It was bad enough that her feelings for him had resurfaced. She'd been ignoring them, but she didn't want to be attracted to him on top of that. He smelled different now. The pheromones of puberty had been replaced by musk, sweat, and a touch of oud. Her eyes widened. She could smell him. Even though he wasn't in the room, his scent lingered.

Asha shook her head, got out of bed, and stood where Neel had. Millie was close, and Asha's nose recognized oleander and the sea.

"What is wrong with you?" Millie asked.

Asha cleared her head. "I just . . . I can smell your perfume, all of it. Lili Bermuda." A fragrance Asha had once deconstructed down to the molecular level. The life she thought she'd lost was slowly coming back.

"That's great." Millie grabbed her hand and squeezed.

Asha squeezed back. "Maybe. I hope. I don't want to get too ahead of myself." She'd been making do in a dull world and needed to sit with this, understand her level of recovery.

Millie straightened the bedcovers.

"Don't put it in the group chat," Asha warned. "I have to figure out what's happening, how much of it is back."

"I won't." Millie fluffed the pillows. "But you should let Leela ba know. She can help with the rest of it."

Asha smoothed down the foot of the bed. "They shot warm castor oil up my nose." Besides, she didn't want to be pushed to go back to France sooner than she planned.

Asha went to the window and looked down on the quiet street. The rows of attached houses with pretty facades reminded her of Paris. San Francisco was newer, without the wear and tear of history in the same way. "A week ago, I would have booked my flight and rushed back. But right now, I want to stay. Finish out my holiday." Her work didn't seem as urgent anymore. The loss of Guerlain wasn't as devastating.

Millie stood next to Asha. "That's not like you, soon-to-be master perfumer."

The anvil pressed down. "Yeah."

"I get that you needed a little break," Millie said. "Apparently, burnout is a thing. Neel keeps sending me books on it because I work twelve-hour days. But I love what I do, and honestly, getting out of the financial hole of the last few years has been exhilarating. I was able to prove myself not just to my dad but to me. I mean, I have a healthy ego, but it's nice to validate it."

Asha nudged Millie with her shoulder. "You never miss an opportunity to brag about yourself."

Millie nudged back. "Well, I'm not going to wait around for compliments when I can give myself the best ones. Shower and get dressed—I'll make Neel cook us breakfast, and you have a choice of cha or coffee. But I don't have a fancy espresso maker like your mom since I'm barely here and my assistant brings me whatever I want whenever I want it."

Asha stretched her body and rolled her neck as Millie headed toward the kitchen. "Must be nice."

"It is. And he's very attractive, so I make him run a lot of errands just to keep his arrogance in check." Millie headed out of the guest room. "You should get one of those."

Asha went to Millie's bedroom and looked through her closet to see what she could borrow. She'd brought up her travel bag despite Millie's orders but felt like something light and flirty instead of her minimalist monochromatic wardrobe. The Desais were a tall family, all of them, and at five ten, Millie was only a few inches shorter than Neel, so length would be an issue.

Her best friend's collection was either corporate suits or billowing dresses. All of them in vibrant colors. Asha opted for the simplest long-sleeve maxi dress. She'd swim in it, as Millie was also curvier at the bust and hips. She found a cloth belt in a paisley pattern that would work to hold up the hot-pink dress with tiny flowers embroidered around the hem of the skirt and sleeves. She decided to use Millie's master bathroom instead of going in after Neel's hot shower. She didn't want to bathe while his scent lingered in the steam.

Once back in the guest room, she put her hair up in a messy pony-tail and took a deep inhale through her nostrils. She rarely wore per-fume because she swam in scents all day, but today, she brought out a small vial of something she'd been playing with before she'd gotten sick. She dabbed a drop on her wrist and rubbed it on the other. The halo exploded in the room. Earth, honeysuckle, and a touch of sandalwood at the base. She took another sniff. It wasn't quite right. The ratio was off, a little too sweet, and the sandalwood didn't add depth the way it should. Her brain was lost in calculations as she moisturized her skin and added a touch of mascara.

There was relief on her face as she glanced in the mirror. For the first time since she'd lost her sense of smell, her jaw was relaxed and some of her frown lines faded. It was working; there was hope that she would actually be able to keep her career. She stared into her own eyes.

Yet instead of excitement, all she felt was weariness.

CHAPTER
TWENTY-THREE

Neel was dressed in jeans and a T-shirt as he whisked eggs in Millie's kitchen. His sister was at the counter stool on her laptop. Asha took in the heaviness of green peppers, a mild tang from the tomatoes, and the pungency of chopped onions.

"What are you making?" Asha poured cha for herself from the ceramic teakettle.

"I'm messing with a recipe," Neel said.

"Hope you're not hungry." Millie sipped from her mug but didn't look up from her laptop screen. "He's taking a long time to make eggs. Sometimes, scrambled with butter is just fine. Not everything has to be a culinary event."

"Mill, be more like Poppy in the mornings," Neel said. "Quiet."

Millie stuck her tongue out at her brother. Asha craned her neck to see what was cooking in the pan on the stove.

"Poppy, grab naan from the oven and butter them."

She moved around him and was close enough to put her hand on his back as she got to the stove. She had the sudden urge to touch him, to inhale his skin.

He turned and caught the look in her eyes, raised an eyebrow.

Asha cleared her throat. "Naan and eggs? Not very original."

"You've been in France too long," Neel said. "Sorry, Mademoiselle Poppy, no baguette and brie. I didn't have time to go to the boulangerie this morning."

She jabbed him with the handle of the butter knife she'd pulled out of the drawer before heading to the other side of the granite-topped island. The kitchen was bright thanks to the floor-to-ceiling windows that framed two walls of the shared living room and kitchen area. The furniture was spaced out but cozy with a deep couch, a few short, comfy chairs, and a chest that served as a coffee table. Where Millie's office was austere and intimidating, the apartment was warm and inviting. The front door was framed by abstract paintings by an artist Millie had commissioned for a few of DHG's boutique properties. Fresh flowers sat in a bright-blue vase near the console table by the entryway, with a hook for Millie's purses and a place to drop her mail and keys.

Neel scrambled the eggs in the onion-pepper mixture and brought the pan to the counter. "Ta-da! Fix your own kathi rolls. Millie, close that laptop. You know the rule."

"No electronics while eating," Millie parroted.

"That's still a thing?" Asha asked. "Mimi and Leela aren't here."

"They'd know," Millie said. "Because Neel would tell."

He winked as he handed Asha a plate.

"Unlike you two lazybones"—Millie placed a naan on her plate—"I have to finish a few things before Poppy and I head to Sausalito for shopping and lunch."

"You're going to go blind from the screens you stare at all day." Neel added the egg mixture to the top of his plated naan.

"Aww, are you worried about me, big bro?"

"Only because you're my retirement plan," Neel said.

Asha plated for herself. The eggs were in folds and glistened with butter. There were little chunks of potatoes along with the onions and peppers. She'd missed identifying them with her nose but didn't beat herself up over it. Instead, she sprinkled shredded mozzarella, then added slices of avocado and a touch of salt. Before she rolled the naan, Neel stopped her and added a dollop of green chutney and raita.

After her first bite, she silently thanked him for his skills. The fresh cilantro, the tang of lime, and a hint of garlic in the yogurt blended perfectly with the eggs and naan. The dish was too complex and shouldn't have worked, but it was delicious.

As they ate, Neel and Millie went from bickering about Millie's work to her grilling her brother about his previous night's activities, which turned into him telling her exaggerated stories about boys'-night-out shenanigans. For all their back-and-forth, there was deep love between them. As an only child, Asha had always envied their relationship. They would fight each other but were impenetrable when they joined ranks.

"My cooking not to Parisian standards, mademoiselle?"

"It's fine." She wasn't about to stroke his ego when she'd rather . . . she cleared her throat to dismiss her runaway and highly inappropriate thought. "It could be better with brie instead of basic mozzarella. From a bag, no less."

"First, that would be too oily and would throw off the fresh flavor." Neel talked as he chewed. "Second, let's see you make something. When's the last time you cooked?"

She couldn't remember. "I don't know."

He sighed. "You're staying the weekend, right? Tonight, I'm going to teach you the basics."

"Can't," Millie said. "We're having dinner at the parentals'."

"Tomorrow morning," Neel said.

"Early brunch," Asha added.

"Excuses, excuses," Neel said.

Millie finished off her breakfast and slid her plate away. It was a quirk where she couldn't have a dirty plate in front of her after she was done eating. Since she wasn't allowed to leave the table until everyone was done with the meal, she'd gotten into the habit of moving it. "If you want to spend more time with Poppy, ask her out on a date."

Asha glared at her friend. "Ignore her."

"I always do," Neel said.

Asha refused to look at him. Didn't want to see his lack of interest.

"Don't worry, you'll get your chance to spend more time with Poppy at Goldfield," Millie added.

Neel turned to Asha. "You're going to take your dad up on his offer?"

"Millie and I talked about it last night." It was likely a mistake, but it would give her a way to spend more time in Napa before she headed back to her life. Besides, she still needed to fully recover her abilities. If Millie let slip that there was more progress, her mom would drive her to the airport and shove her onto the plane.

"I convinced her," Millie said. "Poppy was like, 'But I'm on vacation,' but then reason prevailed. We're best when we're doing things, and it's not bad to have a backup plan."

"It's not permanent." Asha turned to Neel. "Don't worry, I'm not going to be a threat to your eventual takeover of Goldfield."

"Wait, what?" both said at once.

"I'm not naive." Asha scraped her plate into the trash before rinsing it off for the dishwasher. "I figured out why Neel spends more of his time there than here. He has an office at Goldfield. It makes sense, especially since he doesn't want to head up DHG. He's the best candidate and, in a way, the hotel stays in the family."

"Wow." Millie put away the phone she'd been checking. "That's a lot of dots you've connected."

"Thank you." Asha wiped her hands on a kitchen towel.

Millie started laughing. "You're so wrong. First, this one here"—she pointed to Neel—"has zero interest in the hotel business and couldn't cut it either at Goldfield or DHG. Second—"

"Knock it off, Millie." Neel shoved her phone toward her. "Go work."

"Fine, but let her in on your plans."

Asha pushed away her plate. "There's more?"

"Ignore her," Neel said. "She was raised right, but it didn't take."

"Just tell me." Asha bet the group chat was fully aware of what was happening.

"I'm working on doing something of my own." Neel took the towel from her and hung it on the stove handle.

Millie loudly cleared her throat.

"With my sister's help," Neel said, "I'm opening a brewery."

His words didn't compute. Asha's first thought was that he was a stranger. She had no idea he'd been interested in doing something on his own, or that he even wanted to do something like this. How had she missed this? How had she been *that* out of the loop? "Huh?"

"For beer," Millie called out. "He's going to make ale or lager or whatever. I'm just an investor and prefer dirty martinis, but I reviewed the plans, and as long as I turn a profit, I don't have to drink it."

He put his hands in the front pockets of his jeans. "It's fun. Going slow."

"At Goldfield?"

He shook his head. "No. I want to do it in Napa. Another option among all the wineries. I'm just using the hotel as a space to work. Apparently, there are a lot of meetings and a ton of paperwork when starting a business."

"Some even require a tie," Millie said.

"I'm currently working out the concept. There's a back area where your dad's let me set up some brews I'm testing. I want to add a restaurant as part of it."

"I have the perfect name for it too," Millie chimed in. "Beer Bros. He just hasn't agreed to it yet."

"Because it's a terrible name." He pointed to Millie. "She's better at ordering lamps and carpets than marketing."

"I don't understand," Asha said. "When did you know that this was what you wanted to do?"

He furrowed his brow. "About four years ago. A while before I left DHG."

"Fired," Millie said.

He sighed and turned his back to his sister. "I left because my dad kept telling me I needed to do better, work harder. Like a broken record of the things I heard all my life. He's still mad about it."

"So much so," Millie added, "that I'm the one who is investing in Beer Bros."

"Along with a few others," Neel added. "And stop calling it that."

"My dad?" Asha asked.

"No," Neel said. "He doesn't want to get in the middle of it and has his own financial stuff to deal with. But the ba promised to have the Nanis of Napa throw a big launch event once it's open."

"You're very far down the road."

"All I need is a location," he said. "Which is proving to be tough."

"But it'll sort itself out," Millie said. "And as lead investor, I'm going to make a killing. Especially when he adds the restaurant."

Asha could see the pride in Millie's eyes. Neel and his dad never had a good relationship, and Millie always sided with her brother even if she didn't agree with him. It's also why Leela and Mimi favored him more than the girls. They tried to make up for the friction between father and son.

"Congratulations." She was happy for him and a little sad for herself. Last night she'd basked in the idea that no matter how much time had passed, she and Millie could pick up where they'd left off.

That wasn't true for her and Neel. She'd missed the last fifteen years of his life, and that couldn't be made up.

CHAPTER
TWENTY-FOUR

Two hours into Asha's "shift" at the front desk, she thought it wasn't too bad. Kini, who had been assigned to train her, was friendly and cheerful as she answered guest questions, mainly concerning requests for late checkout with an occasional lost key card. Asha didn't have much to do except answer any phone calls, and once she'd learned how to transfer calls to reservations, room service, and housekeeping, the job was pretty easy. In between guests, Asha chatted with Kini, who had moved to the area from Texas after earning a degree in hospitality management. Kini told stories about her family, who had emigrated from Trinidad when she was three years old. She loved her job, and the time passed quickly as she talked to Asha about her ambitions, her future.

Asha thought back to her time at ISIPCA, where she got her master's in perfume making. A job at IFF was the natural next step, so there hadn't been the nervous anticipation of what came next after graduating. It was merely a shift from student to working professional. She'd been trained and had the proper skills required for a role as tester, then lab technician, before consistently moving up. Because of a lifetime of preparation, there was virtually no performance anxiety or impostor syndrome. The first time she felt unsure about something was after she'd lost her sense of smell.

She'd relied on the science and her nose to guide her, to help her succeed. When her sense was gone, she'd clung to the idea that she could power through, fake it until it all fell into place again. She realized now, though, that what had once been so devastating had become freeing. She gave a quiet laugh as she looked around the serene lobby. Never in her planned-out life had she ever imagined being behind this desk. She'd learned more about herself, her family and friends, and her skills in the last few weeks than she had in the last fifteen years.

She hadn't even written down her schedule for the week in her planner. Sonanum in the mornings, a few afternoons at Goldfield, and the rest was open to whatever came next. She might even ask Neel for that cooking lesson one evening this week, hear more about his beer-making plans.

Kini's expression was eager. "I've been going on and on; your turn. I know you're a temp, but what do you want to do?"

The question stumped Asha. She'd never been asked in that way, nor had she asked it of herself. *What do you do?* was easy—she was a chemist and a perfumer. The way Kini had framed it made her the agent of choice. She answered honestly. "I'm not sure."

Kini nodded. "That's exciting."

"Is it?"

"Hang on." Kini answered the phone.

From the sound of it, someone had a question about their bill for a past stay, and Kini efficiently looked up the reservation and then transferred the call to the accounting department.

"If you don't have a job right now, it means you can try out different things." Kini didn't miss a beat as she returned to their conversation. "See what sticks."

Except Asha had a job. Two of them. "I bet you don't believe in planners."

"Are you kidding?" Kini said. "I have so many. Right now, I'm into the Hobonichi, which is a Japanese system."

"I've been loyal to Franklin for over fifteen years."

"Wow," Kini said. "But you know what? You found the method that works for you, just like you'll find the next thing."

"Yeah." Kini's enthusiasm was contagious. "Maybe I will figure it out."

"Kini." A woman in a coral tailored skirt suit and a hotel-staff name tag rushed up to the other side of the front desk. "I just got out of a meeting, and Jennifer Kim is about to show up any minute. I need to be here to meet her. Can you please help me?"

"What do you need?"

"There's a luncheon for a board meeting that's supposed to be set up outside of the Anand meeting room, but I haven't had a chance to make sure it's all done."

"Sure, I'll go check it out. Asha, are you okay to watch the desk for a few?"

Asha was not but nodded, and Kini rushed off.

"New?" the woman asked.

"Sort of," Asha said.

"I'm Marta Malloy, director of sales and meetings." The tall woman looked Asha up and down. "Not in uniform?"

"I'm pitching in." She'd worn a white shirt and black pants, but Goldfield staff uniforms for the front desk included a black blazer, and there hadn't been a spare one for Asha.

"Marta!"

A petite brunette in UGGs, dark leggings, and a bulky neon-green sweater rushed to the front desk.

"Jennifer. How nice to see you," Marta said. "I didn't have you on my calendar until later this afternoon."

"I know." Jennifer glanced around the lobby. "I couldn't wait. I want to look around the garden and take pictures to send to Pierre

Luc. He's going to do fabulous watercolors for each table to add to the centerpiece."

"I see." Marta kept her expression blank. "We have a list of all the items on each table; I'm not sure we can spare the space for more."

Jennifer pulled off her slouchy beige hat. "Oh, you'll manage to handle it. Pierre is an incredible artist, and I knew I needed to commission some work. I mean, how could I possibly have a French country theme without art?"

"How indeed."

Asha kept her laugh in check. Marta didn't strike her as someone who could be easily pushed around, but running events meant accommodating client wishes.

Jennifer pulled out her large cell phone and tapped some keys. "Here, read this email. You'll need to send him the things he's requesting in addition to the pictures."

"I don't read French."

Jennifer waved her hand. A giant diamond gleamed in the soft light of the hotel lobby. "I'm sure you'll figure it out. Just make sure everything is sent by tomorrow. He needs as much time as possible."

"Jennifer." Marta's voice was flat. "The wedding is this weekend. With so much left to do, adding something like this with such short notice might not be possible."

"That's why I have you," Jennifer said.

Asha felt sympathy for Marta, who had clearly been dealing with brides for quite some time. "I can translate the email," she offered.

Both of them turned and acknowledged her presence.

"You can read French?" Jennifer asked.

"Je parle français," Asha said.

Jennifer clapped her hands. "I love it. I don't understand it, but you sound *très* French." She turned to Marta. "Have her help you. There! I solved your problem with the email and with not enough time."

"It doesn't work like that," Marta said.

"And I don't know anything about wedding planning," Asha added.

"My fiancé is the founder of a tech start-up, and he always says it's important to pivot." Jennifer pointed to Asha. "This is a great opportunity for you."

Asha and Marta exchanged looks.

"I have a few more appointments today and then I'm heading to Calistoga for some pampering," Jennifer said. "Let's go to the gazebo; I want to take some photos to send to Pierre Luc."

Marta mouthed *thank you* to Asha before guiding her client toward the atrium that led to the garden area.

It was interesting to be behind the front desk, Asha mused as she watched the two leave. She'd never been allowed out here when she was a kid. The lobby area smelled different now. In her memory, there had been an earth scent, more grass with a hint of sweet grape from the nearby vineyards. Now, there was musk and citrus. The fresh trees in the corners emitted a woodsy aroma that added texture to the fruitiness.

She found a notepad and pen in one of the drawers and jotted down ideas. Not a potential fragrance combination, but tea blends. A green base with berries instead of the citrus. Would a touch of *Salvia verbenaca* from Sonanum round it out? She wanted to get back to her parents' house and play around with the ratio. Lately she'd been focusing on the color, not just taste. It was important to have the tea look appealing. Her blends weren't merely medicinal; she wanted to convey calmness, relaxation, giving the leaves and herbs time to steep, brew, open up the flavors.

For the first time, Asha imagined what her life would be like if she spent most of her time focused on her tea hobby. If it maybe could turn into more than just a hobby.

No, that was ridiculous. She had a job, and now her sense of smell was returning.

The sensible thing would be to go back to Paris.

Of course it would be.

CHAPTER
TWENTY-FIVE

Two days later, Asha had become Marta's assistant and was ticking off the list of tasks she'd been assigned for the Kim-Wilson wedding. There were so many moving parts, and everyone tagged in wherever help was needed. Marta and Sapna led their staff in ways that empowered them to make decisions and simply get things done. Asha saw a different side of her mother. At Goldfield, Sapna was friendly, congenial, at times even funny, which came as a shock to Asha. Her mom didn't present herself as the head of anything but instead worked alongside the team, including ironing tablecloths or any other thing that needed to be done, from checking with vendors to confirming orders and delivery timelines.

While Sapna wasn't happy that Asha was helping at Goldfield, her mom kept it to herself and treated her like a team member. Asha mainly worked with Marta, though, and spent early afternoons in the garden mapping out how the altar would be decorated. A few hundred feet away on the lawn were forty "ten tops." She grinned at the new hotel shorthand she'd learned.

Now Asha was on her way to meet the pastry chef who was providing desserts and the croquembouche, the traditional French wedding cake. She'd attended a few weddings of friends and colleagues during her time in France and was a fan of the tower of sugar-coated, cream-filled puff pastry balls. She grinned at the thought of a "cake tasting" as she drove through the narrow, winding roads that were now becoming familiar again. Since she wasn't getting paid, her perks came in the form of food. The hotel staff had figured out Asha was Sanjay and Sapna's daughter, but they didn't treat her any different. Only teased her about how she looked like her mother but didn't resemble either parent in personality.

It was new for Asha to see herself in the context of her parents. A few of her French colleagues and friends had met Sapna, Mimi, and Leela but didn't know them well enough to see where Asha came from or how she was like or unlike them. Her father had never made it over to Paris. Not even for Asha's multiple graduation ceremonies.

Asha pulled into the parking lot and found a space near the door of the bakery. It was nondescript with elegant tiny letters in black calligraphy on the glass floor-to-ceiling window next to a black door. *Patrick's.* The window display had dainty confections in a rainbow of colors. Neel would hate it. He was the only person she'd ever known who hated cake. In any form. Asha wondered how he would handle the idea of a wedding cake when he married.

She didn't like the thought of that, or of seeing him with someone else. It was better to not wonder in that direction. She was curious, though, as to whether he'd ever fallen in love again. What they'd had was real, she didn't doubt it. But they'd been so young.

She'd had a few relationships in the last decade—Micha being the longest. Her work took priority, and eventually things just fizzled. She'd cared about the men she'd dated, some she believed she loved. But she hadn't really experienced the yearning, the angst of it all. Asha left the car. She was too practical for it, she supposed.

No grand gestures for her.

She passed another storefront attached to the bakery. Napa Valley Interiors seemed to sell only throw pillows with grapes on them, based on the window display. As she walked along the concrete sidewalk, she felt the pinch in her toes and was glad this was her last meeting before she headed back to her parents'. Leela and Mimi were cooking dinner, and Asha was looking forward to it because eating sandwiches in between work for the past few days was getting boring.

"*Bonjour*, Patrick." She'd spoken to the chef on the phone twice before meeting him in person.

"I'm so happy to meet you." He wore a white coat over dark jeans. His salt-and-pepper hair was swept back with a headband. "Marta told me you live in France, and I have to know if I'm making this—well, I can't even pronounce it—cake right. It's my first time doing something like this. Not that I'm not up for it. My husband, Leo, is an urban planner, and he mapped out measurements for the ball sizes and how many it would take to make a four-foot-high tower."

They chatted as he led her through the shop and into the kitchen. It smelled heavenly with sugar, vanilla, burned caramel, chocolate, and a mix of nuts. She could even pull apart the nutty aroma with her recovering nose.

"Voilá. Did I pronounce that right?" Patrick laughed.

"Perfect."

"I need this wedding to go absolutely perfectly," Patrick said fretfully. "Jennifer Kim is a huge lifestyle influencer. If she likes me, my business will take off from a single post on her Instagram account. Did you know she has over a hundred million followers?"

Asha was surprised—she knew this wedding was a big deal, but not *that* big a deal. "I didn't. I think my last Instagram post was over two years ago."

"My account is just for professional stuff—all my creations. Leo posts about the rest of our lives, including our two new puppies."

Patrick unlocked his phone and showed her the background photo of the couple, each holding a small chocolate Lab.

"Adorable," Asha cooed. "Don't worry, Jennifer is going to love this cake."

"And I hope Sapna too. Goldfield is a very important client. And to have an in with the Visit Napa people would be great. I hope you don't hate it."

"I won't." Asha looked at the tray of puffs. "These look fantastic."

"I'm not sure the color is right." He brought over a pan with syrup. "Should the fried balls be lighter or darker? It's hard to tell from all the pictures I've seen. But I also don't want them to be underdone or overdone. Jennifer has very discerning tastes." He picked up a puff with tongs and dipped it in the syrup before serving it on a small plate to Asha. "The syrup is warm. But it shouldn't burn."

Asha took the sticky pastry and bit into it. It was sweet and doughy and delicious. It would go perfectly with a strong Assam with cloves and cinnamon. "Amazing."

"Whew. These aren't stuffed yet. I have a few different types of cream because the bride wants the guests to experience a surprise in each puff." He moved her to another counter. "Here I'm working with vanilla, strawberry, and chocolate, but that feels too conventional."

Asha dipped a small teaspoon to taste each one. "They're really good, though."

"Yes, but they won't be mentioned when the press covers this wedding," Patrick said. "I want to wow the guests so that when *Town & Country* writes it up, they'll say, 'And the wedding cake by Patrick was the perfect ending to the dinner.'"

"I see." Though she didn't. "What about pistachio?"

"Too common."

Asha racked her brain for dessert flavors and all she could remember were the sweets she used to have with Leela. "Cardamom, sage, rose? Maybe a tea pairing?"

"Oh, interesting." Patrick tapped his chin with his index finger. "I can do something with that. Sage is a bit tricky but unique."

They spent a little more time brainstorming, then covered the logistics before Asha headed home.

She was tired, in a good way. She liked the routine of her days but also appreciated that not every afternoon was the same at Goldfield. Her task list changed, sometimes from hour to hour. She smiled as she pulled out onto the two-lane highway and headed toward her parents' house. She called Millie through the car speaker.

"What are you, fifty?" Millie said. "Anyone younger than that doesn't call without a text first." Millie didn't do hellos.

"I'm driving and took a chance," Asha said.

"I have five minutes before I need to head out for a dinner meeting with a potential new supplier."

"I had an awesome day today."

"Do you need me to send you a 'you go, girl' GIF?"

"Funny, and yes. My phone barely pings now." Her email had been silent since she was on leave, and her Paris friends didn't message her since she wasn't around to be included in their plans. Most of her friendships, she thought regretfully, were based on proximity. Her Paris friends were all from different places—some from elsewhere in France, but many from around the world. Each had their own lives outside Paris, so when they were together, it was out of wanting company and a social life. They had inside jokes, but most of their conversations, because they worked in the same sector, centered around workplace gossip.

"Fine, I'll add a meme to each morning's word of the day."

"Thank you. Anyway, I wanted to share my day with you." Like they used to when they were young and one of them got an A on a hard test. "I'm actually enjoying working in events for the hotel."

"Said no person who has done it for more than a month," Millie said.

"The Kim-Wilson wedding is a ballyhoo." Asha refused to dampen her joy.

Millie laughed. "Well done."

"I wish you were closer so you could come for dinner. Mimi is cooking."

"That sounds more fun than talking soap," Millie said.

"Come for the weekend. Stay at my parents'. And now that we're grown-ups with wheels, we can even go out and do stuff."

"Listen to me carefully," Millie said. "Stop spending all your time with the ba; you're taking on their slang. Find people our age who do not say 'wheels.'"

"Then come save me."

"I'll see what I can do," Millie said.

"Please." Asha switched lanes to let the car behind her pass.

"I'll check my calendar."

"It's okay," Asha said. "I'll ask Neel to block it out."

"I changed all my passwords," Millie said.

"He'll find a way."

"I'm not sure I like this chipper side of you," Millie grumbled. "It's annoying."

She grinned. "You should try it; it's great for your skin."

"So is water. I have to go; my rideshare is downstairs." Millie disconnected the call.

Asha stared past the headlights at the winding road and grinned. For the first time in a long time, she felt something close to contentment.

CHAPTER
TWENTY-SIX

Mimi and Leela had prepared a feast, a traditional Gujarati thali with fifteen separate items. Each bragged about their specialty, teased about the other's dish being too simple or not spicy enough. There were laughs and jokes. Asha sat at the table, surrounded by her family, with only Millie's parents and her best friend absent. It was an unfamiliar pleasantness. In Paris, it was usually Asha with a bowl or a plate at her tiny table for two near the window as she ate alone.

Tonight, she was included as the conversation flowed. Everyone shared memories of the three "kids" and the trouble they used to get into. Since Millie wasn't there, both Neel and Asha put the blame squarely on her. Her dad teased Asha about how long it took for her to learn how to check a guest in because she couldn't figure out how to use the property management software. He added that he was proud of her and that she was a hotelier by blood. She basked in the attention and the approval. Until her mom reminded Asha of the temporary nature of it all.

"It only seems like fun because it's not your permanent job," Sapna said.

"Poppy has been wonderful helping at Sonanum in the mornings," Leela chimed in. "I would say she's almost seventy-five percent recovered. In a week's time, she'll be ready to be back in the lab."

"I heard Jennifer Kim spent an hour chatting with you about your work," Sanjay said.

Asha nodded. Done with her meal, she sipped the fruity pinot noir Neel had opened. "She wanted to know how perfume gets made."

"No one is interested in how the occupancy rate is calculated," Sapna said. "The business side of hotels is the least glamorous of all careers."

A few weeks ago, Asha would have read that comment as her mother's envy, but she'd seen how Sapna enjoyed her job, was good at it. So now she saw it as an indirect way to remind Asha that her life was in Paris, not here.

Asha twirled her glass as the conversation moved on to Neel and his brewery. Her father enjoyed the samples and gave him tips on the type of menu he should explore. Sapna and Leela asked about progress, and Neel was, in his usual way, noncommittal. After dinner Asha helped clear the table, load the dishwasher, and wipe down the counters along with Sapna, then slipped out for a walk.

She used her phone flashlight to guide her through the fields until she returned to the back porch, where she'd left her glass of wine. The night was cool but not brisk as she sipped to warm her insides. She felt comfortable in the long-sleeve blue-and-yellow maxi dress she'd changed into as soon as she'd gotten home. It was a treat for herself from her shopping trip with Millie. Asha appreciated the quiet, with an occasional chirp from crickets.

"You're back."

She smiled as Neel came out on the porch. "Were you coming to look for me?" Her heart did a little somersault. "You didn't have to. I stayed on the path and managed to not get lost."

"I'm getting air. I just got back from dropping Leela and Mimi off," Neel said. "They'll drive over in the morning to pick up Mimi's car."

"Too many glasses of wine."

Neel sat next to her. "Mimi kept trying to get me to go barhopping with them."

"They're going to demand their own reserved table at the brewery."

"Mimi already asked for a designated Nanis of Napa booth," Neel said. "They said they would pay for a plaque in exchange for a permanent reservation."

"They'll be your biggest promoters." She stared out into the darkness, thinking how she wouldn't be there to see it. She would miss them and him.

His hand was next to hers as they sat side by side. If she moved hers less than an inch, their fingertips would brush. She wanted to do just that. A slight touch, then lean over and rest her head on his shoulder. He'd grown big and broad. She wanted to know what it would feel like now that he wasn't as bony as he'd been as a teenager. Maybe she would lift her head and they would lock eyes. He'd lean toward her and their lips would lightly brush. Had his taste changed in the same way as his scent?

"Don't," he said softly.

"I'm not doing anything."

"It's the expression in your eyes. Your breathing changed. I can see what you're thinking."

"And would it be such a bad thing?"

Neel leaned away. "You're going back to Paris at the end of next week."

She hated the reminder even though it was true. He was being practical when she didn't want to be. To cover her embarrassment, she took a verbal swipe at him. "I get it—you're not in the market for something casual, a vacation fling. I shouldn't be so surprised that American puritanism has seeped deep into your veins."

He raised an eyebrow.

She looked away toward the dark night.

He leaned over. "There is nothing"—his breath touched her cheek—"between us that will ever be casual."

She closed her eyes. His smell was heady, tinged with earth, ink, and soap. If she turned slightly, she could brush her lips against his. Revel in his taste. Salt, sweet, spice. Risking it, she tilted her head toward him and saw the glimmer in his eyes. It was a dare. Despite his protests, he wanted her to do exactly what she'd been thinking. Time froze. If she did what she wanted, he would respond in kind.

Except he was right. They weren't designed for a fling.

Before she could lean away, he pulled back and rose.

Asha looked away so he couldn't see the hurt in her eyes. She finished off her wine to coat her dry throat. Her body itched in frustration, so she stood and passed him to stand near the porch swing, her arms on the railing. She was grateful he stayed by the steps.

"How was your walk?"

She was glad to hear similar frustration in his voice. He wasn't immune.

He'd been her first kiss. For over a year in high school, they were boyfriend and girlfriend. But she had not been the best version of herself with Neel. She'd constantly pushed him to study more, to try more, to *be* more. It embarrassed her now.

And he'd put up with all of it. Would still tell her he loved her. Sadness at who she'd been enveloped Asha. It was only right that he was weary of her. He deserved better. She looked over toward him. "I'm sorry I made you do homework during our weekends together."

He laughed. "You made me earn every kiss and make-out session. I think my GPA went up by a point and a half that year."

"Except we never did things you wanted, like kayaking or camping," she said. "It was always on my terms."

"We were kids, Poppy. Keep it in the past." Neel started to head inside.

She stopped him. "I'm also sorry for the way I ended things." Here and there during their senior year, Neel would bring up the idea of Asha staying. At least for undergrad. There were plenty of excellent chemistry programs in California and after that she could go to ISIPCA. But that had never been the plan. A few days before her flight to France for university, she'd gone to see Neel, told him it was best they go back to being friends. She'd rehearsed it so many times that it had become a practiced speech absent of all emotion. She hadn't given him time to talk, simply said her piece and left him to accept it. She saved her tears for her eleven-hour flight to Paris.

Neel turned back. "No need. It wasn't a secret you were leaving. You'd been accepted to the Sorbonne."

"And a few safety schools here."

He shrugged.

"You wanted me to stay," Asha said.

He stepped closer. "I was a hormonal teenager."

"That's all it was?"

He kept his eyes on hers. "Wasn't it?"

She'd loved him. With her whole heart. So much so that she'd never spent any time repairing it, had let it scab over, but the wound was still deep, and if she peeled off the top layer, it would bleed. She turned her back and looked away.

He stepped up to stand next to her. "I wanted you to stay."

Her breath caught in her throat as something shifted inside. This was the closure she needed. Proof that he wasn't like everyone else who'd pushed her to leave.

They stayed still, said nothing in the silence of the night. Finally, she broke it. "I like working at the hotel. It's so different. I've never done anything other than what I do. Even summer temp jobs were in labs."

"Your dad keeps telling everyone how quickly you've picked up on things."

"And my mom tells them about when I'm going back," she said.

"You know this is all temporary." Neel put his hands in his front pockets. "You like it because it's a distraction."

"What if it's more than that?"

He didn't respond.

A need so strong rose in her that she had to swallow unexpected tears. "I don't want to leave again." She'd whispered it. It felt impossible, but it was there. She was starting to see how different her life was in Paris than how her family lived without her here. In the last weeks, she'd been less lonely than she'd been in the past ten years.

Neel took her hand. Held it. They stood side by side, and she recognized that what she felt at Sonanum was the same here, with Neel's hand in hers.

Belonging.

CHAPTER
TWENTY-SEVEN

A few hours before the Kim-Wilson midafternoon wedding ceremony, Asha attached antique-treated place cards to small padlocks with twine because the bride wanted to pay homage to the love lock bridge in Paris.

"I cannot wait until tomorrow." Kini sat next to her at the large table and placed stems of wildflowers into small mismatched bottles that would be at each place setting. "I have three days off, and I'm going to sleep through two of them."

"You say that now, but you'll find something to stay busy." Asha appreciated Kini's energy.

"Like recognizes like." Kini gave Asha a fist bump.

Asha's work relationships here felt natural even though she'd only just met everyone. Patrick regularly texted her pictures of the cake along with photos of him eye-rolling at his husband's Instagram posts. It had taken months to build rapport with her colleagues at IFF, and even then, there was more competition than camaraderie.

Perfumery was a big endeavor, but her portion was very much just her and her formulas, experiments. She consulted with other scent scientists at times, but it wasn't an environment where they joked or teased one another, or even bonded in times of stress. She wondered if it was cultural or indicative of the profession.

"We're going to miss having you around," Kini said. "I bet you're excited to get back to Paris, though. I'm planning a trip at some point."

She nodded and focused on her work. It had been a couple of nights since she'd confessed her deepest, darkest thought to Neel. It was out there, between them while they made small talk as they passed each other in her parents' house or at Goldfield. Though he never mentioned it. On the one hand, she was annoyed that he didn't press her to stay. On the other, Asha was grateful that he hadn't said anything to anyone. She'd asked Millie about conversations in the Patel-Desai group chat. The current drama was around where the Ambalal Patel Honorary Fundraiser would be hosted during the Asian American Hotel Owners Association annual conference.

"Weddings are so romantic," Kini said. "But this one isn't my thing. Too over the top. I want one of those sunset weddings on a Maui beach."

"With?"

Kini shrugged "I'm working on it, but nowhere near close to a ring. I went out with this gorgeous woman last week. I'm still swooning."

"That sounds fun." She couldn't remember the last time she'd been excited over a romantic prospect.

"I don't think she's that into me, though," Kini said. "I'm eight years younger, and she's probably looking for someone more mature."

Asha put the lock she was holding down on the worktable she and Kini shared. "You're an old soul. You're also ambitious, intelligent, and very hot. If she's not interested, it's not because of you."

"I'm going to spell it out for her using those exact words." Kini made a note in her phone. "What about you?"

Asha waved away the question and returned to tying bows of rope around the lock and place card. "That's not a priority for me right now."

"Could he help with that?"

Asha looked up to see Neel walk into the back room that served as command central for the wedding.

Kini called him over. "Neel, what are you up to?"

He shrugged. "Doing whatever Marta tells me to." The white T-shirt underneath his unbuttoned flannel stretched just enough for Asha to take notice. "What's all this?"

"Padlocks," Asha said.

"I see that," Neel said. "An interesting choice for a wedding. Does it have something to do with the couple being under permanent lock and key?"

"Wow," Kini said. "That might be the least romantic sentiment I've heard today."

"It's a reference to the Pont des Arts bridge in Paris where couples used to put their names on this." Asha held up the bronze lock. "Then they lock it to the side of the bridge. Parisians hated it. They removed over forty tons of locks because the weight compromised the bridge. They even changed the railings to make it difficult for tourists to add any."

"And that is the second-least romantic thing," Kini said. "The two of you are perfect for each other if you're looking for a practical and non-swoony relationship."

"I'm not looking." Asha said it fast.

"Appreciate the update." Neel gave a small wave and headed toward Marta, who was on the walkie-talkie giving instructions.

"I know this is all a bit much." Asha changed the subject. "But I saw the gazebo and the reception area, and it's going to be beautiful. Marta has an amazing touch."

"No, your mom did that," Kini said. "She's more of the artist, and Marta is logistics. I sent a few pics to my mom, who wants something like that for my wedding. I haven't told her about my beach plan. How about you?"

"I don't know. I haven't thought about it."

"You didn't play wedding when you were little or dream about the perfect dress?"

Asha shook her head. She and Millie usually played school or hotel, where they could badger Neel into being a bellhop so he would move the toy chest and other items from one end of the room to the other. Her parents hadn't pressed her about marriage or even relationships. Her mother and grandmother were more invested in Asha's career than her personal life. Mimi was the only one who asked about Asha's dates and wanted details of grand romances.

Asha watched Neel on the other side of the room and wondered if he thought about such things. As if he sensed her stare, he turned to look at her, his brow furrowed in question. She looked away.

CHAPTER TWENTY-EIGHT

A few days after the Kim-Wilson wedding, Asha sat at the kitchen table, tea in hand. The house was quiet, so she took the opportunity to spend time with what she thought of as her tea bible. The notebook was down to a few blank pages, as Asha had filled it with thoughts and recipes.

She had a week before her flight, and just two more shifts at Goldfield. She wanted to spend time with her blends, not with any smell therapy. The most successful recovery method proved to be Asha leaving it alone, letting the sense heal at its own pace. She would figure out how that translated to her work when she was back in Paris.

The mere thought made her want to shake her knee and bite the inside of her lip.

To brush it off, Asha tapped her pen to the open page of her notebook. She'd been playing around with various teas. She'd picked up more base like Assam, Ceylon, and Keemun and deconstructed their strength based not just on volume but also steep time. She'd made notes on how various blends worked together and, when the recipe didn't work, set about trials to improve it.

"Asha." Her mother entered the kitchen, iPad in hand. "I'm so glad you're here."

"Where else would I be on a Sunday morning?"

"Who knows?" Sapna placed the tablet on top of Asha's notebook and tapped the screen. "There are write-ups of the Kim-Wilson wedding in *Vanity Fair* and *Town & Country*."

Asha scanned the articles. While she hadn't witnessed the ceremony because she'd been wherever they needed extra hands, she'd seen Jennifer in her long lace-covered gown with flowers in her veil. The bridesmaids were in pale lavender, and groomsmen and the groom wore matching silk ties.

"The hotel looks beautiful." Asha was impressed at how well the photos captured the elegance and stature of Goldfield. Having spent more time there, she appreciated all that went into the upkeep. She'd learned that Goldfield didn't cater to tourist buses or offer deep discounts. Even as it struggled. That was one of the reasons why it had been hard to financially recover. But her father was dead set against devaluing the hotel by slashing rates.

"And look at this." Her mother increased the size to show the text. "My quote is in there."

Asha took the iPad from her mother to read closer. Overall, it was positive and full of Jennifer gushing about the perfect day, the romance, and how she was able to bring a bit of French countryside to Napa Valley. Toward the end of the piece was a quote from her mother, and Asha stopped breathing.

We were happy to give Ms. Kim the wedding of her dreams. So much so that we even had our daughter help make sure there were authentic French touches. Asha (Patel) lives in Paris, and it was serendipitous that she came for a visit just in time to help with this wedding. And our daughter knows elegance, as she is a master perfumer at IFF who creates luxury scents for Louis Vuitton and Hermès. At Goldfield, we try to not just meet our guests' expectations but exceed them.

Asha read it again in case the words were not there. Seeing it laid out like this felt icky and exploitative. Especially considering her current status at work. What was worse was disclosing the inner workings of the industry. Sure, if people looked, they'd find that IFF, Firmenich, Givaudan, and Symrise were the creators of most fragrances. But luxury brands would never go to market as such.

"Mom." Asha's voice shook. "How could you say this? It could get me into a lot of trouble at my job just to be associated with this kind of blatant promotion."

Sapna didn't seem to hear her. "I'm so happy that Goldfield is getting mentioned in these write-ups. It's going to be great for business."

"Why did you have to mention me?" Her mother had spent most of Asha's life keeping her away from Goldfield. This made no sense.

"Because you helped." Sapna began making an espresso for herself. "And because you've lived in Paris for so long and what you do is so unique, it made for a great talking point to show how we go above and beyond for our guests. It was an inspired angle, if I do say so myself."

"Except you never asked me," Asha said.

Her mother stirred the espresso with a tiny spoon. "Why should I have to? You joined the events team temporarily, and your expertise helped us pull off the best possible wedding we could based on the theme. You should be happy for this mention. Who knows? It may even help you when you go back to work."

Asha's jaw dropped at her mother's naivete. "This is so bad." She stood and paced. "It's going to be the opposite. If Celeste sees this . . . This is horrible."

"Calm down," Sapna said.

"I'm going to get fired." Asha talked aloud to herself. Nerves tingled in her whole body. She knew the rules of the industry. And the perfumer's reputation had to be built based on excellence and achievements, not self-promotion.

"Of course you're not," Sapna said. "Brands care about influencers. Even luxury ones, because they need to sell their products, and any publicity is good."

Her body shook as adrenaline-fueled panic rose in her chest. "No, it isn't. First, I'm not a master perfumer, so that's a lie. My boss is going to think I'm trying to be bigger than the company. Making it all about me." Asha counted the strikes against her. She was already dinged for being brown, because diversity in French perfumery still had a long way to go. Add to it her American origin, which was consistently looked down upon. That her fall was expected had made her rise that much harder. Now she would have to not only prove herself again but deal with the looks and aspersions of those who would assume Asha believed she was better than them.

"Calm down," Sapna said. "You're worrying for nothing. I read about the annual perfume awards, and the name of the perfumer is right there. When you win for Guerlain, your name will be mentioned along with IFF. There will be press releases."

"Why do you care so much about this?" Asha stopped and wrapped her arms around herself to stop the shaking in her voice.

"I'm your mother," Sapna said. "Your success reflects mine. I want the world for you, I always have. I want your name alongside Dominique Ropion and Patricia de Nicolaï."

"They are not household names, Mom."

"No, but they are known in your field, sought after." Sapna scanned the article again. "You're still off-balance because your nose isn't back to its full potential. You'll see. This is a good thing. The world revolves around influence. You can't buy publicity like this."

Asha couldn't listen to any of this. "Is it just in the US editions? Or are there any French blogs or any international outlets that could pick it up? You didn't call any perfume industry outlets, right?"

"Honestly, I don't understand this reaction." Sapna closed the cover before going to the espresso maker. "And no. This is for Goldfield; you're part of one quote, a mere passing mention. Not the whole story. We don't have global reach, but Jennifer has a worldwide footprint, so maybe. And even if she does post about it, she'll focus on her wedding, not you. I only hope she mentions the hotel."

"I don't want this." Asha modulated her voice. Panic and tantrums weren't going to help here even though she wanted to stomp her feet and run away. This was just like her mother. Sapna did what she believed Asha needed—it didn't matter whether her daughter wanted the same. And she never asked her daughter. That's what bothered Asha the most.

"I don't understand you," Sapna said. "When you were young, you loved that we shared this passion. We would snuggle on the sofa and rip out the fragrance strips from magazines. You would describe different elements in the scents. It was our special time together."

"Yeah, well, I can't remember the last time we hugged, much less snuggled." She couldn't keep the bitterness out of her voice. "You see me only for my career. You never once asked if this is what I want or if I even like what I do."

Sapna stopped the milk steamer and put the metal pot to rest on a hot plate. "Honestly, where is this coming from? It's all you ever talked about. From the time you ran around with that sari tied around your neck, you wanted to live in the world of smells. You and Leela spent all your time with flowers and scents. Leela still has the little mortar and pestle from when you two would mash up different petals and stems like your version of Play-Doh. That's why I bought you chemistry sets and essential oils. I read books about your interest, nurtured your passion."

"You pushed me towards becoming a perfumer." Asha stared through the glass of the french doors. "As if I had no other option."

Sapna sipped her coffee. "I know it's typical to blame the mother."

Asha shook her head. "That's not what I'm saying."

"It's what you think," Sapna said. "Except you were the one who wanted to study in Paris, to be in the heart of the industry."

Asha whirled on her mother. "How did I even learn about it? The story goes that it's all I talked about before I even turned ten. What kid knows those things?"

Sapna looked defiantly at Asha. And then, suddenly, her shoulders slouched. The fight seemed to leak out of her.

It was all too much. Asha needed to breathe, so she opened the doors and went out onto the porch. The heat and humidity were stifling, and Asha reveled in it. She was uncomfortable on the inside and glad the air matched it. Some sort of stasis. Her knee shook, and she didn't even try to still it as she sat on the porch swing.

It was over. Her career, her reputation. If her colleagues saw this piece, they would think she was trying to recover from the Guerlain fiasco with PR. Style over substance was a cultural no-no. She should have never come here.

CHAPTER
TWENTY-NINE

Asha was annoyed and surprised her mother came out to the porch. Their family never talked things out. They understood each other based on what was left unsaid. Eventually, it was expected that anger would fade, hurt would heal, and they would carry on as if nothing ever happened.

Not this time. Asha couldn't let it go. "You never asked me if I wanted any of it."

Sapna handed Asha a glass of water and sat next to her. "You were so enthusiastic and happy about your superpower. All I wanted was to nurture it."

"I was a kid," Asha said. "Not every eight-year-old becomes a veterinarian because they love animals."

"You weren't like that. It wasn't a playtime fantasy. Scents were your world; your nose was always in the air or in a box, jar, or even the compost. Every other sentence was about what you smelled. We would go to the supermarket, and you would close your eyes in the produce section to see if you could find where the strawberries were with your nose."

"That's a big jump from enjoying something to making it my life's work."

Sapna shook her head and stared out past the window boxes to the hills beyond. "Maybe it *was* my fault. I pushed you into it. When Leela told me about your potential, I realized this could be a way for you to have a big life." She gave a short laugh. "You could live beyond this small town and do things besides becoming a hotelier. I didn't want a typical career for you. I wanted you to be something other than a doctor, engineer, pharmacist, or computer scientist. You had talent to create and put your name, our name, on something different."

"There's nothing wrong with any of those careers."

Sapna nodded. "They weren't glamorous. Not to me. I wanted to give you the world. Perfumes were so exotic. You could have a steady profession and still be creative. So I worked more, saved up for French lessons and private tutors." She stared into her coffee mug. "I ruined my marriage."

Asha hadn't expected that. "What?"

Sapna shrugged. "You know why your father has never asked you to be a part of Goldfield until now? It's because we made a deal. He would leave you alone, and I would help him make the hotel into the world's best."

Asha couldn't process the revelation. She was a bargaining chip. "I don't understand."

"I didn't want you to become like him. You were supposed to take over Goldfield, but I couldn't bear that. Your father has never forgiven me."

The bickering, the underlying animosity all these years between the two of them, had been because of Asha. She stood and clutched the edge of the porch railing. "Did you ask him to stay out of my life?"

"No," Sapna said. "Only to not pressure you."

Asha stared out toward the fields and held back emotions that rose in her throat. "So if I wasn't going to be his heir, he decided to not be my father."

Sapna came to her and laid a hand on her shoulder. "I don't believe it was intentional, merely a circumstance of our choices."

"You mean yours," Asha said. "I didn't have one."

"Maybe," Sapna said. "I married young, and I know that's not enough reason, but it's the only way to explain. My parents, they had a bodega in Jackson Heights. All I saw was how hard they worked. Ten hours, seven days a week. I helped out after school, did my homework while at the counter. And every free moment, I dreamed about leaving, doing something more than what they did. My mother and father had to survive, and I wanted to live."

Asha had never heard her mom talk about her childhood this way. She'd met her maternal grandparents a few times when she was a child and remembered visiting them in their fourth-floor apartment. Sometime around Asha's time at ISIPCA they'd retired and moved back to India. "Did they force you to get married?"

Sapna smiled. "No. Not like that. I'd started modeling, saris and salwars. I was on posters in store windows and even did some catalogs. I'd always been told I was beautiful, and with those pictures I had proof. I wanted to go to Milan and Paris, be the next Christie Brinkley or Brooke Shields."

"But you married Dad instead."

Sapna nodded. "My parents didn't think it was a proper career, modeling. They started showing me boys, educated, from a good family, the right caste and all of that. They were very conservative in their view of how women should behave. I was trained to be a dutiful wife. Education and dreams weren't a priority. Marriage was the end goal. Then I met your father. He was the most handsome one of all, and he was different. He'd been born in America. He lived in California, and I had never traveled west of Michigan. I was so excited to leave the East Coast, move to this area. I'd heard all about Goldfield and how I would be marrying into history. If I couldn't go to Europe, this was the next best option, away from my crowded and noisy neighborhood."

Asha felt as if she were listening to a stranger's life. She'd never known of her mom's restricted upbringing. It wasn't how Asha was raised. "You wanted the adventure."

"I did." Sapna sat back on the swing. "I thought I was special because I was beautiful. All the aunties told me I would make a great match because of my looks." Sapna laughed. "I was nineteen when I met Sanjay."

"You didn't make your parents see what you really wanted?" Asha couldn't imagine her mother cowering to anyone. "It's not like you don't stand up for yourself."

"I was sheltered when I married your dad," Sapna said. "I hadn't quite grown into myself."

"But you resent all this, the hotel," Asha said. "This place where I grew up. Is that why you sent me away?"

"I was naive." Sapna tapped the side of her ceramic mug with her red painted nails. "It was a shock when I learned what Sanjay's and his parents' expectations were of me. They were working hoteliers. And that's what I had to become. Within a month of my marriage, my days were full. I scrubbed toilets, did laundry, so many sheets and towels. I filled in for staff who quit or called out. And I still helped Leela make dinner, cleaned the house, and saw to Sanjay and his father's comfort. My days were exhausting, the same each day. Weekdays blurred into weekends. The only rest I got was the first three months of your life. Then I had to turn you over to Leela's care so I could go back to the hotel."

Asha sat down next to her mom and offered her a sip of water.

"Thank you." Sapna gratefully accepted it. "During that time, I was so angry about my circumstances, my choices. One day, as I was leaving, you cried in my arms. Not for me but to reach for Leela. You were so small, and you wanted to be in your grandmother's arms, not mine. I knew it was irrational and not your fault, but it broke me to see that my own daughter wanted someone else to care for her. I cried all the way to the hotel. I fantasized about taking you away. The two of us would go to Europe, and I would find a way to support us." Sapna laughed again. "Can you imagine? I was so naive. Instead, I decided you would be the one who would be free. I went into your father's office and told him I didn't want his life for you. That you didn't belong here. Goldfield wouldn't be your albatross."

And you decided on a different one.

"Why perfumes?"

Sapna furrowed her brow. "You know, I don't remember. When Leela told us of your gift, I must have seen a commercial or an ad for perfumes. It was magical; the models gave off this idea of a luxurious life. I must have put it together that your sense of smell could be your way out of here."

"And you could live through me." It had always bothered her, but until now, she hadn't realized why her mom wanted to so badly.

"That's how it sounds, doesn't it?" Sapna said. "I don't think I was consciously doing that. I mean it is fun to think about, you have this incredible life. I love it when we travel, even though I know you don't always want to spend a lot of time with me."

"It's not that."

Sapna put her hand on Asha's knee. "It's okay. I haven't really been a mom to you. You will always be Leela's."

It hurt her to think that way, but Asha couldn't deny it. She always gave her grandmother more deference, more grace, more acceptance for the way Leela was. Asha had only seen her mom as someone to put up with.

"Did you ever love Dad?" Asha suddenly felt she bore the responsibility of both her parents' happiness.

"Of course." Sapna stroked Asha's hair, tucked the heavy curtain behind her ears. "I still do. That's separate from all of this."

"I don't understand," Asha said. "You said you ruined your marriage for me."

"Yes," Sapna said. "It was selfish of me to give your father an ultimatum. But he eventually accepted it, mainly because Leela sided with me. Your grandmother wanted you to do what you were meant to do with your talent. She had more sway than I did. But your dad and I made our peace. Then we fell in love. It wasn't a burst or like in the movies, at first sight." Sapna brushed out Asha's hair with her fingers, then began to pleat it in a thick braid. "We had made a commitment to be a family, to share a life, to have a child. And there was attraction between us, we started to care for each other, then at some point along the way, it became love. There was no actual aha moment."

"But you argue all the time."

"Because we're very different people," Sapna said. "You only see us when it's us three. We have our shared moments, intimacy."

"Nope." Asha covered her ears. "You don't even like each other."

"Lately, it seems that way." Sapna finished the braid and left the end untied. "That's for us to sort out."

"But it's because of me," Asha said.

"Because of me," Sapna said. "I had you when I didn't even know how to be a wife, much less a mother. When we learned of your natural talent, I thought your nose was your way out of the hotel life and it might also be a connector between us. I thought if I motivated you, helped you, took an interest, you and I would have that at least. I suppose I thought then we'd have something to talk about every week."

There was a giant lump in Asha's throat. She finally understood her mother. It was so painful to realize how much it must have hurt her mom that Asha always went to her ba first—as a child, and even when she'd come home recently, it was to the cottage first. Sapna found out about Asha's arrival via a text from Leela, not from her own daughter.

She couldn't make up for the past, but Asha could try to change their relationship going forward. "Thank you for telling me."

"I guess some things need to be said out loud."

"Do you still hate your life?"

"No. Of course not. I've lived longer as this version of me than the teenage life in Queens. This is what I know. Besides, it's easier now that I realize that I'm good at what I do. I kept my promise and helped your father grow Goldfield, and even through this financial downturn, we survived. We work hard, your father and me. The hotel is now a part of me too." Sapna stood. "Wow, I wasn't aware of how much I had to say until I sat down next to you."

Asha stood. "For what it's worth . . . it shouldn't be all on you to have a relationship with me. I will do better. I promise."

"Just be happy." Sapna clasped Asha's hands.

Asha pulled out of her mom's grasp and wrapped her arms around Sapna. It was a long-overdue hug. And for a few minutes they both stayed that way. It was only when Sapna cleared her throat that Asha let go.

"Do you want me to make you a café au lait?" she asked her mother in French.

Sapna grinned. *"Oui."*

CHAPTER THIRTY

Asha had a restless night because of all she'd learned from her mom. She felt guilt and regret, but also a closeness to her mother that came from understanding, woman to woman, instead of merely mother and daughter.

In the morning, she checked with Kini to make sure there was enough coverage. Then she sent her father a text that she was going to spend her last full week on official vacation. She couldn't go back to Goldfield, not now.

Asha didn't know how to feel about her father given what she'd learned. The realization that he'd turned away from her because she was no longer the heir to the hotel . . . it wasn't easy to accept.

What was best for her final days here was more time with Millie. They'd become close again, and she wanted to soak up as much time as possible. Her goal was to make Millie pinkie swear that they'd make an effort to stay connected, no matter how busy life got for them.

When she walked into Millie's office a few hours later, the first thing Millie said was, "Did you bring lunch?"

"I thought you had a hot assistant to do that for you," Asha teased, but held up a paper bag.

"You were on your way over," Millie said. "Josh has more important things to do. He's reviewing training modules for our general managers to make sure they're compliant with brand guidelines and DHG expectations as well."

"I passed a sushi burrito place a block from where I parked. You have a choice between satori or a salmon samba."

"Sushirrito is one of my go-to places!" Millie went over to the sofa where Asha set up their food.

"Busy day?"

"Every day," Millie said. "The group chat is buzzing with you quitting Goldfield."

"It wasn't a real job," Asha said. "I didn't even get paid."

"If you really wanted to take a vacation, why are you here instead of at the beach or in the woods, or basically anywhere else?"

"Ingrate. I want to spend more time with you."

"I'm not buying it." Millie unwrapped her burrito. "We talk every day now."

"Promise me we'll do that when I'm in Paris." Asha reached over and touched her friend's arm. "Or at least text with life stuff. I don't want us to fade away."

"We're family, dost." Millie didn't often use Gujarati. It only slipped in when she was around a lot of uncles and aunties.

"I'm also here to do another big haul from Imperial." The oldest tea shop in San Francisco was in the Ferry Building nearby.

"This is turning into an obsession."

Asha shrugged. "I'm enjoying it."

"You can do cha delivery service like the chai-wallas in India," Millie said. "Though I'm sure the French are too snobby for that."

Asha chewed on a small piece of salmon and rice. "First, I do blends, not cha. Though I'm close on a rose masala that's going to be incredible. Second, the Parisians are not snooty, they're discerning."

"I think those two words are synonyms." Millie scanned her phone.

"I don't need a ruling from the dictionary," Asha said. "Anyway, I've signed up for classes at the Palais des Thés; they have a tea sommelier program."

"That's a thing?"

Asha nodded.

Millie tapped her pointy red nail to her chin. "There *are* a lot of tea shops, and luxury tea is an interesting concept."

Asha shook her head. "It's just a hobby."

"Oh, not for you," Millie said. "I was thinking about my problem around a signature something for DHG."

Asha shook her head. "Do you do anything but work?"

"For your information, I have a date tonight."

Asha clapped. "You're just now telling me? Who?"

"Don't get so excited. My mom wants me to meet a friend's son. A suitable boy."

Asha's eyes widened. Millie hated setups, especially by parents and well-meaning family. They were worried that, left to her own devices, she would never prioritize a partner.

"The only reason I agreed is because he's a nonprofit lawyer and not a tech bro," Millie said. "And he's hot."

"There it is." Asha laughed.

Millie leaned back in her chair and patted her soft belly. "I'm stuffed." Asha loved the lime-green pantsuit Millie wore with a gold belt. Not a style she could ever pull off.

"What's his name?"

"Who cares?" Millie said. "I've only seen a photo and scanned his résumé."

"I almost kissed Neel," Asha blurted out. "Twice."

Millie sat up. "That explains it."

"What?"

"He's gone quiet in the group chat, more so than before," Millie said. "Especially if your name comes up."

"How often do you all talk about me?"

"Lately?" Millie scrolled through her phone. "You're a topic at least once every other day."

Asha picked at her food, trying to push away the left-out feelings.

"I take it you and Neel didn't . . . and ugh, I'm not finishing that thought."

"I don't know why it's so weird and complicated between him and me. We were friends and then more, and now we're people who live in the same house but spend most of our time avoiding each other. When we do talk, it's intense and all these feelings come up and he's so attractive now, I still can't get over that. And it rankles that he keeps rejecting me."

"Maybe because you don't know how to eat." Millie took in the mess Asha had made and gathered it all up to place back in the bag. "Look," she said, "I love him, and I love you, so I'm going to tell you something, and you can't ever let him know I spilled."

Asha braced herself. "Is he seeing someone?"

"No, dingus." Millie crossed her legs; the black stiletto pump dangled from her toe as she let her foot slip out of the heel. "You hurt him."

"I know," Asha said. "But it was high school, you know."

"One of the things Mimi constantly tells my dad is that while I'm the hard one, Neel is soft," Millie said. "Dad doesn't get how awesome that is. Neel has always been more sensitive than all of us. He adopts puppies he finds on the side of the road. Will turn his life inside out to be there when anyone needs him, especially if it's Mimi or Leela. He doesn't recover from dents to his heart very quickly, if at all."

"I'm so selfish."

"No," Millie said. "You just see him as one of us. As kids, we were still forming, and there were differences, but we were the same in that we did everything together. I only started noticing who my brother really is once he and my dad started having issues around DHG. I don't think their relationship will ever recover because he's caused Neel so much pain and self-doubt."

"I didn't realize things were that awful between them."

"They don't speak," Millie said. "Only spend time in the same room if it's a family gathering. That's why he didn't join us for dinner at my parents' a while back."

"And lives at my parents' house instead of here in the city."

Millie nodded. "All I'm saying is, if you want a fling or to scratch an itch with an old flame while you're here for a few more days, don't do that to Neel."

"What does it say about me that I can moan about wanting him, but I don't even know him?"

"That you've been gone too long."

Asha's throat constricted. And in a few days, she'd leave again.

Mille stood. "I have two meetings at the same time and need to pick: HVAC systems or revenue forecasts?"

"HVAC, because that sounds more boring," Asha replied.

Millie sighed. "Revenue management it is." She headed to her desk. "Go hang with my mom if you don't want to go back just yet. I'm tied up for the rest of the day."

Asha nodded. She didn't feel like any more conversations. "I'm going to spend a few hours in Imperial instead. I'll head back to Napa after so as not to crash your date." She cleaned up their trash from the coffee table. Before leaving, Asha pulled out a satchel from her tote. She'd planned to spend the evening here, but her friend had a life, and it would be best to head back to Napa.

"Millie, want me to make you a cup of tea before I go? You can try one of my blends."

Millie looked up. "What flavor?"

She sorted through a few packets. "I have Earl Grey with jasmine and vanilla or green with ginger and cinnamon."

"Which one has more caffeine?"

"I'll make you a cup of green."

Asha boiled some water in the office kitchen, then said goodbye to Millie when she dropped off her tea. She wondered how else she might make the most of her last week of vacation, with Millie so busy.

And realized, for the first time in her life, that what she actually wanted was to spend more time with her mom.

CHAPTER THIRTY-ONE

There was a strong tomato-and-cumin aroma when Asha let herself into her parents' house and made her way to the kitchen. "You're here."

Neel diced white cubes that looked like tofu at the island. "Yup. Where were you?"

"I had lunch with Millie." She dropped her tote on the counter stool. "Are you staying for dinner?"

He furrowed his brow. "It's kind of why I'm making it."

"What?"

"Mutter paneer and paratha."

She nodded. "My parents?"

"They should be home any minute."

She glanced to her right as the front door opened and both her parents came in past the hall and into the kitchen. "Neel beta, that smells heavenly."

"It's your favorite, auntie."

Sapna gave him a wide grin. "I'll set the table. How much longer?"

"Forty-five minutes," Neel said. "I have to make the dough and then the parathas while the paneer is simmering."

"Asha," Sanjay said. "Help him."

Everyone stopped what they were doing.

"What did I say?" Sanjay asked.

"I don't cook, Dad."

"Sanjay uncle," Neel said. "We don't really want to burn the kitchen down. It's probably best if Poppy sets the table."

Asha stuck her tongue out at him.

"It was a dad joke. I'll wash up, then make cocktails." Sanjay left the room.

"Lychee and pomegranate martinis," Asha called out after him. "Since we're having Mom's favorite meal, we should also have the drink she likes best."

Sapna fished out her phone. "Is it my birthday? Why are you being so sweet to me?"

"I can be nice when I put my mind to it." The fact that it was not typical for Asha to be considerate of her mom didn't sit well. She would fix it.

An hour later, her parents had changed out of their work clothes into more casual wear—a polo and khakis for her father and a short-sleeve sweater and slacks for her mother. They were seated around the table with half-finished cocktails and a fresh mutter paneer and parathas on the table.

"Buon appetito." Neel served her a ladleful. "Correction. *Bon appétit.*"

Asha helped herself to a paratha, delighting in how the ghee glistened on the wheat roti.

"We missed you at the hotel today, Asha," Sanjay said. "It was quiet, and no one's check-in was mixed up."

"I'm sure the guests were happy their room keys worked," she said. "But in all seriousness, it was fun working at the hotel. The people there are great, especially Kini, who had to fix all of my messes."

"I knew it." Her father pumped his fist. "You had it in you all along. I had given up hope, but here we are."

"What are you talking about?" Sapna said.

"Goldfield is in our daughter's blood," Sanjay said. "With more experience, she could grow into it."

"Absolutely not," her mother said. "Asha, if this is some plan to tell us you're quitting your job to work at the front desk, that's not going to happen."

Asha looked at Neel in confusion. "I don't . . . that isn't my plan."

"Maybe not now," Sanjay said. "But if your smell doesn't come back, you know there is another option. Goldfield is yours as much as it is mine."

Even though she had enjoyed her short time there, she knew it had been a mistake to give her father this opening. Goldfield was not hers, no matter what he wanted. Sanjay rose to get another drink, and her mom left the table to begin clearing up their dishes. Sapna had once again closed herself off—one confession apparently didn't break a lifetime of the same pattern.

Asha leaned over to Neel. "What just happened?"

Neel shrugged. "You gave your dad hope."

"And made my mom miserable."

They finished their meal, and Neel declined her offer to help clean up. So Asha took her wineglass and went to the porch swing.

She'd wanted a simple family dinner, and somehow she'd wound up in the middle again, the rope in her parents' tug-of-war for her life.

"Refill?"

Neel brought his glass and the bottle out with him.

She held hers up and he topped it up. "Thanks."

"You okay?"

She wrapped her gray sweater tight around her with one hand. "Just thinking about how my parents can turn a simple meal into a minefield."

"They suck."

She laughed. "I've never heard you criticize them. Ever."

"I'd never seen it from your point of view until recently," Neel said. "When we were younger, I thought you and your mom were tight because you two had the same plans for you. Your dad was always busy at the hotel. Living here, seeing the way the three of you interact, I get it."

"My mom told me she pushed me to be a perfumer because she never wanted me to take over Goldfield." Asha took a sip and savored the sweet, tart grape on her tongue. "That she developed an interest in my work to bond with me. Now she's upset again because she thinks I would turn my back on everything because I thought working at the front desk was fun. Even though that's not true."

Neel sat in silence for a few minutes before he spoke again. "What do you want?"

She stayed quiet for a long time.

"Did you mean what you said the other night? About wanting to stay?"

She was about to brush him off, tell him she'd just been in her feels. But this was Neel, and he was the one person she could tell the truth. "Yes."

He nodded.

Nerves buzzed in her stomach. "I have to go back. You know that. Especially now, knowing how much my mom sacrificed. And it's not that bad. I like what I do. I mean sure, I have boss problems and the politics of corporate life, but I know how to navigate that. And even if I don't fully recover, I have enough of my sense back that I know I can do my job well." She took another fortifying sip. "But I still don't know what I should do." There was the *have to* and then there was the *want to*, and she didn't know how to reconcile them.

Neel didn't look at her. "Poppy, the one thing I know about you is that you find your fulfillment in work. Always have. People are secondary."

"That makes me sound cold and unfeeling."

He turned toward her. "Not at all. It means you need purpose. You have an ethic that drives you to succeed. I've watched how out of sorts you've been these last few weeks because you didn't have things to do. You made your checklists even though there were only three things on them. You're not good at relaxing or winging it."

She laughed. "You know me better than anyone."

"We know each other."

"Even after all these years apart?"

He shrugged. "Yeah. We know what makes each other tick and what buttons to push. It's like in this physics article I read about valence shells."

Asha gave him a surprised look.

He gently shoved her with his shoulder. "What? I read."

"Physics?"

"*Anyway*, it's the outermost part of an atom and interacts with other atoms. My point is that we know each other at the atomic level, we just haven't kept up with what we've been doing this past decade and a half."

Asha often overlooked how smart he was, mainly because he never revealed that about himself. Neel was fine with letting everyone think he was unmotivated or that he lacked ambition. It was more that he took his time, did things his own way. "I forgot how stubborn you are."

"I'm laid back."

She laughed. "Yeah, it's all a facade, like the valence shell."

"Yeah no, that's not how it's defined."

"What I mean is, you give off this go with the flow vibe," Asha said. "But the truth is you only do what you want. On your terms."

He put his finger to his lips. "Shh. Don't tell anyone."

She looked into his dark-brown eyes. There was so much behind them even though he rarely shared all that he was with anyone. His face was older and more handsome. "If I stay, what happens with us?" It was the scariest question she'd ever asked, and she braced herself for the answer.

He didn't respond right away, and she pressed her lips together to keep herself from taking the question back. She'd asked it.

"You have to decide what you're going to do," he said.

"If I stay?"

He leaned over and brushed his lips against her cheek. "You're tenacious."

Then he stood. "I want you to be happy, Poppy. And I know that means you need to be doing something you want. Without passion, you will make yourself miserable. Your sense of smell is what defines you, always has. You haven't dealt with losing it or getting it back again. You've been back and forth, indecisive, and uncertain. That's not you."

"Then help me."

He shook his head. "We're grown-ups now, we're not talking about getting rid of violent ducks. This is something you have to figure out yourself. I have faith in you." With that, he went inside and left her alone with her thoughts.

The jerk didn't even give her an answer. Then she forgave him, because she knew why. He didn't want to be a catalyst or a crutch. Neel was right. It had to be her choice. And she didn't think she was wired to make the wrong one.

CHAPTER
THIRTY-TWO

Asha rubbed her nose as pungent smells of soap, alcohol, and lavender irritated her enough to wake her from deep sleep. Eyes closed, she lay there, unable to escape the odor. She turned to her side, and the crisp tang of lemon and cotton assaulted her. She sat up. Her heart raced.

It was back.

All of it. It wasn't just her nose, but her sense of self, her confidence, her assuredness. It was just there again. She'd been navigating the world in black and white for months, and now there was lush color. Salt and sweat on her skin. Sweetness and spice from the uncapped moisturizer on the small table by the window. Citrus and cotton from the towels drying on the hook behind the door. She laughed as she recognized herself.

She wanted to sniff everything, from the herb garden at the side of the house to the teas she'd gathered these past three weeks. Relief relaxed her shoulders. She would give herself a few moments to revel. She'd never appreciated what she'd had until she'd lost it. She'd believed it was forever. Now that her sense was at the level she was familiar with, Asha had a new understanding of her gift. Her eyes wet, she allowed herself to finally release all the weight, uncertainty, fear, and doubt she'd been laden with these long months.

The search for what came next was over. Her life could restart. Asha was whole again. There was comfort, though she couldn't understand why she wasn't elated. She should be twirling around the room, texting Millie, running down the stairs to tell anyone who was home. But her relief at realizing she could return to her old life was mixed with a heavy sadness. In all its messiness, Napa Valley had become her home again.

Asha rose and stood for a few minutes to take it all in, then began the day. She made the bed, showered, and took her time getting ready. She was a bit off-balance as she adjusted to all the overwhelming smells that surrounded her. She no longer had to reach for them. She opened the window, and the outside and inside meshed to create a more complex odor—grass, wood, and earth from distant vineyards, alongside the steam from the heater, the unlit pear candle on the desk. It was all there for her to parse out at will.

She walked barefoot down the carpeted steps. The house smelled like her mother—vanilla with notes of caramel. It was quiet, and no one was in the kitchen. She glanced at the clock. It was almost 10:00 a.m. She'd slept for eleven hours. That was impossible. Somehow her daily 6:00 a.m. alarm hadn't gone off . . . or it had, and she'd turned it off. Which was unlike her. She didn't even snooze and was usually naturally awake a few minutes before it was scheduled to sound.

She checked her phone and saw a missed call from Celeste. Asha had scanned her emails here and there when she'd first arrived, but there hadn't been much. It had been close to two weeks since she'd last logged in. She should check the voice mail, but if Celeste had somehow found the article about the Kim-Wilson wedding and Sapna's boasts about IFF, she wasn't quite ready to deal with the fallout from it all.

Asha noticed the change in herself. She typically never avoided anything related to work, but right now, she had to come to terms with the return of her super nose before the rest of it.

Instead, Asha took the tea tins out of the small drawer she'd cleared out for supplies and heated the kettle. As she waited, she sniffed each tin, then grabbed her notebook to jot down her thoughts next to the recipes, then added ratio adjustments. It was familiar, comfortable, and it grounded her as everything had reshifted.

Neel had said she was happiest in pursuit of her passion, but what was that? Questions swirled in her mind. Was it still perfumery? Could she pursue it here, or would she need to be back in Paris? If she was about to be fired, then her decision to stay would be made for her. Except that she didn't want to lose her job or career. She'd worked too hard, and she enjoyed it, that much was true. Was it because if she succeeded, became a master perfumer, it would mean her time in Napa would be back to annual visits?

She let out a frustrated sigh. Too many things were happening inside her brain. She had to get out. Asha grabbed two travel mugs and her tote and hopped in her rental car.

She was happy to see Neel's truck in the side lot of Goldfield and pulled in behind it. She headed for his office, then stopped abruptly in the hallway. She wasn't here to make him drink tea. She was here because she wanted him to know before anyone else. Not Leela, not her mom. It dawned on her that he had a different place in her heart. He wasn't just a shoulder, a part of her past, a sounding board, or even a boy she'd once loved. He was more. He was her present and she couldn't imagine a future without him being firmly rooted in her life. Feelings overwhelmed her even more than the smell of carpet cleaner.

She knocked on Neel's open door. "Are you alone?"

He held his arms out as if to ask her if she saw anyone else there.

His familiar response made her grin. His office was very different from her father's, which was on the other side of the narrow hallway. There was no organization; chaos ruled the space. Books were stacked on the chairs that surrounded a circular wooden table. A pair of mud boots, with one toppled over, sat by the door. The beige walls were bare except for a section where he'd stuck Post-it Notes. He was at a table with pandemonium around him in the form of books, papers, folders, and a few mugs. She resisted the itch to organize his desk. "I brought you tea." She handed him a mug.

"Your tea or real cha?"

"Mine is better. And I added honey for you. Don't complain until you try it. You might actually like it."

He grimaced but took it from her. "If you say so. But don't be upset if I don't; it's not personal. You already know my feelings on brown water."

"And beer is what?"

"Robust, bright, complex, balanced," he said.

She closed the door behind her. "The same could be said for tea. And they're both brewed."

Neel put his hand on his chest in exaggerated shock. "Do not compare the two. My heart can't take it."

"Comedy again?"

He took a hesitant sip, then put the mug down on the table. "It tastes like backyard."

She dropped her tote in the empty chair. "It does not, you philistine."

"Hey, take your fancy words to my sister," he said.

Close to him, she could get leather, wood, sweat, grass, and something new . . . hop, malt. Memories rushed through her. It was the Neel she'd always known, but with more depth. She closed her eyes to etch him into her brain. If she lost her sense again, she didn't want to forget this version of this man.

"You okay?"

She shook her head, then nodded. "I'm fine. Better actually." She leaned against his messy desk. "Super Nose is back in action." It was bittersweet to admit.

He rose and faced her but stayed silent.

"You switched up your soap," she said. "There's moss in it now."

"It's whatever is in your parents' guest bath."

She nodded. "Of course. It has to be different than what your mom buys."

"The least exciting cold war."

"I don't know why I'm not more enthusiastic," she confided. "It's a good thing, right? I'm happy. I feel like my old self. Except."

"You don't know who that is."

"Exactly." Could a person change so much in a few months, weeks? "Maybe it's the shock, the suddenness of it. In a day or two, I'll be me again." Her eyes welled up. "I missed it so much."

He pulled her into his arms. Ink. Cotton. And Neel. Asha hadn't been held in so long that another wave of emotion roiled through her, and she clung to him. It was Neel who finally let her go.

"Sorry," she said.

He grinned. "You only cry when you're alone."

"It's embarrassing."

He leaned against his desk, next to her. "Guess what, Poppy? You're human, and we're a messy bunch. It's nice to see you like this."

She cleared her throat. "Don't get used to it."

"I know better."

To avoid giving in to the urge to lean her head on his shoulder, Asha went to the table and grabbed her mug. The tea was still hot. "I have to tell Leela and my mom."

"Say the word and I'll post it in the chat."

"No. I have to do it." The damn chat. "My boss left me a voice mail," she added.

"That's a good thing, right?"

She shrugged. "I haven't listened to it yet."

She was worried about the message. Did she want Celeste to tell her Simon had messed up Guerlain and that Asha was needed back ASAP? Or did she want Celeste to say that she'd been fired because of her mom's quote? Yet she loitered in Neel's office. The force that drove her was absent.

"Don't make this hard for yourself, Poppy."

She looked at him. Unsure of what he meant.

"You know what you're going to do," he said. "So do it."

She knew that tone. He was ready for her to leave. He'd been expecting it. And he was right. This back-and-forth, wavering, was an exercise in futility. She'd woken up with her sense of self and purpose. That's who she was. Asha Patel would not leave her career midstride. She had commitments and obligations. Then there were expectations. She was who she'd been, and that meant going back to Paris.

And Neel wasn't going to ask her to stay.

She nodded. She suppressed all emotion in her voice and went for a matter-of-fact tone. "I have to go give Leela ba the news in person." Then to soften the severity, she added, "I just hope she and Mimi aren't sunbathing topless again."

"I told them to knock that off," he said.

She could hear his effort to keep things light. "You caught them too?"

He slowly shook his head. "I can never unsee it, Poppy."

She had to agree.

"Your mom is likely in her office. You can stop by on your way out," he said.

"You really want me to leave, don't you?" She couldn't help herself.

"It's not my decision," Neel said. "It's your choice."

"I hate that word."

CHAPTER THIRTY-THREE

Before Asha left Goldfield, she walked down the path to Sonanum. She passed the cypress trees, then paused to take it all in. There was so much here, and this was likely her final goodbye to the place that had come to mean so much. It was painful to know the beauty and splendor of it would be replaced by buildings. In a little over three weeks, the garden had altered, dramatically. Buds had turned to blooms, the herbs were taller, the rosebushes full. The vegetable patch lay bare, merely tilled soil, likely because nothing would be planted for the season. Or ever again.

Asha walked through the paths, memorizing the surrounding aromas. She stopped at the blue sage and silently thanked the plant for giving her nose enough of a jolt to revive her. On her knees, she cleared off some dried leaves and fanned out the stems to show it love. Then she sat in the dirt, not minding the dust on her long dress. Asha stayed there until the sun became too hot and the skin on her sleeveless arms singed. With eyes closed, she said her final goodbye. From the top of the path, near her car, she thanked the place that had given her so much.

Twenty minutes later, she found Leela alone on the back deck of the cottage. She was reading a Gujarati novel; the large green hat on her head gave her shade.

"I'm glad you're wearing a shirt." She'd sent Leela a heads-up that she'd be stopping by.

"I'm protecting your sensibilities."

"Where's Mimi?" Asha took a seat on the empty lounger.

"Dentist." Leela put the book on the small table between them. "You're here to say something. Out with it."

Asha took a fortifying breath. She should just share the news and be done with it. Instead, she needed to know something first. "Did I always want to be a perfumer?"

Leela turned toward Asha. "What kind of question is that?"

"I don't recall how it all happened." Her mom had explained, sure, but she wanted to know how much her grandmother had influenced the outcome. "I was so young. It was always something I knew I was going to do, but I don't know how I knew that."

"Smells made you happy," Leela said. "When your mother was getting ready to go to a function, you would want her to spray a little perfume on your skin."

"I remember that," Asha said. "I felt so grown-up even though I was, what? Four or five? Is that when I said that's what I wanted to do?"

Leela stared out toward the garden and the fields beyond. "No. You didn't know that could be a career. A year or so later I read a biography of Coco Chanel, and I was fascinated about how her life was captured in No. 5."

"I see."

"Sapna and I thought we could channel your gift into a profession beyond our dreams. You embraced it. Why does it matter now?"

Asha stood and paced. "Lately, I've been thinking about whether it's something I would have picked for myself. Did I love the idea first, or was it because I loved you that I became interested in those things?"

"Use your words, Poppy."

Which meant get to the point. "I'm wondering if I became a perfumer because that's what the two of you expected." It was the most direct Asha had ever been with her grandmother.

Leela stood and stopped Asha's pacing. She cupped her face. "Does it matter? You loved it and still do. Look how hard you're fighting to get your smell back. It shows how much you care."

Except they'd urged her, pushed her, shoved leaves up her nose. Asha had accepted the loss and had come back to find something different.

"If I had a say, what would that have looked like? I don't even remember liking anything else. Maybe coloring or puzzles? The only after-school activities were ones that would help my college applications." Cross-country running had been her least favorite.

"A say in what?"

She shrugged. "I don't know, chemistry tutors, weekend-long programs on aromatics, the Sorbonne, ISIPCA—it was all mapped out, one thing led to the other. I never considered anything else."

"You never objected."

Asha nodded. "I didn't know that I could."

Leela grabbed Asha's hands. "I didn't raise you to be timid. I encouraged you to speak your mind."

You raised me to pursue your dreams. "And to be obedient. Not talk back, not question my elders and all that."

"We instilled values for you to have a strong foundation," Leela said. "This deciding for yourself, that's a very Western notion. My parents never had any options. They were farmers in a village fifty miles away from Ahmedabad. If I hadn't been married off, I would have been a farmer's wife. I built a life from decisions that were made for me by the adults in my life. They knew what was best; they'd learned the same way. That's how I raised your father. You. Your mother and I guided you, channeled your talents, and gave you the ability to aspire and achieve."

Asha wanted to feel gratitude; instead, it chafed. "In high school, my friends were taking personality tests to figure out what they wanted to do with their lives."

"They were purposeless," Leela said. "You were happy to have direction."

Leela wasn't wrong. Asha used to feel smug that she didn't need a personality test to see what career suited her best. She wondered if she would have chosen to live so far away if that hadn't been the plan. "Mom told me she never wanted me to work at Goldfield."

"Sapna saw it as a sort of prison." Leela wandered down to the small garden.

"What about you?" Asha said. "Why did you help Mom keep me away from the hotel?"

Leela picked off a few dried leaves. "What is the point of all this? It's done. I gave you a foundation, you worked hard to build on top of it. This way of thinking, the questioning, it'll lead you to a life with regrets, constantly second-guessing what you do. And anyway, the one thing I've learned in my eighty years is that nothing is permanent." Leela bent down to pinch off a dried flower and dropped it in the dirt.

"Is that why it's easy for you to let Sonanum go? You created it from nothing to something beautiful. And in a few months, it will be gone as if it never existed."

"Come here." Leela called her over to the far area that was lush with short trees and tall shrubs. "See this? California buckeye. A favorite of the butterflies, bees, and you. I brought the shrubs over from Sonanum, as I did a few others, and now they grow here. Just because they live somewhere else doesn't mean they are gone. It's not the location that matters."

"They survive for hundreds of years." Asha gently caressed the pale-pink flowers that bloomed on the long, thick tips of the shrub. She could smell their sweetness.

"Even when your body turns to ashes, the soul finds another place."

"And your life, the way you live it, is enough?"

Leela took Asha's hand and squeezed. "It has to be."

"You never had dreams."

"There's a futility in doing so," Leela said. "I don't have disappointments because I live the life I have, not wish for something more or different."

There was value in dreaming. To have aspirations meant to strive toward something more meaningful than present circumstances. "I'm fully recovered."

Her grandmother smiled wide, reached out and embraced Asha. "I knew we would do it. See? Even your loss wasn't final. You found your way back."

Back to where she was. Neel had once said that she only looked forward, yet somehow, she felt as if her life were going in reverse.

"The Nanis have a wager going, and Mimi and I bet on you," Leela said. "We'll be collecting big. All the money will be donated back to the foundation, of course."

"I guess congratulations are in order." Asha went back to the deck. That her future had become a gambling chip didn't sit well. "I should go."

"When do you leave for Paris?"

She still had five days left but knew that her mom and Leela would urge her to go back early now that the reason for her to stay was no longer valid. "I'll let you know."

"Poppy," Leela called out. "When you know this is what life is, you find ways to create joy within that. Your mother eventually came around on Goldfield, so much so that she wears her name tag with pride. Your father embraced his destiny and has built something he is proud of. I accepted my life here and found my happiness in the garden and in raising you. When you get back to your lab at IFF, your surroundings will help you realize you're where you're meant to be."

Asha nodded and left her grandmother. Acceptance.

It was such a defeatist word.

CHAPTER
THIRTY-FOUR

Asha spent the afternoon in the guest room with her planner. She had yet to listen to Celeste's voice mail. It loomed over her, but she couldn't make herself face that reality quite yet. She wanted to enjoy her last few days. When she looked through her list for next week, it overwhelmed her. The daily meetings. Then a list of personal errands she would need to catch up on. The empty spaces would fill up with new projects.

Vanilla. Which meant dinner. Her mother didn't like the smell of cooking, especially anything that was pungent like onions and garlic, so she always lit a candle to ward off the aromas. In yoga pants and sweatshirt, Asha headed down the steps, surprised to see both her parents at the small dining table by the kitchen island.

"It's like that dog experiment we learned about in high school," Sanjay said. "Your mother lights the Diptyque and Asha comes downstairs for a meal."

She rolled her eyes at her father's attempt to tease.

"I only lit one," Sapna chimed in. "I know how sensitive your nose is."

"You heard."

Sapna rose and hugged Asha. "Leela put it in the group chat, and we're all celebrating. I'm so happy for you."

Her irritation grew. She didn't even get a chance to tell her mom before it was blasted to everyone. And she hadn't even known it had been sent.

"Hope you're hungry, Poppy." Neel came into the kitchen from the pantry room with a jar of chili flakes.

Asha pulled out of her mother's arms. "What's for dinner?"

Both her parents and Neel paused and stared at her.

"Can't you smell it?" Her mom looked at her with concern.

"Garlic, tomato, onion, dairy, some sort of peppery heat. Either Italian or Indian. And stop treating me like a party game. I'm not your trained monkey."

"Desi lasagna," Neel said.

"Her nose really is back." Sapna gave her a pat on the arm as she moved past her to the bread on the island.

"How much longer before we eat?"

Instead of answering her, Neel reached into the oven to pull out the clear glass casserole.

"Wine, Asha? I have a very nice bottle of Peju cabernet." Sanjay took out a bottle from the wine rack that sat above the temperature-controlled fridge in the adjacent dining room.

Asha joined her dad at the formal dining table that had already been set. Her mom sliced fresh baked bread as Neel grated a wedge of Parmesan over the resting lasagna before they both brought over the food and sat across from Asha. A family dinner. This was likely the last one; next week she would probably be eating alone.

"This looks delicious, Neel beta," Sanjay said. "You spoil us. Stay as long as you want. Don't tell my wife, but your cooking is much better."

Sapna took her seat. "Your wife agrees."

At least her mother was in a jovial and friendly mood. Then she realized *why* her mom was so happy: it was because Asha's nose was back.

"In that case," Neel said, "I'll stay forever and pay rent in the form of food."

Once Asha's plate was full, she dug in. The chili, coriander, and cumin hit her tongue. There was something here. Her mind wandered. Peppercorn, maybe with cardamom, and chicory. She thought about ways to round out the blend she'd been working on.

"I added artichokes, Poppy, because you love them," Neel said. "But eat it like regular people and the way it's meant to be, don't pick at little chunks so that your meal looks like a decimated carcass missing only the things you like."

"I don't always do that." Asha dug her fork into a corner and ate all three layers at once. "See?"

Sapna turned to Neel. "It's my one failure as a mother. She's been doing that since she was a toddler. Remember, Sanjay? We had to separate her food on her tray. Peas in one corner, carrots in another. If we gave you khichdi, you'd pick out the onions and potatoes and eat them before you ate the rice and lentils."

"That one time I took her to a business dinner when she was ten," Sanjay added. "She ordered minestrone soup, and I knew it was going to be a problem."

"Her poor pink-and-white dress," Sapna said. "It had so many splatters on it, even hand-washing couldn't remove the stains."

"Stop picking on me."

"See, after one forkful of lasagna," Neel said. "Now you're picking out green peppers and eating them one by one. It's not how you're meant to eat my food."

"Bell pepper overpowers everything," Asha said.

"That's an insult to my cooking skills."

"Children," Sanjay said. "Let's just enjoy a nice meal."

Sapna pointed her fork at Asha. "How many trials are you in for Guerlain? Where will you pick up the process?"

"Mom, I have an NDA," Asha said. "You know I can't share anything specific."

Sapna made a motion to zip her lip. "Whatever you tell me will stay in the vault."

"Sanjay uncle, can you pass the bread?" Neel changed the topic. "And the salad."

Her mother passed the bowl to Asha. "I bet the sea is part of the scent profile, right? Tahiti is an island."

"Speaking of." Asha cut her mother off. "The Nanis went kayaking last weekend."

"Mimi put the photos in the chat," Sanjay said. "They had a great time. Ming Na lost her hat and jumped out of the kayak to get it, which scared the guides, who lectured her on not doing that. Then Yulie lectured the 'young men' that Ming Na was a strong swimmer and could have gone to the Olympics if she hadn't become a doctor."

"They raise such a ruckus when they're together," Sapna said. "Mimi and Leela are supposed to be in white saris like traditional Gujarati widows. Stay at home and pray."

"Why should they?" Sanjay said. "I can't imagine you giving up your high heels and pencil skirts at any age."

Sapna pointed her fork at him. "You would be the first to complain."

"Your legs are your best feature." Sanjay raised his glass to her.

"Please stop." Asha didn't like them fighting but didn't want to hear them flirt either.

"You're not the one who has to deal with it when one of them gets hurt," Sapna said. "I had to take an entire day to sit with Mimi when she thought she hurt her foot. Jaya couldn't spare time away from DHG to come help her own mother-in-law. Thank God it was only a sprain. She shouldn't have been on a ladder when they can afford to pay someone to clear out the gutters."

"I've been doing that since then," Neel said.

"You are such a sweet man," Sapna said. "I don't understand why you're single."

Asha coughed, then cleared her throat. "Yes, Neel, inquiring minds want to know." It was better to needle than think about him being with someone else.

"Same could be said of you," Neel said.

"Oh, I don't think anyone, even in this room, would say I'm sweet." She put her elbow on the table and rested her chin on her hand since Leela wasn't here to scold her.

"Asha will think about that after she's a master perfumer."

Her mother's words deflated her, and she tried not to show any outward sign. "We were talking about Neel."

"This was a nice dinner." Sanjay pushed back his chair and stood. "Not the most scintillating conversation, but the food and wine were great. Sapna, why don't we go for a walk and let these two clean up."

It annoyed Asha to no end that her father never once brought his plate back to the sink after he was finished with his meal. "Aren't you forgetting something?" She pointed to the empty plate.

He gave her a smile. "I have a daughter and a son." He pointed to Neel. "I'm sure the two of you can manage." And with that he took Sapna's hand, and they left through the french doors.

"It's weird to see them hold hands," Asha said. "They've been fighting nonstop and now they're fine?"

"I guess they sorted themselves out." Neel put leftovers in containers to store them.

"Will you wait until the brewery gets going before you date again?" Asha kicked herself for asking.

He was close as he added a spatula to the sink where Asha was rinsing off plates to load in the dishwasher. "I'm not a planner, remember?"

"Right. If someone cute comes along, you'll drop your plans to pursue her."

"Is that what I said?" He added the casserole dish to the sink and, in the process, touched her back with his free hand.

"I'm inferring."

He moved away from her. "The worst about me, as usual."

She winced.

Neel wiped off the dining table and the counters, then disappeared into the small half bathroom to wash his hands.

She'd done it on purpose. She'd been irritated but more, she was hurting. It was time to leave them again, and her heart wasn't ready to let everyone go—not Neel, not Millie, not even Leela or her mom. She'd spent so much time here and rediscovered her family and especially her love for them. And deep inside, she knew that next time she came for a visit, they would go back to being acquaintances at a distance. The group chat would go on without her, she would miss the daily happenings, she would be kept out of inside jokes. Everything would go on here, and Asha would go back to being alone with her life in Paris.

CHAPTER
THIRTY-FIVE

Everything was laid out on the bed, folded, and organized by the way the clothes would be repacked. The empty suitcases sat open on the floor. Last night, she'd finally listened to Celeste's voice mail, and it was for Asha to get back to work immediately. No further details. Obeying the order seemed logical, since based on yesterday's events, it was as if everyone was ready for her to leave.

It was time.

Long goodbyes were painful; she'd learned that the first time she'd left for Paris and they'd spent weeks celebrating her departure. With each interaction, it had become more daunting to leave. Each going-away party had made adjusting to university that much harder.

She'd changed her return ticket for an early-afternoon flight that day, which meant leaving Napa in a couple of hours. All she had to do was repack, shower, and head out. No one needed to drive her since she had to return her rental.

"Well, this won't do," said a voice from the doorway.

Asha turned around, and Leela and Mimi came into her room, followed by Sapna.

"It's slow going," Asha said, though that wasn't exactly true.

"We're here to help." Mimi sat on the floor and began putting the piles into the suitcases.

"Not like that." Leela took them out and reordered them.

"I messaged everyone," Sapna said. "They all wish you a safe return."

Asha had planned to talk to Millie on her drive, but it seemed as if everyone had been informed. She wondered how Neel felt about the news.

Leela moved a stack of shirts on top of a stack of pants and sat down on the bed. "You don't have to stay away for long. Come back for Diwali."

"If your work allows," Sapna added.

Asha nodded. She knew she'd probably fall back into her aggressive schedule, especially if Celeste needed her for a new project. Eventually, all of this would fade again. Including the relationships she'd rebuilt.

"Oh, beta." Her mom rubbed her back. "I know this is hard. You've been through so much, but it will all work out. You'll see. Once you're there with your friends and in your apartment, you'll remember how much you love Paris."

She nodded and steeled herself. "Okay. Let's get to packing. I have a long drive and an even longer flight."

Mimi took a small baggie out of the pocket of her caftan. "Something to help you."

"Pills?"

"They will knock you out," Mimi said. "Throw them back with one of those small bottles of wine and you'll wake up in France."

Leela took the drugs away. "She doesn't need lorazepam. Stop being a pusher."

"See? This is why I'm the favorite grandmother and you're not." Mimi took the baggie back. "Here, beta, you're an adult. You can make your own decisions."

"Not when it comes to doing drugs," Leela said.

Asha put the little bag in her tote and hoped her grandmother didn't notice.

"I also have a bag of your favorite things so you don't have to eat airplane food," Mimi said. "There's batata pauva and handhvo. I also added the sweet sakarpara you love so much."

Half an hour later, the four of them were at the big table having cha and nasto. Asha sipped the sweet, milky tea but skipped the snacks; her stomach was not settled enough for food.

The mood was somber. Asha wanted to make it better. "All of you should come for a visit, over the summer. We can catch some of the Tour de France if we time it right."

"Oh yes." Mimi clapped her hands. "I would love to see those skinny boys in bike shorts ride around everywhere. We can rent a camper. I've seen it on TV, and that's how people go watch."

"I'm not living in a van with you," Leela said.

"That's a good point," Mimi jumped in. "It would be a murder-suicide waiting to happen."

Then they argued about who would be the worst van driver. The mood lightened and there was more laughter, this time as they reminisced about the fun they all had during Asha's visit, including the e-bike tour that turned into day drinking, the movie marathons, and all the times the Nanis of Napa tried to corrupt their Poppy. Sapna asked questions about the work Asha would be returning to, and this time, she knew it was because her mom was interested in her life, that she was trying to connect.

When she left, Asha clung to each of them for a long time, taking in their scents to etch the memory in her mind.

As she loaded her suitcases into the car, she was so lost in thought she jumped at the sound of Neel's voice.

"Sorry," he said. "Didn't mean to startle you."

"It's okay." She closed the trunk with her luggage inside.

He shuffled his feet, his hands in his pockets. "I see you're taking off."

"My boss called," she whispered.

They stayed in silence. She didn't know what to say and he clearly didn't either.

"I guess you were right," she finally said. "I was always leaving."

He said nothing.

She bit her lip. "I'm nothing if not predictable."

He didn't look at her. "Sticking to your plans isn't a bad thing. I hope you know that."

She did. Except it shouldn't have been this hard. "You know, a while back, Millie made me think about a value equation. About how to assess the cost and benefits."

"It's a weird way to look at life."

She could see that, but part of her had always made decisions this way. "I can't seem to make myself do what I really want." It was the most honest sentence she'd ever spoken.

He finally looked at her. "It's okay."

She leaned against the driver-side door. "God, I've never been this sappy."

"It works for you, even the splotchy face." He came to stand next to her and nudged her shoulder.

"I have an excellent skin-care routine."

"I know," he said. "I've been using that eye wrinkle cream you kept in the shared bathroom. Send me more."

And with that she leaned her head on his shoulder. "I'll add it to a postcard of Notre Dame."

He put his arm around her. Then kissed her on the top of her head. And just once she wanted to know what it would be like for them as adults. Not fumbling teenagers. She looked up and let him see her, all of her, the want, the love, the entirety of what he meant to her.

She saw it all reflected back in his eyes just before he leaned over and touched his lips to hers. She sank into his kiss. It was gentle and filled with tenderness. It wasn't heat but heart. They stayed in each other's arms for a long time.

He was the one with enough strength to let her go. Neel reached around and opened the car door, waited for Asha to slide into the driver's seat. He stepped back as she started the engine. She backed out of the drive, then turned the car around. She saw his small wave through the rearview mirror and let all the tears she'd held back fall over her warm cheeks.

CHAPTER
THIRTY-SIX

Two days later, red-eyed from lack of sleep and jet-lagged, Asha sat in front of her computer and scanned her inbox. Her cubicle was way smaller than she remembered. She'd been gone so long, she had no idea what awaited on her plate, but she'd gotten to work early in the hopes of seeing Celeste and getting started with whatever was next.

"*Bonjour*, Asha."

Celeste sounded unusually chipper as she came over to her. "Come to my office. I have coffee and pastries to welcome you back."

Asha was surprised. She and Celeste hadn't been on the best of terms when she'd been asked to leave.

"How was your holiday?"

Asha helped herself to a mug of coffee from the tray that was laid out on the small table. She poured milk and added two spoons of sugar. "It was nice." An understatement of all that had happened.

"The weather must have been wonderful there, no?"

Asha couldn't remember the last time her boss made small talk with her. "Yes."

"It was like this most of the time. Wet," Celeste said. "We only had sun a few times."

Maybe Celeste was trying to soften the blow of firing her. She'd spent her sleepless night thinking about all the reasons she'd been asked to come back so urgently. At first, she thought Simon might have made a mess of the Guerlain account. A few weeks ago, she would have reveled in the fantasy of Celeste begging her to come back and fix his mistakes. Now she hoped that wasn't the case. She'd made peace with that account and didn't want to revisit it. She was here to move forward. She had planned to confess all—losing her sense of smell, getting it back—and apologize for not telling Celeste sooner. Then she would fight for her job.

There was a sigh. "I'm sorry to ask you to cut your leave short. But something has come up and we need you."

Those words didn't make her happy in the way she'd hoped. Asha sipped the mediocre coffee. The blend had been the same over her entire tenure at IFF. She wondered if her mom had made herself espresso this morning or just had cha because it was easier.

"There has been a development," Celeste said. "We have an opportunity to create a celebrity fragrance. Someone huge approached us."

"I see." It wasn't common for a manufacturer to work directly with a client, but celebrities were an exception. Beyoncé had been their last big get.

"I must say it was naughty of you to speak about being so lofty in your position at IFF," Celeste said. "I read that magazine article."

Asha shook her head. "That was my mother. I had no idea, and you know I would never assume."

Celeste waved her off. "Mothers brag about their children, very easy to understand. It's all water under the bridge. Especially as Jennifer Kim's team reached out to see if IFF would be interested in partnering with her on a signature fragrance."

Asha set down her mug. "Really?"

"She is an influencer with hundreds of millions of followers, and she wants to partner with you," Celeste said. "Jennifer spoke highly of your meeting and requested you to be the perfumer for her fragrance."

There were so many things to process. Never in all her scenario planning did she think *this* would be her second chance. And it was even bigger than going through a known brand. This would be her creation. Of course, the client would inform what she was looking for, but it would be for Asha to execute on that vision. She could do for Jennifer Kim what Clement Gavarry and Laurent Le Guernec did for Sarah Jessica Parker when they created Lovely.

"That's incredible."

"I know," Celeste said. "Isn't it wonderful? And you having a personal relationship with her makes it that much better."

"I barely know Jennifer Kim." Asha wanted to manage Celeste's expectations. The pressure made her feel weighed down. She had to take this step-by-step if she was going to deliver her best.

"Don't be so modest," Celeste said. "It is very un-American of you. Now go get started on your background work. You have calls with her team later this afternoon. It is an initial conversation, but Jennifer plans to be in Paris later this week for her first meeting with us."

Asha left Celeste's office with her mug in hand. Back at her desk, she started reading through anything she could find on her client. There was a lot. She got lost in the recent articles about her wedding when she came across the photo spread of Goldfield. In two dimensions, it was elegant and austere, but the pictures didn't capture the warmth. She wondered if Kini would be on shift today, or if Neel was busy in his messy office.

"Bon soirée."

She looked over to see her friend hovering over the cubical separation.

"Lisle."

"It's so nice to have you back," Lisle said. "I've had no one to gossip or walk to have a coffee with in the middle of the afternoon."

Asha laughed. "The entire office is your friend."

Lisle was always cheerful and knew everything about everyone, from birthdays to anniversaries to who had children and what they were like. She was a digital designer who worked with the brand team. Asha wondered if Lisle would be on the Jennifer Kim project. Since she didn't know if it was confidential, she kept quiet.

"Have you seen Simon?"

"I just got in." Asha minimized her browser.

"He's been locked up in the lab," Lisle said. "Is probably still there. I've never seen so much pressure on him."

"Are people still talking about how he took over the account?"

Lisle hesitated. "When you left for holiday, Celeste made it known that while your pitch won it for us, you were not the right perfumer for the project, that you lacked the necessary expertise."

"That is not true." Asha clutched the computer mouse.

"Some of us didn't believe her," Lisle said. "You're talented. But something must have happened."

Asha nodded. "My ratios weren't well balanced in the last round." There was no point in talking about her loss of smell. She was recovered and it wasn't relevant.

"Simon shared the scent you presented with everyone," Lisle said. "It was off, I must say. But then he also started to have problems with his version."

She released her hold on the mouse. "If he wants, I can help him."

Lisle laughed. "Simon's ego would never allow for it. Anyway, rumor has it that Celeste needs you. She's been excited to have you back. She told everyone that you were so dedicated to IFF that you offered to cut your holiday short."

Asha kept her face neutral, as the compliments felt hollow. Celeste went whichever way the wind turned. There was no loyalty except to Celeste. Asha was wanted for a high-profile project, and Celeste now planned to ride on her coattails. The politics of her job left a lot to be desired.

"Do you know what it is?" Lisle asked.

Asha didn't know how much to share, but a part of her didn't want Celeste to control the narrative. Still, she wasn't going to upend anything. If she upset her boss, then Celeste would find a way to steer Jennifer Kim to another perfumer. Her relationship with the client was loose at best. "I guess I'll find out. All she said to me this morning was that there was another project on the horizon and that it would be a good opportunity for me."

"She's going to make a big production of revealing it," Lisle said. "I have a meeting without much more information on Monday. Maybe we'll be on this together."

"That would be fun."

"How was it being away?" Lisle sat down in the single chair in the small space. "It's been so humid and rainy. I haven't been able to let my hair out of its bun for weeks."

Just the thought of Napa Valley gave her an energy boost. "It was incredible. Lots of time outside. I think I'm three shades darker."

Her friend compared her dark-brown skin to Asha's. "You're getting closer to me, but that's because I've barely seen any sun. Did you do any shopping?"

"Some," Asha said. "Most of my time was with family and my best friend."

"No vacation lovers?"

Her heart skipped a beat at the thought of Neel. "No."

"That's a missed opportunity," Lisle said. "*Pas de problème.* I met one of Adan's friends from Angola who recently moved here. The four of us can have dinner."

The thought of dating made her cringe. "Let me readjust first and see how much work this new project will be before making plans."

"Fine, but this Saturday," Lisle said, "the group is going to Le Chalet. You're coming. We want to hear all about your trip."

Asha nodded, rolled her shoulders back, and reopened the browser. She switched away from the Goldfield article. Time to make notes on Jennifer Kim's life and brand.

CHAPTER
THIRTY-SEVEN

Two weeks later, Asha tapped her pen on the page of her tea bible as she sipped Milky Blue Absolu at Mariage Frères in the fourth arrondissement. It was forty minutes away by metro from where she lived in the seventeenth arrondissement of Batignolles-Monceau. It wasn't typical for her to leave her neighborhood except for outings with friends she'd made over the years. But it was Saturday, and instead of spending it in the office, she'd made the trip to her favorite tea shop.

This area of Paris was different from where she lived. On the right bank of the river Seine, she was in the Hôtel de Ville section, which was dense with locals and tourists navigating around each other. The stores were busier, as were the cafés.

Where Asha lived, the shops had become her go-to places, from the *boucherie* for meats, the *pâtisserie* for sweets, and the *fleuriste* for her weekly supply of blooms. Her apartment was located on the edges of Paris, and the neighborhood was small and familiar. While she didn't know her neighbors, she liked recognizing faces and nodded greetings. Asha usually found the more touristy areas of the city overwhelming, with a combination of cigarette smoke, the Seine, the cafés, and car fumes. She preferred the little leafy garden near her small residence, with its inviting aromas and relative quiet.

She brought the mug to her nose and reveled in the richness of aromas: cotton candy, coconut, brown butter, and floral undertone. It was a carnival in a cup. Since she'd been back, tea had replaced work in the evenings. Her tiny kitchen didn't have counter space, so she used her coffee table to spread out her precious leaves. It was the only time she could relax. It even helped her miss Napa less, because she could bring herself back there through the blends she'd made from local herbs.

What was new was old again as Asha was right in the thick of things. Her daily schedule was filled with meetings and lab time. Her list of tasks was long and growing by the hour. Thanks to Celeste.

Three days ago, while at her desk, she'd seen Esme Moreau and her team pass by as they holed up in the conference room with Simon and Celeste. She wanted so much to put her ear against the door and listen. Asha smiled as she thought that if Mimi were here, she'd find a way.

But Asha had stayed in her chair. When they left, the team looked satisfied, which meant Simon likely delivered where Asha couldn't. It was disappointing to see but didn't bother her as much. Likely because she had Jennifer Kim's perfume to prove herself, which began to feel daunting because while Asha's nose was back, her creative well seemed to have run dry.

Last week, she'd spent a few hours with Jennifer, who wanted to talk in the Tuileries Garden, a high-traffic area because of its location between the Louvre and the Place de la Concorde. Asha had learned that as much as Jennifer was obsessed with French history, she wanted a fragrance that was an East-West mix between her European and South Korean ancestry. It was a complex challenge, and at any other time, Asha would have been excited to pursue it. But her mind wouldn't stay on the task at hand.

Instead it wandered, and always to what was happening back home. Asha would try to snap herself out of it. She wasn't a homesick college student. But she missed everyone.

Since she'd been back, Asha had chatted with Millie at least once every few days. Her friend was knee-deep in work, but they managed to navigate the time difference. Asha was happy that Millie's fix-up had now turned into a relationship. Her friend even confessed to leaving work early to make him a home-cooked meal. Well, to have Neel make the meal and for Millie to serve it. Asha wished she were there to meet this person her friend was prioritizing over work.

Then there was Neel. She didn't want them to be distant again, but their last kiss left a mark on her heart. It hadn't been one of goodbye or closure. It had been an *I will love you forever*. So instead of avoiding him, she'd resorted to texting him photos of areas she passed with captions about how beautiful Paris was as a way to poke at him. To her relief, he responded with pictures of vineyards, hills, and open landscapes. No captions, which was his way.

Her mom, Leela, and Mimi called her on video chats. Sapna had booked another high-profile wedding and a *quinceañera* for a tech mogul's daughter. Leela and Mimi told her about the hot-air balloon trip the Nanis of Napa were planning. Everyone was back to their lives and happy. It didn't seem as if they missed her as much as she pined for them.

She'd thought getting her sense of smell back to full would be the key to having everything revert to normal, but something was still missing. Her world was less vibrant because the people who brought it to life were nine hours behind her.

Asha put down her teacup as her phone chimed. Incoming message from Celeste. She typed off a quick response, irritated at the intrusion. Her boss had a way of inundating her with work.

She rolled her shoulders. They were stiff from all the to-dos on her list. Next weekend she was accompanying Jennifer to Grasse to explore lavender fields and spend time near Côte d'Azur. Celeste had suggested Asha give Jennifer a daylong crash course in building a scent at the school there, so now Asha had to carve out time for that.

The mid-April sun reflected on the glass pane of the café and warmed her enough that Asha tugged off her multipatterned Hermès scarf. It had been an ISIPCA graduation gift from her mom and a way to acknowledge her budding future career at IFF. It was strange to miss the woman whose calls she'd begrudgingly answered for over a decade.

Asha closed her notebook. There was no point in doing anything, as she had no focus thanks to her mind ricocheting between work and memories of home. She took out her planner and scanned the rest of her tasks for today. On the way home she needed to stop at the market for staples. She would pick up eggs, along with cilantro, tomato, and cumin if she could find it, to make herself Neel's omelet. She was sure she could figure it out, and with enough butter, it wouldn't stick to the pan. She had yet to renew her metro card and had simply been adding money as she went. Committing to a month seemed daunting, even though it was practical.

Asha finished off her tea, then stopped at the counter to buy a small batch for another cup later. Tonight, she was supposed to have dinner with a group of friends, including Lisle, and even though it was not too far from where Asha lived, she found the idea of heading to Montmartre exhausting. She'd seen the group the last weekend and had caught up on all the local gossip. Some had relationships end, others had found someone new. One of them had been promoted in their role. All in all, she hadn't missed much.

She left the shop and boarded the metro, bound toward her tiny top-floor apartment in a building with yellow painted stone facade. Half an hour later, she emerged from her station onto the familiar quaint, colorful street where she lived. The sidewalk, shops, and cafés were dotted with residents, not tourists. She breathed in the mild air.

She headed up her building's narrow steps and unlocked the door of her flat. It was dark and claustrophobic compared to the bright glass windows and spacious rooms of her parents' home. Asha glanced around the living area that flowed into a small kitchenette. She hung up her jacket in the closet next to the bedroom with a full-size bed. It was functional, the whole of it decorated in black, white, and gray. The color came from the fresh flowers she'd displayed in every room and the art on the walls.

Her bookshelves were stacked with texts and tomes from her school days along with anything that was related to work. She couldn't remember the last time she'd read a novel or anything for fun. She needed to diversify her shelves, possibly redo the apartment. It had been a place of shelter, somewhere to be when she wasn't elsewhere. It didn't feel like she lived here.

Asha logged into her laptop and started going through family photos. It was a habit she'd begun lately, and she wasn't sure it was good for her—but she couldn't stop herself. The photos weren't just from her recent trip but from all the other vacations and the captured memories of her childhood. She laughed at the pictures from the e-bike tour with the Nanis of Napa. There was one of Millie and Neel from a wedding a few years ago that Asha had skipped. Neel was in a gray-and-silver kurta with Millie in an emerald lengha. She'd rarely seen him in desi clothes, but she admired how handsome he looked, even with his hair slicked back, which must have been Millie's doing.

She promised herself that she wouldn't miss any more events. She'd spend the money for travel and make no excuses, even if it hurt to leave them again and again.

Asha sat back on her small white sofa and closed her eyes. The afternoon sun warmed her skin as it filtered through the sheer curtains of her small windows. It was dark when she woke, and Asha realized she'd taken another nap, a habit she'd fallen into whenever she had time and wanted to do nothing else. She hadn't made it to the market, and her fridge was empty save for a block of cheese. There was bread on the counter, and she ate enough to sustain herself before she crawled into bed.

Today was a lost day. She'd done the most necessary things on her task list but was uninspired to do more. This would fade, she told herself. She'd gotten over it before, and she'd been eighteen. She was an adult now, and missing home was silly. Her life was here, and she'd chosen to leave. She just needed to get back into her routine, and with time the ache in her chest would fade. Tomorrow, she'd restart and accept what she was here to do. She'd go to the office and spend time in the lab. On Sundays there was rarely anyone there. Once she started working on a few formulas, she would get that familiar feeling. This maudlin version of herself was unacceptable.

CHAPTER THIRTY-EIGHT

The lab had done the trick. A few days later, everything was humming along. Asha was back in form. The initial batches she'd tried were raw in the best sense, but she had a direction to explore. That morning she'd met with the business team, who laid out the budget and the parameters around which types of ingredients to use. Jennifer Kim was adamant about natural over synthetic, but Asha knew that IFF needed to manage the margins, which would be helped by using synthetic ingredients to make the fragrance more accessible for a broader target market.

Asha wanted to evoke an industrial feel with Jennifer Kim's fragrance. The woman was a powerhouse and had built her brand by understanding how to leverage technology. After spending time with her, Asha learned that Jennifer liked the idea of flowers for their aesthetic beauty but was drawn to smoke and charcoal in scents.

"I'm thinking coal and steam, volcano," Asha said.

"It feels too masculine." Celeste, who was ever present in all conversations, objected.

"I would soften it with chocolate, apple, and a touch of citrus. It's still very much a work in progress, but that could be enough to work with for a mood board."

Lisle, who had been taking copious notes, added her thoughts. "I like it. It's different, more current. I can see deep colors, metal, brass." She began to sketch in her notebook.

Once the meeting disbanded, Celeste called Asha into her office.

Her boss sat behind her large teak desk and invited Asha to sit opposite her. "I have to say, you're finally stepping up."

"Inspiration takes time." Asha steadied her knee by keeping her heels planted firmly on the thinly carpeted floor. She was back in her suits, and while it took getting used to after weeks in casual clothes, it made her feel more like the old version of herself.

"I'm glad you got there," Celeste said. "As you know, the nominations for master perfumer are due soon."

Asha forced herself to relax. There were about six hundred master perfumers in the world, and sixty of them were at IFF.

"I understand it is something you've been striving towards," Celeste said.

"I've never been secretive about my ambition."

"No, you have not," Celeste said. "When I reviewed your interview notes from when you first joined the company, it was mentioned."

Asha wondered where this conversation was going. Right now, Celeste was a fan of Asha's, and this perfume was gaining more momentum within the ranks of the company.

"I know it is your expectation to be nominated." Celeste folded her hands in front of her. "But that will not happen this year."

Her stomach sank.

"I don't want this to derail you," Celeste continued. "The reality is your performance this year has been, well, below average if you take in what happened with Guerlain. And you have yet to prove what you can do with Jennifer Kim."

Neel always said Asha didn't have a poker face, but right now she could prove him wrong as she sat silently. Even her knee resisted the urge to shake. She acknowledged to herself that Celeste spoke only what was true.

"You're still very young," Celeste added. "At least a decade or more away from maturing into your craft before you're considered for such a lofty title."

A decade. A few months ago, she would have argued with Celeste, figured out a plan to cut that time period in half. Now she was more pragmatic and understood that the title was given to the most experienced and talented. You needed to have dozens of successful fragrances in your portfolio before even being considered. Asha had thought she was being determined and that by sheer will and hard work she could achieve it sooner. The reality was she would have to dedicate her entire career to reach such an achievement. She'd been ready to do that a few months ago; it didn't sit the same way now. "Is there anything else?"

Celeste leaned forward. "I know this is upsetting to hear, but you need to have realistic expectations. I've been meaning to discuss this with you ever since I read the article in *Town & Country*."

Asha stood. "I appreciate your candor, but it isn't necessary. I am well aware of what it takes to earn such an esteemed title. It is very much aspirational."

"I do believe you have the talent to get there," Celeste said. "Experience is where you must focus."

Asha thanked Celeste and left her boss's office. Instead of going back to her cubicle, she left the building to get some air. Experience was code for more work, vying for high-profile projects, competing with her colleagues, being more visible. All in service to a big corporation.

Behind the building was a small well-maintained garden with benches where she would often take a few minutes to eat or walk. The day was warm, the blue sky dotted with large puffy clouds. Painter's sky. It's what Neel called it when they'd lie in the grass and stare up, the three of them banished from the house on summer afternoons so Mimi and

Leela could watch their soap operas. The kids would be allowed back in for a snack only after *General Hospital* was over.

Asha wandered around the hedgerows. The plants within had yet to reach bloom. In late summer they would overflow with red, orange, and yellow flowers. For now the colors were muted, even among the lush greenery.

She found a bench in a small copse, away from others, slipped out of her heels, and put her bare feet in the grass. After a few minutes of breathing, she called Millie.

"It's four a.m. Are you in the emergency room? Because that is the only reason to wake someone up this early."

Asha winced. "I forgot to calculate the time difference. Go back to sleep, I can call later."

"I'm up now."

Asha heard her friend shuffle around.

"The man is still sleeping, so I'll go to the kitchen and make coffee."

"He has a name," Asha said. "And you must like him very much if you're actually being considerate enough to not disturb him."

"Guess it's another milestone in whatever it is we're doing," Millie said. "Now why are you bothering me?"

"Just having a career crisis. No big deal." Asha pressed her toes into the cool grass.

"What's up?" Millie said.

"Turns out, I'm not an exception or a wunderkind," Asha said. "I'm just like everyone else in my profession. To even be considered for master perfumer will take another ten or more years. In terms of my portfolio, I'm actually behind, so it could be another twenty, and there's no guarantee. And all I keep thinking about is whether I can last that long."

Millie blew her nose before she replied. "Well, that's quite a lot before I've had coffee."

"I know I should have all this figured out by now," Asha said. "But losing my nose and spending so much time in Napa, it messed with me."

"Honestly, being Super Nose warped your expectations. You were a success right out the gate, but you work in an old industry; there are norms and rules, paths to follow. You can only break through up to a point before it gets more difficult to join the ranks of some of these pedigreed people. And you're not French, so that's going to make it tougher."

"Yeah," Asha said. "There are a few Black and Brown people who are making inroads, but it's still predominantly white."

"It's not a barrier," Millie said, "just another hurdle to have whoever decides these things see you as one of them. You have to overcome it through the work."

"Yeah." If she still wanted it, Asha knew she'd be ready to put in the effort. "Sorry I woke you."

"I'll allow it," Millie said. "As long as you don't make a habit of it."

She let the phone drop in her lap as she glanced around the garden. People dressed in business casual milled around, and she was one of them. But did she still see herself as one of them?

CHAPTER
THIRTY-NINE

Asha had barely looked up from her computer. The calculations were making her eyes cross. There were so many rows of ingredients, their dilution percentages, whether the base was ethylene or propylene, costs per amount used, and many other things that went into the formula. Celeste stopped by and interrupted her concentration.

"I just spoke with Jennifer," Celeste said. "There are some concerns."

Asha removed her blue-light glasses and rubbed her eyes.

"Come into my office and we'll talk through them." Celeste left.

Asha was expected to follow. This past week her boss had interrupted her a dozen times a day with little things. There was constant poking and prodding while she added more work to Asha's already-full plate.

"I spoke with Jennifer for over an hour." Celeste took her seat behind the desk.

It was unusual for someone to have this much direct contact with a client. There were layers of teams involved—Jennifer's people, IFF's team, legal, and more. Her mind went back to the calculations.

"Asha," Celeste called out.

"Sorry. Right. Concerns." Asha focused.

"She conveyed to me that she is not a fan of your initial direction," Celeste said.

That was news to her. Lisle said Jennifer's team liked the mood board and the industrial theme. "When did that change?"

Celeste ignored her. "She doesn't think iron and steam are on-brand for her."

"Did you tell her it's inspiration, a layer, that they wouldn't be the dominant notes?"

"I thought it best to ask her what she enjoyed, her preferences. The client loves champagne with strawberries."

Asha clenched her jaw. Simple and derivative. "Isn't that a Bath and Body Works soap?"

Celeste flattened her lips. "It would be a new take, a luxury version. I can see the bottle, bubbles and maybe a cork for the cap."

"Calvin Klein did a peach bellini," Asha said. "We should look at the sales numbers to see how well it performed. Marketing should test whether that's something her segment would gravitate towards."

Celeste leaned forward. "You're not thinking. Her name alone will sell volumes. This is the opportunity for us to put our artistry forward."

"I want to give Jennifer something that speaks to who she is, the way she's achieved success. Not an Instagram version of a fragrance."

"It is too masculine. Jennifer agrees."

Asha shook her head. "Did she come to that conclusion, or was it something you mentioned to her? I know you're not a fan of the direction I'm taking."

Celeste tapped her red-painted nails on the leather blotter. "I am trying to help. I don't want you to fail. You should want to stand out."

I'm not going to do it with strawberries. "At least let me send a few vials to her to give her a better sense of what I'm building."

"If you're determined, I want to review them first. But I'm asking you to also explore my concept. After Guerlain, I don't want to be in a position where you don't deliver again."

The trust was gone. The truth settled in. No matter what she did, how innovative her ideas, Celeste would always remind her of that failure. It hadn't been the blip Asha believed it to be. It now defined her in Celeste's eyes.

Rationally, she knew she wouldn't always work for Celeste, but the woman was an institution and would direct the next few years of Asha's career.

A career she no longer wanted.

Everything in her body stilled. Her shoulders relaxed, and her chest rose and fell as she took full, deep breaths. This was the truth she had been avoiding, afraid to admit to herself since before she left Napa: her passion for the work was gone.

And without it, Asha couldn't dedicate sixty hours or more per week on this one part of her life.

She was in a different place than her grandmother or even her mother had been. She had the privilege of their sacrifice. Leela had to survive in a new country; for her, acceptance had been the only option. Her mom had to toil because she'd been sheltered and had been raised to obey her family's choices. Asha only had the burden of expectation.

She could carve out her own path. Leela and her mom would be disappointed, but their approval shouldn't be the reason for her to continue doing something that felt more and more like someone else's weight to carry. Fear rose in her chest at the idea of an uncertain future.

Asha stood and planted her feet firm on the floor. "Celeste, I don't believe we will ever be on the same page when it comes to this project, or, likely, future ones. I don't think I'm the right person for this account. I'm sure there are others who will be more than happy to explore champagne and strawberries. It won't be me."

"This is not a request," Celeste said. "I expect you to follow my direction."

Asha nodded. "I appreciate the time and experience I've gained here. I learned a lot. Unfortunately, this is no longer what I want to do.

I'll email you my letter of resignation by end of day. If you'd like me to work through the notice period, I understand. However, I'm sure you won't want me around for morale and confidentiality reasons."

"This is ridiculous," Celeste said. "Because we don't agree?"

Asha shook her head. "I've changed."

"You have another offer?"

"No. I just need to figure out what I really want." With that, Asha left her boss's office for the last time. She went to her desk, saved her personal documents on a thumb drive, then typed up the letter and clicked send before shutting her computer down.

She didn't have a lot of photos or anything that wasn't work related, so she grabbed her tote and coffee mug and left the building. It wasn't until she was halfway home that the reality of what she'd done sank in. Adrenaline coursed through her. She was euphoric and scared at the same time. She'd never done something so spontaneous or irrational. As she rehashed the conversation in her head, she couldn't even figure out what had happened from one minute to the next.

She was tired of dealing with Celeste, but her boss hadn't done anything particularly egregious. It was typical push/pull. Yet she knew she couldn't do it for another minute, much less for the rest of her professional life.

Asha stopped inside the café where she usually had coffee on week-end mornings. There was a painting on the wall in front of her that she'd never noticed. The lavender fields in Grasse. The first time she'd gone there, Asha had been excited and full of ambition. She'd vowed to take on every challenge, to become known in the industry, be someone notable.

She'd been so young and naive. She remembered Neel's comment about the valence shell and looked it up on her phone. She didn't under-stand most of the physics terminology, but one description resonated. It was about how when the atom gained energy from an outside force, it broke away from the parent atom and became a free electron. It was likely not an appropriate comparison, but somehow it fit.

She waited for regret to settle in as the server brought over a frothy café crème and a chocolate croissant she'd ordered on a whim. But it didn't. She grabbed her planner. It was bursting with notes and tasks. She leafed through it. She removed everything personal or confidential, then tossed the planner in a nearby bin before she indulged in her late-afternoon snack. Through the open floor-to-ceiling windows, the sky was bright and clear. A few people passed by in a hurry. They had places to go.

Asha grinned as she licked the milky foam from her top lip. She had nowhere she had to be. The idea of nothing to do no longer made her stomach lurch. She bit into the flaky, sweet pastry and savored the rich, buttery taste. Either she was experiencing a break with reality, or she'd finally done what she wanted to. For herself.

She was proud of her choice. Away from everyone, she'd made this choice on her own, without backup plans, and not for anyone else. She gave herself a small pat on her back and noticed that she didn't even have to roll the tightness away. From there, Asha leisurely strolled back to her apartment. There were so many things she hadn't noticed. The buildings were densely situated, many with street-level shops. Window boxes were overflowing with flowers. The side streets were narrow, the road just wide enough for a single car and a motorbike. She stopped at Kebab Élysée, where she'd gotten many takeaways but hadn't realized the stools for the outdoor tables were bright yellow. On a whim she stopped to pick up a bottle of champagne and laughed at the irony.

In her apartment, she removed her gray jacket and went to find a glass to pour the chilled bubbles. Then she put her socked feet up on the coffee table and took a sip. The fizz rippled on her tongue, and she grinned at her own silliness. The air was musty from the windows being closed. She'd hardly been here, except to sleep. So she opened them all to let in the fresh air. It wasn't like Napa. There was more pollution, less greenery. But still, it was breathable.

She grabbed her travel bag that she hadn't fully unpacked from San Francisco. She remembered there was a sleeve of STARBURSTs in there she'd picked up at SFO, and a strawberry-flavored STARBURST would go perfectly with this solitary celebration. She came across Mimi's baggie of drugs and laughed. She didn't want to knock herself out. She would save that for when she came down from this high.

She opened up the zippered pouch to see if she'd slid the candy in there and noticed an envelope. Her heart sped up. Maybe Neel had left her a note and she'd missed it. She hurriedly opened it and then laughed again at how much she'd wanted it to be a love letter. Instead, it was a printout of tea sommelier courses in San Francisco with a Post-it from Millie that said, *if you come back.*

She clutched it in her hand, the candy forgotten as she poured another glass. She was still euphoric from what she'd done, but it was lonely that no one was around to congratulate her.

She reached for her phone. It was a day of being impulsive, and she wasn't going to stop now.

CHAPTER FORTY

Nerves jumped around in her belly and she held back a giggle. Asha knew she was being ridiculous, but the cocktail of adrenaline, fear, and champagne was having an unfamiliar effect. The line rang and rang, and Asha was about to hang up. Then she heard the voice that made her feel like home.

"Poppy?"

"Did I wake you?" She twirled the stem of her wineglass.

"It's eleven a.m."

She bit her lip. "The question still stands."

"You okay?"

"I'm celebrating." Her voice shook, as if she were trying to convince herself.

"Yeah? So am I."

"Did you make the perfect IPA or something?" She put her legs up and curled them under her on the couch. Then she stood to pace. Then sat back down again.

"Listen to you using beer speak," Neel said. "What do those letters stand for?"

"Hold on, let me look it up." She pulled the phone away from her ear. Then realized she couldn't talk to him so put it back. "I can't do it while we're chatting."

"Have you been drinking?"

"I told you. I'm celebrating." She finished her glass and went for her third refill.

"Are you out?"

She heard concern in his voice and urgency. "No, I'm in my teeny-tiny apartment. Are you worried about me?"

"Can I call you in an hour? I need to go back and finish up a meeting I walked out on."

"To take my call?" Asha put her hand on her chest as her heart swelled. "You're making them wait just for me." She wanted it to be for her, except deep down, Asha knew that was Neel being Neel when it came to those he cared about. Though it was nice that she'd made the list.

"I was worried. It's not like you to call me."

"Millie would say something like, 'People in our age group text first.'"

"Poppy, drink some water and then go to bed. We can talk later."

She laughed. "Look at you trying to take care of me from nine thousand miles away."

"I need to go," he said. "There's a room full of people waiting."

"Wait, I have news." She could sense his frustration, which was unlike him. Neel never rushed. "I want you to be the first to know because you're important. You're the best person I know, Neel."

There was silence on his end. Finally, after what seemed like a long time, he responded.

"Get some sleep, Poppy. I'll call you later to check on you."

She was so disappointed, her heart cracked. "I quit my job today." She'd said it. Out loud. And it sank in. "It's not what I want to do anymore, so I went into my boss's office. Well, I was summoned. We had a difference of opinion, so I offered my resignation, then took my ISIPCA coffee mug and left."

"Look—"

She cut him off. "Then I threw away my planner."

"This isn't like you," he said.

"No," she said. "It isn't."

Asha knew he had to get off the phone, go back to his meeting. But he was there, on the other end of the line, and she didn't want to let him go. "Come visit. I'll take you to all my favorite spots." She picked at a chip on her pedicure, then smoothed it out. "We can go on a boat tour along the Seine, and you can see all the usual sights. I promise not to make you eat snails, but they are delicious and you should try them at least once. It's like chewy calamari but instead of fried, it's drenched in butter, garlic, and herbs."

"I can't get away right now," he said. "Maybe in a couple of months."

She put her glass down. Her buzz was wearing off, and all that was left was fear of an uncertain future. "You go with the flow, so get a ticket and spend the weekend with me, a whole week. I'm not busy."

"*I* am," he said. "I'm in the middle of sorting out some really big things for the brewery."

She retreated to soothe the pain in her chest. "Right."

"I have to go."

"I understand." She covered her hurt with anger. "Your hobby, one you've been working on so slowly that you don't even have a location. If you don't want to come to Paris, say so. Don't use work as an excuse. That's a little hard to believe coming from you." She'd gone too far and needed to take the words back. "I—"

"Yeah, your opinion of me will never change. I haven't been that guy in over five years." She could hear the hurt and disappointment.

"Neel, I'm sorry."

He didn't hear her. "I have commitments, responsibilities. I'm trying to get my business off the ground. But you don't want to know that because you only see me as who I once was. I have to go. I don't know what you need, but I don't think it's me. Call Millie."

With that, he disconnected the call. She dropped the phone on the sofa and placed a hand on her stomach. The burn and churn weren't because of alcohol. Asha walked to the window with champagne in hand. It was dark, and the streetlights gave a soft glow to the narrow avenues. It was quiet—most everyone was likely home or tucked away in a restaurant. She turned her face to the cool breeze. It gave her small comfort. If Neel's reaction was shock, everyone else's would be disapproval.

Fighting back her tears, she raised her glass to the night sky. She'd done it for herself. Tonight, she would be happy. Tomorrow would come soon enough. And with it, regrets.

CHAPTER
FORTY-ONE

Every new planner Asha started, she wrote down her favorite quote. *If you want to be successful, seek competence, empowerment; do nothing short of the best you can do.* It was from Sadhguru. She'd read his book *Inner Engineering* as part of her self-designed personal development curriculum.

The two weeks following her resignation had been a hailstorm of doing. After her impulsive call to Neel, she'd woken up with resolve. Neel had sent her a text to call him back. Instead, she sent him a tourist photo, keeping up pretense that all was fine. He'd replied with a thumbs-up emoji. They'd gone backward, and she knew it was her fault. But she needed to fix her life before she dealt with her heart. And his.

Celeste had accepted her letter and did not request that Asha work through her notice period. Then Asha had spent a day making lists of pros and cons of staying on her career track or hopping off. She was a citizen of the EU, having lived for so long in France that she could apply for roles at Coty or Givaudan. All the pros of staying were practical and safe.

There was only one con. She wouldn't be able to explore whether she had a passion for something of her own choosing. That's what she really wanted to do. If she was going to try a new challenge, the time was now. So she'd packed up her tiny apartment with her art, personal items, and a few mementos and shipped them to San Francisco. She'd taken Neel's advice and had called her best friend the following day. Millie was the second person to know Asha had quit her job, and she had made her promise not to post it in their group chat. Her friend was worried, and Asha had reassured Millie that she would figure it out but had left out any details until she could put things in motion.

Then Asha booked a one-way ticket, said goodbye to her friends with promises to stay in touch and to host their visits to Northern California. On her last day, she had taken one last walk. As she crossed her favorite bridge, the Pont au Change, she paused to take in the incredible views of the city that had given her a home, one she only appreciated when she looked up from her beakers and vials.

It had taken a lot of action for everything to fall into place. Unlike the last time, she was going back with a solid plan for her future. She'd purposefully packed up her life in Paris and left so that they couldn't push her back. As for the rest of it, it had taken a lot of thinking and learning. And research. Every spare moment had gone into having a solid foundation, making pro/con lists, and reassuring herself that she could do this. Once everything was in order, she'd landed in San Francisco with determination.

And with a lighter heart.

Instead of staying with Millie, Asha had decided to get a hotel room. Millie would have a thousand questions. Worse, she'd want to help, and Asha needed to do this on her own. For herself first, without input or help. She would succeed or fail by herself. The day after her arrival, she made the phone call, one that was necessary for all her plans to work out. She'd ask for secrecy, just for one more day. This wasn't something she could do over the phone. It would need to be an in-person conversation.

With her documents in order, Asha was situated in a coworking office space she'd rented for a few hours. It was important to have a neutral venue for this meeting.

The office was small, with adjacent corner windows that looked out over other buildings in the district. It had a simple desk, two chairs, and a lamp in the corner. Two generic paintings of compasses and clocks hung on the beige wall. It wasn't pretty, but she appreciated its functionality.

Asha smoothed down the bottom of her gray sheath dress as she received a call that her guest had arrived. She resisted the urge to shake her leg or tap the heels of her red pumps. Instead, she took a few steadying breaths. This wasn't do or die, and if it didn't work, she would think of something else. There was no one path; it was just what she planned to do next.

"Asha."

She stood to greet her father. "Dad. Have a seat. Close the door."

Sanjay nodded. "This should be interesting."

Cardamom. Violet. Peppercorn. His cologne perfumed the air as he crossed one knee over the other. Asha wondered if they would ever get to a place where they hugged each other. She'd made her peace with this man. He was tangential to her life, and she no longer expected anything more. "Thank you for meeting me."

"I couldn't resist," Sanjay said. "Especially with so much mystery and secrets."

She smiled. "I want to do this in the proper order, which I'm sure you will appreciate."

"Or it is something that your mother and mine will not approve of and you want to test the waters." He adjusted the cuffs of his coral shirt and navy suit. "No matter, I managed to schedule a few meetings while in town."

"I'm not going to ask you to take sides," she said.

"No, I am well aware it's you three ladies versus me." He toyed with his silver cuff links.

She redirected the conversation. "I don't want to waste your time, so I'll just say it. I'd like you to give me Sonanum."

The only sign that her request registered was a slight raise of his brow. "Give?"

"Yes," Asha said. "Just like dada gave you Goldfield. I only want the garden."

He picked something off his knee. "Is this your way of saying you'd eventually take over the hotel?"

She shook her head. "No. Right now that's not what I want to do."

He gave her a questioning look. "So, it's not out of the realm of possibility."

"Don't get your hopes up, Dad. I'm not going to work for you. All I want is Sonanum."

"Why?"

Instead of looking down at her notes, she kept eye contact. "It's a working garden. I'll tend to it."

"It costs money to keep and maintain," he said.

"I know. I want to use the herb garden for my start-up tea business."

He nodded. "The little hobby of yours. Interesting."

"It's more than that. I've done the research—there is a market for boutique blends."

"Do you have capital?" Sanjay asked.

"My savings. I have enough to support me and my business for two years before I would need to turn a profit."

"And you would lease the garden."

She leaned forward and crossed her arms. "That's not in the budget. I want you to give it to me outright."

He laughed. "Do you know how much that land is worth? I'm not in the position to give away four acres."

"Did you pay dada for Goldfield?" She wanted him to see her as a worthy adversary.

He rose to stare out of the windows. "I didn't ask him for a piece of it for a hobby. I worked at Goldfield since I was a child, got my degrees in hospitality management while I continued to grow in the business. It wasn't given to me, as you put it; it was turned over with the expectation that I would run it, build on it."

She moved to stand next to him. "Dada told me that his father wanted to buy the original motel but couldn't, so he worked for the seller in exchange for half his salary back to the original owner, then that owner willed the hotel to dada's father."

"The laws back then didn't give us opportunities."

"He wanted to do something on his own," Asha said.

Sanjay looked at her. "It's a Patel trait. We were patidars in India. Landowners. Patels don't like to work for others; we prefer to control our own destiny. We need to be self-made."

"That's what I want too."

"Do you have half a million dollars to spare?"

"Of course not." Asha went back to the desk. "Just like dada's father had help, I'm asking for yours. Pass down a piece of our history to me."

He rubbed his chin, then went back to his chair. "Why the sudden interest? As far as I know, you have a thriving career. This is a big change."

Asha decided to be honest. "You always knew you would take over Goldfield. Did you ever wonder if there was something else for you? Were there things you were interested in that you let go because there was no other option?"

Sanjay looked at his hands. "Poetry. I loved listening to the ghazals my parents played Sunday mornings. I would try and write my own. I used to read Pablo Neruda and Langston Hughes. Now I enjoy seeing what poets of current times are doing, like Amanda Gorman and Saeed Jones."

It shocked her that she'd never known this about her own father. But then, she hadn't asked. Instead, she'd grown comfortable with their one-dimensional relationship. She wondered if it was possible to have something more than civility between them. "My brain doesn't get poetry, not unless it's the rhyming kind."

"It's about subtext. The beats in between the words, the pauses. The space and cadence within the sentences. That's the genius of it. Like your perfumes, there are layers, and the more you become familiar, the more you understand."

She made a note in her planner. "I'll pick up a few books by the people you mentioned."

"I have a shelf in my home office," he said. "You're welcome to it."

"I guess I spent most of my time in the kitchen and the guest room when I was there." Asha put down the pen and crossed her hands. "What do you think about my offer?"

He smiled. "It's a request, not an offer. You're not giving anything in return."

She'd been prepared for this. "You're right. What is the most valuable part of Goldfield?"

"I'm listening."

"The name. It has history and legacy that goes beyond the buildings and levels of service. It is what has lasted from its very beginning."

She was encouraged by his nod. He was interested. "My years at IFF, I've learned a lot about branding and expanding the market. Millie mentioned that hotels have signature smells and items. I know you would never franchise Goldfield. It is inherently the hotel in a specific place, on a specific piece of land. But what about what grows in that earth, at Sonanum? Imagine 'Sonanum Tea from Goldfield.'" She leaned back in her chair.

Her father steepled his fingers under his chin. "A boutique tea from a boutique hotel."

Asha nodded and smiled. "You said Patels prefer to go into business for themselves. That's what I want to do."

"How big is your operation? What do you estimate as your margins? What's your timeline? Do you know if you can generate enough volume? Do you have suppliers and distributors? Selling it merely at one hotel isn't sustainable."

"This is a pitch," Asha said. "Without Sonanum it can't happen."

"You do realize that this won't be easy."

She got the sense that she had his support. "I'm a hard worker. That's one thing I've never shied away from."

"Your mother and Leela ba."

She waved him off. "I plan to talk to them, help them understand. And I'd like to do it myself if you can hold off on letting them know about our meeting."

He agreed.

"What do you think?"

"The idea has merit, and I like the way you incorporate Goldfield. If this takes off, the reach could go well beyond the hotel."

"Exactly," she said.

He shook his head. "Unfortunately, Sonanum isn't mine to give anymore."

She didn't think she heard him. "What do you mean?"

"I sold it."

The words sat heavy between them.

Sanjay paced. It was the first time she saw her father ruffled and unsteady.

"I needed an influx of cash," he said. "For Goldfield. The land was too valuable. I had tried everything to keep it part of the complex."

"You were going to build cottages on it," she said.

He shook his head. "We can't afford it. The recovery from the pandemic is tough, peaks and valleys, and I couldn't continue to overextend, not without serious risk."

"You sold the whole plot?"

He nodded. "Your idea is solid. You can find another source, other gardens you can buy herbs from, and you can use the Goldfield name."

"So it's all upside for you." She couldn't keep the anger out of her voice.

He raised his brows.

"You get the benefit of branding without having to invest in anything," she said. "It's always and only about the hotel for you. I have never once asked you for anything, and still you're okay with taking."

Sanjay sighed, then went back to his seat. "You and I, we don't know each other very well."

"Not my fault."

"Maybe," he said. "Though as adults, we stayed out of each *other's* way."

"I was a bargaining chip you conceded to Mom."

"She told me about your conversation," he acknowledged. "I haven't always handled things well. I have no other heirs. You are the one who is supposed to take over Goldfield after I'm gone."

She crossed her arms. "I'm a person in my own right, not someone who exists simply to fulfill a path I never chose."

He stood. "That's how history works. That's what being part of a family is. You can go on and on about being an individual, but we are who we've come from. We must honor the past, preserve it for the future. This is what your mother failed to teach you."

"She sees it as wanting something more for me." Asha couldn't believe she was defending her mom.

"More?" He spread his arms. "You had a career, which you don't want. Now you're going to try your hand at tea making, a saturated market. Boutique teas? Ours is a culture of cha, milky and homemade. Not this watery concoction full of flowers that you plan to create. And you want Sonanum, the legacy you toss aside."

"You talk about history," she said. "Indians have been drinking herbal teas since before the British arrived. You might want to look up Ayurveda."

"This is pointless," he said.

"Agreed." Anger receded as hurt settled in. He would never understand her, nor she him. He was so rigid in his view of the world, single minded. He had no room for a daughter who wasn't useful.

"Use the Goldfield name or don't," he said. "I leave it to you."

With that, Sanjay left the office, and Asha sat back in her chair, defeated. She stared down at her notes. She'd been so sure that it would work out. She'd planned for a scenario where he would say no to the whole garden, so she had sketches of how keeping the herb area would be aesthetically pleasing to cottage guests. She'd never thought he would go through with selling a part of something that meant so much to him.

Or that it would leave her without even a small piece of where she'd felt at home.

CHAPTER
FORTY-TWO

That evening, Asha had replayed the conversation over and over again in her head. Her plan had evaporated before she could even get to the next step. She'd spent the night with a bottle of wine and dinner, flipping channels on the large-screen TV in her hotel room. After a few hours of wallowing, she called Millie.

"What did I tell you about texting before calling?" Millie said.

"And still you answered," Asha said.

"Only to lecture you about telephone etiquette in the twenty-first century."

"I need to borrow your car," Asha said. "Yes, I'm in town. No, I don't have time to go into all the details."

"Lucky for you, neither do I," she said. "I'm with the man, and we're heading to his place after a nice meal. I'm too mellow for all the questions."

"I promise to fill you in soon," she said.

"My precious is in my parking space." Millie ran through instructions and texted the codes for the garage and her apartment. "You will not scratch it or get even a speck of dirt on my baby or you'll have to deal with me."

"It's an inanimate object," Asha said.

"I'm texting the door person to not let you in."

"No," Asha shouted. "I'll take care of it. I promise."

Millie softened her voice. "If you need me, I'm here. You know that, right?"

Asha nodded even though her friend couldn't see her. "I love you, Mills."

"Not a speck or scratch." Millie disconnected the call.

Asha played back the conversation the next morning as she drove Millie's fiery-red Audi TTS. Her friend could be nosy, bossy, and all the other things, but she could also give space if Asha needed it. Right now, instead of burdening Millie with the uncertainties in her own life, Asha knew she had to get herself on track.

Bend and adapt was her new approach. And while this was a major setback, she would figure it out. Sonanum was no longer an option, so she would think. The business plan was solid, but her differentiator was gone. While she sorted it out, Asha knew she had to let her mom and Leela know the whole of it from her, before her father let slip about their meeting.

As she crossed over the Napa County line, the hills were greener than when she was last here, the countryside more vibrant in greens and reds. The cloudless sky was bright blue, and she let out a contented sigh. It felt right to be here. This was where she wanted to be. She saw wineries dotted on both sides of the road, each with distinct architecture, and her mind automatically went to Neel. They had yet to talk.

She hoped he'd found a location for his brewery. It would add something unique and very Neel to this area. She smiled as she stared at the brake lights of the car in front of her. He'd found a way to do something on his own terms, and she was proud of him. Nerves fluttered at the thought of seeing him again. She should have sent him a message, but a part of her just wanted to show up, surprise him, see his reaction. And hope there was happiness in his eyes at the sight of her.

Once back in her parents' house, she put her suitcases in the guest room before composing a text to Leela and her mom. She steeled herself for the emotional pressure they would unleash to force her to stay on her path. But even though her plan hadn't worked out, she wasn't going back to Paris. That part of her life was done. She wanted to be here, and she would do whatever she needed to stay.

With every change there was opportunity. She would figure out what was next, but first she would stop hiding. Asha put the kettle on and heard the multiple beeps of incoming messages. All she'd said was that she was home, had news, and looked forward to seeing them soon. Their questions would have to wait until they were in person.

Thirty minutes later she heard a car in the drive.

Leela came through the front door. "Are you sick?"

"Did you win the lottery?" Mimi followed her. "Do they have that in France?"

She hugged them both. "No. I wish. And yes."

"Did something happen?" Leela took both her hands and held on.

"Can we wait until Mom gets here so I can say it all at once?" Asha pulled her hands from Leela's. "It is nothing bad, there is no tragedy. How about I make us some tea?"

"I'll make cha," Mimi said. "I want something kadak."

She knew her grandmother was watching her. "I'll go pick some fudino from the back for you." Asha left through the french doors and walked toward the side herb garden. The smells were heady in the soft breeze. She spotted the mint with its textured leaves, smooth to touch with their brown stems. It was used to help with digestion and was often added to cha as a way too cool the effects of the warm masala spices. She picked a handful and took her time before heading inside.

Leela had raided the pantry and put out papdi ganthia, a fried snack made of chickpea flour and tossed in red chili powder. There was khari puri, another fried savory treat, as well as sev mamara, a puffed rice mix seasoned with peanuts and tossed in hot oil and mustard seed. There was always a stock in every Gujarati pantry, their version of potato chips and popcorn.

"I canceled my lunch meeting." Sapna rushed into the house and dropped her tote on the sofa as she approached the kitchen. "What's the emergency? What are you doing here?"

She hugged her mom. "Everything is fine."

"No tragedy." Mimi strained cha into tall mugs. "And unfortunately no scandalous pregnancy."

"What?" Sapna said.

Asha joined them all at the big dining table laden with snacks.

She kept her hands in her lap and her back straight. "I'm moving back to California."

Mimi was the only one who clapped with excitement. Leela kept her hand on the handle of her mug.

Sapna was the first to speak. "Did you get fired from IFF? Was it because of the article?"

Asha smiled. "No, Mom. I resigned."

"Unacceptable," Leela said. "I did not raise a quitter."

"I know this is a lot and you weren't expecting it, but it is my decision."

"Good for you," Mimi said.

"Is it because you want to live closer to here?" Sapna held her mug in both hands. "IFF and others have bases here in California, though New York is the US hub, and that isn't too far, only a three-hour time difference."

Asha put her hand on her mom's arm. "I don't want to be a perfumer anymore."

"Is this one of those quarter-life crises I read about a few years ago?" Leela said. "That's an American thing. We don't do that."

Asha shook her head. "No. When I went back, I saw my work in a different light. I wasn't an artist; I was a cog in a huge machine. Sure, I was able to use some creativity, but it was in service to profits and shareholders. My art had a lot of fences. If a fragrance didn't test well, it didn't matter that I had put in hundreds of hours; it had to be redesigned for the consumer. And the paperwork and meetings . . . the French invented bureaucracy, and I was drowning in it. I liked my coworkers, but that isn't enough."

"This is all office politics," Sapna said. "Being a part of a big corporation has its pluses and minuses, but you get opportunity and access. And fine, if not IFF, Coty has a huge presence in New York. You have contacts and a solid reputation."

Asha took her mom's hand. The pale-brown skin was smooth, her nails pink and perfectly shaped. The two-carat diamond her dad had given her mom for their twenty-fifth wedding anniversary gleamed. "I don't want any of it." Not right now. But she didn't add that. It would only lead to this being seen as a whim, and they would spend their energy reminding her of all that she would have to rebuild if she went back.

"We helped you get here," Leela said. "You just throw it away?"

Asha took a fortifying sip of her tea, which was still hot and scalded her tongue. "No, I'm building on everything I've learned. I know how to create. I understand ratios and formulas. I have transferrable skills."

"You aren't going to work at Goldfield." Sapna cut her off.

"No," Asha said. "For now, the plan is to see what I can do with tea. I'm going to start a business, of my own. Sell my blends."

"That is the silliest thing I've heard yet," Leela said. "Our tea is cultivated in large regions of Darjeeling, Kangra, Nilgiris, Sikkim. Here people take that and add some potpourri and sell it for five dollars a bag."

"Exactly," Asha said. "You hate that our culture is often co-opted for capitalism. But if I did it, I could highlight the history, the impact of colonialism, incorporate Ayurveda, and showcase the true essence of our culture."

"I'd buy it," Mimi said. "Well, with a family discount."

Asha laughed.

"I don't understand," Sapna said. "You can do the same for perfume."

Asha kept eye contact with Leela. "I can, but that's very dependent on the system, and to scale requires a lot of infrastructure. It could be decades or more before I would have enough influence in a conglomerate like IFF to create a fragrance that honors you. With my own business, I can create something—a tea for you—in a matter of years. We could work together on it, build something that is ours. Not in France or for someone else, but here, with your help and input."

"It's too big a leap," Sapna said. "I think you should stay in fragrances. It's what you know, and if you need a break, fine, take it, but doing something like this, you don't even know if it will work."

Asha finished the last of her cha. "It's a risk. And thanks to you, I can take one. You didn't have as many options as I do. You had to work to make sure I had a home and all the comforts of life. Not only did you help me to become a self-sufficient person but you also gave me a safety net. I know I can do this, and I'm going to do my best to be successful. Tea is what I want to do—it's not the hobby I thought it was, it's a passion. Something that combines my love for Sonanum and uses the skills I've built learning and working all these years."

She looked around the table. Three generations of Patel women. Each had worked to provide for the next. Asha was a testament to their success, not an embodiment of the life they wished they'd lived. The best way to honor them would be to pursue and overcome her own struggles.

"It's risky," Leela said.

"I have the talent," Asha said. "One that you both nurtured in me."

Leela and her mother looked at each other. It was her mom who patted Asha's hand. That was as much as she was going to get for now. Asha knew they were surprised, and it would take time for them to come around. She glanced at her grandmother, who said nothing.

"I'm just happy you're doing it here," Mimi said. "You're still too young for Nanis of Napa, but we can help you. We can start an assembly line to fill the little baggies with your blends."

Asha laughed. "I might just take you up on that, Mimi."

"It seems as if you've decided." Leela finally spoke.

"It's what I'm choosing, for me."

Leela nodded. "Very well."

And that was that. Acceptance. Leela had made peace with Asha's endeavor. With time, she believed, her grandmother would fully embrace it, and so would her mom.

Now there was only one person left who needed to know.

CHAPTER
FORTY-THREE

Not letting any more time pass, later that day, Asha went to Goldfield. Neel's truck wasn't in the drive, and instead of sending him a message, she went down to the garden. She stroked fully mature stems of rosemary. She'd come back with shears and baskets. It wouldn't be poaching. Sonanum was her family's garden, and since it was going to be razed, she didn't want the herbs to be destroyed in vain. Closer to when it was going to be mowed down, she would uproot these precious herbs and repot them until she found a place for her own garden. Engrossed in the smells and scents around her, she didn't hear approaching footsteps.

Neel stood near her, and every rational thought left her mind. Emotion coursed through her—attraction, guilt, regret, and love. Not dormant but fully alive, and in a way that was completely different from when they were teenagers. Her love for him now was laced with history and understanding—it was so deep and overwhelming that she didn't know if she would ever be able to express it with words. She wanted to hold him, have him wrap his arms around her. She wanted them to simply be. Forever.

"I heard you were back," he said.

"Group chat?"

He shook his head. "I muted it. Millie told me you'd borrowed her car. I saw it on the path and came down."

She nodded and took a minute to find her voice. "So you don't know why I'm here." She couldn't look away from him. His hair was mussed as if he'd run his hands through it a few times. It was a warm early May afternoon, and he was in a gray T-shirt and slouchy jeans. She wanted to smooth out the wrinkles on his shoulder but kept her hands to herself.

"I know it's not for me." He laughed and shoved his hands in his pockets.

Asha heard the hurt in his voice. "I . . . there are so many things I want to tell you. I should have handled everything differently. I know that now. When I called you—"

"It's fine." Neel cut her off.

She put her hand on his arm. "I'm sorry." His skin was warm and smooth to the touch. "What I said to you when we talked, it was wrong. I was out of line. I hurt you." It was simple and honest. She would regret her words for the rest of her life.

"Thank you," he said.

"I know you're not all the things your father says about you, what I've said about you," she said. "Even Millie, who does it out of sisterly love. It grates on you, and that's unfair."

He rolled his neck and stepped back from her touch. "What's going on here?" He pointed to the rosemary stems in her hand.

She didn't take his abrupt question personally. Neel wasn't one for long, drawn-out conversations. She would accept him for who he was. "I'm thinking about how to save them all. The plants, the trees. I asked my father to give me Sonanum, offered to name my tea brand after Goldfield in exchange."

He was quiet and became still.

She shrugged. "It's too late. He's already sold it. I want to salvage what I can while it's still here. Can I borrow your truck? One of these days?"

"For?"

"To dig up some of these so they can be replanted. Millie's car doesn't exactly work for that. Besides, she told me she didn't want a single fleck of dirt inside her precious baby. Which is impossible, but I'll find a detailing place before I return it. And I need to find another plot of land, to transplant all of this."

Asha stopped when he cupped his hands around her arms. "Breathe."

She did as he asked.

He let go. "It's not easy in this area. Trust me, I know."

"Right," she said. "You've been looking for a location for your brewery."

He nodded. "I found a place and bought it."

She smiled wide. "That's fantastic. I'm so happy for you, Neel. In this area, I hope."

"In this exact spot," he said.

His words registered. "Here?" There was shock but also a tinge of hurt that she hadn't known. "When?"

"The morning you called me to tell me you quit your job," Neel said.

"I see." Except she didn't. He could have said something. "You know how much this garden means to me. And you just bought it?"

He shook his head and turned away from her. "Since when? It wasn't until a few months ago that you'd even spent time back here. Then you left. Back to your life, career. What did you expect?"

"For someone to give even a thought to how I would feel about losing this place."

He ran a hand through his hair. "I've been looking for a location for over a year. It took me a while, longer than you and my sister, to figure

265

out what I wanted to do with my life, but this is it. And it's mine. Even Millie's investment is structured in the same way as others so that when I'm able to, I'll be the sole owner."

"Did you offer to buy Sonanum from my dad?"

"He approached me." Neel raised his voice. "A week after you left, he said he was scrapping the expansion and needed cash to rightsize the books. Asked if I was interested."

Asha sat down on the ground, her emotions in turmoil. She wanted to be mad at Neel, blame him for taking this out from under her, but he wasn't her punching bag. This was on her father, who would do what was best for his precious hotel, regardless of anyone else's feelings or input. Especially not hers. "Millie knows?"

"She's putting up some of the capital, so yeah." He knelt down in front of her. "Here."

She took the water bottle that he held out and sipped.

"She didn't say anything to me about it." Once again, she'd been in Paris and life had gone on without her.

"It wasn't intentional," he said. "It all happened fast, and she's been busy with work and the guy she's dating."

She nodded. "I'm not mad at her." Asha realized she wasn't. There was only one person to blame here.

"Do you think my dad offered it you as a way to get back at me for not taking over Goldfield?"

Neel laughed. "Have you been watching Mimi's soap operas? No. He doesn't think about business in terms of revenge or payback."

"Or my feelings." Asha glanced around. It took sixty years of effort to make this spot a place of beauty. She'd never associated Sonanum with business. It was always a garden, a place for her to play and learn and be. "When I spent time here, in March, I had this one moment where it was just me and Sonanum. I was completely relaxed, not thinking about the past or future. And this overwhelming feeling settled in the whole of my body. Home. That's what this place became for me."

"I'm no philosopher." He sat next to her. "But home isn't a place."

"Do not say it's where the heart is."

"Ha ha." Neel pulled up one knee and rested his arm on it. "We grew up in the hotel business. Every room is someone's home for the night. We sell hospitality, a way to make a guest feel welcome. It's an idea. Not a place."

"Look at you, being all wise."

"I've been spending too much time with Sanjay uncle."

She rested her chin on her knees. "You don't believe in home?"

"The opposite, really. I live in multiple places—your parents', Millie's, the cottage; sometimes I sleep in one of the guest rooms," he said. "None of that makes me feel like I don't belong where I rest my head. I'm welcomed, fed, loved—that's all that matters."

"Must be nice," Asha muttered. "I've had to fight to stay here. Even when I was back temporarily, people kept asking when I was leaving, how long I was staying. It was constantly a 'don't let the door hit you' feeling. I mean, I'm not even in the Desai-Patel group chat."

"That chat is the bane of my existence. Why do you think I don't carry my phone with me? Even with the notifications turned off, I look at it and there are seventy messages. And Mimi with her videos and GIFs . . . consider yourself lucky."

"You had your phone with you when I called that night."

"I was in a conference room with lawyers and Sanjay uncle. I do use it for stuff other than texting and talking."

She looked up. "My timing really sucks."

"It was too late to undo it," he said. "And I don't want to. I hope you understand."

She tried, but it was hard to imagine Sonanum making way for a brewery. She sighed. "It wasn't until I lost my sense of smell that I realized how much I had built my entire world around it. I thought I didn't know who I was when it was gone. But I learned how to be, because I had to. My whole life isn't around a single dream anymore. I'll figure something out."

Neel nudged her with his shoulder. "I for sure thought you were going to at the very least get in a few arm punches."

"I'm still considering it."

He looked away. They were surrounded by tall plants on both sides, the shade protecting them from the sun. This low to the ground, only the tops of their heads would be visible to anyone looking.

"Come up to the office," he said. "I'll show you the blueprints."

Asha didn't want to have anything to do with destroying Sonanum. "Maybe another time." She rose and wiped down her jeans.

"You're still upset." He got to his feet and did the same.

"It's a little hard to process. I can't imagine all of this gone."

"I hope you know that I'm not the bad guy here," he said.

She shrugged. "I do. It's a business decision." With that she walked away from him. She really didn't blame him, but she wasn't okay with it either, and that was going to be hard to come to terms with.

CHAPTER
FORTY-FOUR

The following Sunday, Asha had been summoned back to San Francisco to drop off Millie's car. She'd spent the past few days looking for land to plant her herbs and hadn't found anything. Leela and her mom were still getting used to the idea, though Asha suspected that they still hoped she would change her mind and go back to perfumery if this became too difficult. She was resolute and made sure that whenever they got together, she continued to show her excitement so that they didn't see any openings to convince her this wasn't viable.

She found a rare street parking spot in Noe Valley, near where Millie had made brunch reservations.

Her friend was seated at an outdoor table under the overhang in the far back corner. As Asha approached them, she noticed Millie had a pink fruity cocktail in her hand, and someone was seated opposite. A very familiar someone.

"I didn't know you were joining us," Asha said to Neel. "What are you doing here?"

"Waiting for Millie to stop hogging all the menus," Neel said.

She sat next to Millie, across the table from him.

"You don't get one," Millie said.

"You're not ordering for me," Neel said.

"I don't need the chef to hate us because you have questions, sub-stitutions, and adjustments. And this one"—Mille pointed to Asha—"doesn't know how to eat like an adult."

Asha snatched one from under the stack in front of Millie. She wasn't going to let Millie be the boss of brunch.

"How's my car?" Millie said.

"Dusty. I brought you some fresh flowers from Sonanum to make up for it." Asha scanned the menu.

"Why did I even agree to this?" Neel sipped from his pint glass of water.

"Because you're here for the weekend and you love me," Millie said.

"Why was she invited?" Neel pointed to Asha.

"I need my car this week. I'm doing some site visits south of the city," Millie said. "And I need details about this tea business from Poppy. By the way, why didn't you tell me?"

"Because I'm still figuring it out," Asha said.

"And I'm the business expert here," Millie said. "I can help you. Send me your plan, including financials, and I'll review it."

Asha crossed her arms. "This is why I didn't come to you. You take over."

"I give advice and offer resources. I'm not asking to be president of your company." Millie sipped her drink, then offered it to Asha. "Here, it's a grapefruit tonic with akvavit. You'll like it."

Asha tried the cocktail. It was fruity and acidic. The hint of straw-berries reminded her of Celeste. "I'll stick with a glass of rosé."

"Just like I told Neel," Millie said. "Sonanum is a great spot for the brewery. Secluded enough, but attached to Goldfield it will have high traffic. There will be cross-promotional opportunities as well."

"You sound just like my dad," Asha said.

"He's not a great father," Millie said. "But he does know how to run a hotel, expand, increase revenue."

"Don't ruin brunch by singing his praises." Asha planned to enjoy the beautiful day instead of griping. The restaurant was busy, and there were groups of friends and families laughing and enjoying the clear, hot day.

"You brought him up," Millie said.

"How about me?" Neel said to Asha. "Are you and I good?"

Asha ignored him and stared at houses on the other side of the street.

Millie rifled through her large bag and pulled out a hairbrush. "I stayed the night at the man's place," she explained. "But this will do. This is the feelings stick. Who wants to go first?"

Asha laughed.

"Put that away," Neel said. "No hair around food."

Millie shoved it back. "Then find another way to make peace, because he's taking you back to Napa after brunch, and it's going to be an awkward ride otherwise."

"Seriously?" Asha turned to Millie.

"How did you think you were getting back?"

"I was going to stay with you and get a rental tomorrow," she said. "I need a car in Napa."

"Borrow Mimi's," Millie said. "They only need one between the two of them."

Asha glanced at Neel. He raised his brow to silently ask her if she was okay with the plan, and she nodded. The server came over and Millie ordered for the table—mushroom toast, sesame flatbread with smoked salmon, sweet potato hash, a salad, and a side of bacon. "It's half the menu, so you'll have something you like."

"Tell me about this man of yours," Asha said.

Millie sighed. "It's awful. He's everything my parents would want. A nonprofit lawyer and a workaholic like me. He's a Patel, of course. Can you get more Gujarati than that? And we go on these perfect dates. Next weekend, we're taking out a rowboat in Stow Lake."

"That sounds awful." Asha's voice was laced with sarcasm.

"Fine. He's great and it's going well."

Asha nudged her friend's shoulder. "I'm happy for you."

"Me too." Millie leaned back and turned her face toward the sun. "Days like this make me really love this city."

"You love it all the other days too." Neel leaned his arms on the table.

"I don't get why anyone would want to live anywhere else."

Neel turned his head to Asha. "It means she still hates the idea of me moving to Napa Valley."

"You're a lost cause, but Poppy . . ." Millie mirrored Neel's pose with her arms and hands. "You would love it here."

Asha tilted her neck. "What are you getting at?"

"I have the best idea," Millie said. "You still want to take those tea sommelier classes, right? So move to San Francisco and do that while you're still sorting out where to set up shop."

"It's expensive," Asha said. "I can't afford to rent a place while I'm living on my savings."

"That's the best part," Millie said. "You can work at DHG."

Asha sipped her rosé. "Also, I don't need a job. I have a plan."

"And DHG will be your first client," Millie said. "That green tea you made me a few months ago? After our Sushirrito lunch, I was thinking about that being the signature item across all of our hotels. It was so calming as I worked. Then I started to do research. Very few brands have signature teas; mostly they're tied to their upscale restaurants, but what if we had our own special blends? You can do some fancy ones for the luxury brands where we can add a high tea offering. For the midrange and economy hotels, we can package a different blend that's available in every room."

Asha's heart raced. An account that big would make her solvent. She began to think through the calculations in her head. "It's a big job, and I don't even have anything set up yet."

"Exactly, but if I put you on payroll, whatever you develop will be for DHG," Millie said. "Win-win."

She looked at Neel, who kept his expression neutral.

"It's an idea." Though working for DHG didn't sit well.

"It can't be that different from creating a perfume," Millie continued. "Instead of scents, it's spices and herbs and things. You'll have an office space, and I'll find a kitchen area that can be converted into a working lab with whatever you need."

"Slow down." Asha held her hands up. "This is ridiculous. I'm not remotely qualified."

"So you'll learn with the tea sommelier courses. DHG will fund it. Then we can pilot. Honestly, I've done the numbers, and this could really work out."

Asha was grateful when their food came. The mere idea of Millie's offer frightened her. She wondered if she could make the leap.

☙

A few hours later, on the drive back, Asha quietly stared out the window. Inside she was freaking out. Neel turned on the radio and she shut it off. Music wouldn't help her right now.

"I forgot. You can't think if there's music," Neel said.

"It's so unrealistic," Asha said. "And Millie has it all planned out."

"That's what she does." Neel rolled in stop-and-go traffic. "So do you."

Except this wasn't the direction she'd even considered. Her plan was to start small, experiment. She wanted to get endorsements from experts who knew teas, build a base of customers who would become advocates, then she would launch the brand.

"What does your gut tell you?"

"The last time I listened to my gut," Asha said, "I quit my job."

"And it worked out. Now you have this opportunity." Neel changed lanes to pass a horse trailer.

"This isn't the way I thought it would go," Asha said.

"Maybe the path is different, but it's still doing what you want."

She crossed her arms and wished she weren't trapped in the truck. Pacing would help. "Is it, though? Remember what you said to me at Sonanum, how you planned to do it on your own? That's what I want."

"I didn't turn down your dad's offer to sell the land," Neel said. "It's kind of what Millie wants to do for you."

She shook her head. "No. It isn't. It's like—" Her brain clicked into place. "I would be replacing IFF with DHG. I'd be working for another corporation. It would be what the brand wanted, what guests liked. It wouldn't be mine. Just my skills and creativity in service to someone else's profit line."

Neel took her hand and squeezed. "Breathe."

She clutched his hand and kept hold. She never wanted to let go. "How are you like this? Always so calm and steady."

"I have my moments." He glanced over, then back at the road. "You've seen a few."

"If my mom finds out about this, she's going to pressure me," she said. "She and Leela have been tolerating my change of plans, but I know they don't like the idea of me taking this risk. I need more time."

"Time is a construct."

She laughed, and it felt good to release some tension. "You're joking. It's finite. Our lives are calculated in seconds, minutes, hours. Then mortality hits and you're done."

"All man made," he said. "We don't know when we're going to die, so it's meaningless."

"Cavemen didn't understand night versus day, seasons?"

"They didn't obsess over how long it took to build a fire." He twined his fingers through hers.

"Slow and steady," Asha said. "That's your pace."

Neel glanced her way and gave her a roguish smile. "I haven't had any complaints."

Her jaw dropped. A different tension took hold within her. "Now? You're flirting with me now?"

"I'm stating a fact."

She stared at him. "Are you just toying with me, or is this some sort of payback for the original sin of hurting you by leaving for Paris after high school?" She'd kept her voice even and matter of fact.

He pulled his hand out of hers, and rejection slammed into her so hard, she had to face away from him to catch her breath.

After a few minutes of silence, he spoke. "Old habits, I guess."

She didn't say anything.

They drove in silence until he turned off the highway and the landscape changed. It was more open and alive, less concrete.

"I do want you," he said. "A part of me still loves you."

She heard him and waited for the eventual *but*.

When he didn't say anything, she looked his way.

"I've never stopped." He didn't take his eyes off the road.

It was Asha who didn't know how to respond. There was so much in those words, but she also heard hesitation. He was afraid of going down this particular path with her again. Yet he'd given her the words. Instead of reaching for him like she wanted to, Asha kept her hands in her lap. Neel turned the music back on, and she let it distract her overworked brain. Forty-five minutes later she recognized the roads. This wasn't the way to her parents'. He turned off into the long tree-lined drive as Goldfield loomed ahead.

CHAPTER
FORTY-FIVE

She looked at him as he turned the truck off in the side parking area. "What are you doing?"

"Kidnapping you." Neel jumped out of the cab. "Let me get the door for you, Princess Poppy."

Asha ignored his hand and jumped down. "I think it's a felony." She was still stunned from what he'd confessed but tried to match his mood.

"Meh," he said. "I'll risk it."

She followed him toward his office. He led her in and closed the door behind them. "If you want, I'll clean all this up. We'll need a large dumpster."

"You can't help yourself," Neel said. "You need to poke at everything. This is how I work. Deal with it."

"I'm only trying to make you more productive."

"And I don't need it."

"But you can use it."

"Here." He led her to a large worktable. "What do you know about breweries?"

It was her turn to be shocked. "They're ugly, and no one comes to this area for beer when there's so much wine."

"Based on zero market research." He leaned against his desk. "You know all those science classes you helped me pass? It sort of worked out. About six years ago, I learned the craft of beer brewing. Started tinkering while I worked at some micro places around San Francisco, then I decided to go out on my own. I finally landed on a name after I closed on the land where it's going up. Wildflower Brewery."

Her heart squeezed. He wasn't even keeping Sonanum the name.

"Here, check this out." He waved her to his side and pointed at the drawings spread out on his desk.

Asha scanned the renderings. "You did these."

"The architect I'm working with, they drew them up." Neel pointed to the top sketch. The building was short, low to the ground, with a flat roof. There were glass railings. "It'll have a seating area on the roof, with cantilevered shade for rain or too much sun." The building itself was dark green and looked as if it blended into the hills behind it. "I've never wanted something stark or intrusive to the landscape. Even at another location, I wanted to build it for this area."

"You always loved the outdoors." She stroked her fingers on the sketch. "This is where the pond is."

He nodded. "Yeah, we'll lose the trees and hedges. Also, the topiaries. Bye-bye, Babar with the wonky trunk."

"Poor elephant."

"But we're going to keep the pond."

She looked up at him.

"This is what I wanted to show you before you stomped off the other day."

She hated to admit it, but it was pretty and not as ugly as she'd imagined. "There's so much open space."

"Yeah," he said. "On the drive over, because music helps *me* think, I had an idea. See this area? Right now, it's sketched out as additional seating with benches spaced out."

"What's this platform?"

"A stage area. I was planning to have live music, and people could wander or sit and enjoy."

"Where the wildflowers are." She pulled her hand away. "The sages are gone too. You took the name but plan to get rid of the actual garden bed."

He grinned. "You want to help?"

"That's your big idea you spent half an hour thinking about?" She was disappointed. "What's with the Desai siblings offering me jobs today?"

Neel crossed his arms. "Beer brewing requires chemistry. You have a degree."

"First, I don't like beer," she said.

"That hurts," he said.

"Second, yeast is pungent. I'd get a headache the moment I walked in the room where all the vats and things are."

"The brew room?"

"See? I don't know the first thing about any of this." Then she paused. Is this what he meant in the truck when he said he wanted her? Instead of being upset, she decided to turn the tables, test him to see how far he would go. If they both got hurt in the process, so be it. Asha didn't want to wonder anymore. No more what-ifs, wishing and wanting. She wanted to know where they stood once and for all.

"What do you know about construction?" he said.

She crossed her arms. "Only that I would look great in a hard hat."

His grin was flirtatious. "Oh, I can see that."

She saw the glimmer in his eyes. And she matched it. Moved toward him. "Can you imagine me in an orange vest around all that big, heavy machinery?"

She saw his Adam's apple move and leaned closer. "It would be hot," Neel said.

Asha grabbed his hands to prevent him from pulling away. She saw the flicker of desire. It would be the perfect time to push him off and leave him frustrated, except she didn't want to do that anymore. She reached up and cupped his face, urged him toward her own, and finally did what she'd been wanting to for a long time. She brushed her lips against his. Waited for permission. Then he kissed her back, took over, and grabbed ahold of her to bring her against him.

Asha poured everything into the kiss, all of her love, frustration, irritation, and apologies for past hurt. She memorized his taste, inhaled the scent of his skin. His arms pulled her tight and still she wanted to be closer. She was the one who tugged his T-shirt off him. She wanted to be skin to skin.

Then there was no turning back. Years of missing each other took over any rational thought, and they took what they needed from each other, gave everything. It wasn't only lust, but love fulfilled. One that had long been dormant that was now impossible to ignore. It was heat and heart, slow and fast, and in the end, they were exactly where they wanted to be. Together.

Out of breath, Neel touched his forehead to hers. "You offered to organize this mess. Instead you made it worse. The files on the desk are all over the floor."

She put her face in his chest, rubbed her nose against his damp skin. "I decided to see what it would be like to be you for a minute."

"And?"

"I'm more of a clean-up person than a clutter maker." She separated from him and picked up the clothes she'd lost. Her dress was wrinkled, and she smoothed it out as much as possible. "When you said you wanted me? On the drive over. Did you mean offering me a job?"

He pulled up his jeans, then took ahold of her hips. "Dingus."

"That's not an answer."

"Yes."

She shoved him.

"Wait," he said. "I mean no. Not a job. I mean I meant what you thought I meant. Didn't I just prove that?"

She reached up and tied her hair in a loose bun.

"I don't want you to work *for* me, but *with* me," he said. "I'll have to run the numbers to see how it impacts projections, but what if I got rid of the music and the outdoor seating? Keep the wildflowers and sages? You can use that area for your tea."

Her jaw dropped.

"I would have to lease that piece of the land to you." He tugged her back to him.

"Right, because it's business." She put her hands on his chest.

"And neither of us has enough money to make this happen on our own. We can redo the business plan, take it to the investors."

"It's important that I have a stake in this too," she said. "I'll see what kind of small-business loans I can get. I can work out a deal with Millie where I'm on retainer for a while as I get started but still keep creative control."

He brushed her lips with his. "Give her hell."

She laughed. "We both will." She kissed him again.

There was a lot of work left to do, but Asha didn't just have a plan now. She had a place.

CHAPTER
FORTY-SIX

A year and change later

It was a gorgeous spring day at Wildflower Brewery and Gardens. Everyone was there for the launch, including Millie and her parents and new friends Asha had made along the way. The sky was blue as people milled around the outdoor space. The roof area was packed, as were the benches around the outside. The servers ran back and forth with food and drinks as guests laughed and chatted.

Neel hopped over the bench seat and sat across from Asha. "Try it."

A beer flight with six short glasses was laid out in front of her.

"The light-orange one is my favorite," Mimi said from the other side of the long table. "If you don't like yours, I'll take it."

"She promised," Neel called over. "At least one sip of each."

Asha made a face.

"Go from light to dark."

She took a lemon-colored one and brought it up to her lips. With a hesitant sip, Asha waited for bitterness and was pleasantly surprised that it never rendered. "Ginger, lemon, and something else?"

"Goji berry." He beamed. "What do you think? I call it Daisy."

He'd named the different brews with different types of wildflowers. "I like it. But can I just drink this one? The Nanis of Napa at the other table look thirsty."

"They're fine," he said. "Millie and her man are supervising."

More like egging them on, but Asha smiled. "I'm proud of you."

That he could still blush made her want to tell him every day.

"You're the one killing it with your Sonanum Tea."

"Leela's Gold is a bestseller," her grandmother said as she sat opposite Mimi.

"I thought old people were hard of hearing," Neel said.

Mimi tapped her ear. "I have a state-of-the-art device that can pick up a whisper from fifty miles away."

"Fifteen feet," Leela corrected.

Asha reached over and held Neel's hand. "Remember when I told you what I most wanted was to stay?"

He brought her hand to his lips and kissed it. "I'm glad you came back."

Sapna and Sanjay sat at the table too, and Neel's parents sat on the other side. They'd all seen how hard Asha and Neel had worked to build their businesses, and while things were still strained between Neel and his dad, and Asha and her father hadn't made much headway except for occasional conversations around poetry he recommended and she read, the one thing that had brought everyone together was Neel and her as a couple.

"Anyway"—she leaned closer to Neel and lowered her voice—"I didn't know it then, but what I meant was I wanted to be here. With family, friends, and you."

He leaned over and kissed her. It was quick because their families were around, but still they lingered long enough for Asha to taste the hops, inhale the scent of malt and cedar, and revel in the way her heart bloomed every time she thought about him.

Her phone chimed and she flipped it over. It was the Desai-Patel group chat. Neel had added her a year ago. Initially he'd suggested he would tag out and she could replace him, but Mimi grabbed him by the ear and lectured him about family until he relented.

Millie: New rule—no PDA from anyone in this group chat.

She laughed, gave her friend a wave, then leaned over to give Neel another peck.

Her father clinked a glass with his fork. "Kirit and I have been thinking."

Asha ignored them and kept her eyes locked to Neel's.

"When these two marry—"

Asha sat back. Her father had her attention. "Let's not go there."

"You're a planner," Sanjay said. "You must have thought about this."

For the last year, busy with work, she and Neel had agreed to simply enjoy being together.

"And since it relates to the family business," he said, "Kirit and I are sorting through the details. Neel will have shares in DHG, and with your marriage there will be a portion allocated to you. When I retire, Goldfield will be folded into DHG but still remain a boutique hotel with its own brand."

Millie came over. "And I plan to oversee all of it."

"Not yet," Kirit uncle said.

"We're still young," Sanjay added. "We're not going anywhere, only working through the best course of action."

"And if we don't get married?" Asha asked.

Neel raised an eyebrow.

"He's more go with the flow," Asha said. "Nontraditional. And I'm very independent."

"You can think how you want," Leela said. "You will still marry."

"Because you said so?" Millie asked.

"No," Mimi added. "I took Asha to my psychic, and Madam Jana all but guaranteed it."

"Well, since Madam Jana saw it in her crystal ball." Neel stood and reached his hand into his pocket.

Asha heard gasps around her, but she kept her eyes on Neel. There was the slightest twinkle, and she relaxed.

He took out a ChapStick and moistened his lips.

Everyone groaned and Millie punched him.

"What?" He sat down and took a swig from Asha's beer.

"What did she say about me?" Millie wrapped her hand around her grandmother's shoulder.

"Oh, child." Mimi slapped her forehead. "All she saw was you telling everyone what to do, including that man of yours. And she didn't see a ring on your finger."

Millie squeezed her grandmother. "Thank you, Mimi. I love your psychic. She's definitely on point. Speaking of, Neel, go get us food. Desi nachos, the ceviche . . . oh, just bring one of everything."

Neel stayed seated. "You know where the kitchen is; you go get it."

She came around and poked her finger in his back. "Please. I'm hungry."

He sighed. "You're going to annoy me until I do it, so might as well." On his way, he grabbed Asha and hauled her with him. "I'll need help."

They walked hand in hand toward the squat building that melded into the facade. "Listen, I know we're enjoying things as they are," he said. "But we have got to move out of your parents' house."

She leaned into his body. "Don't worry, I'm planning on it." She'd found the perfect place and was ready to sign the paperwork once she showed it to Neel. Living with her parents and keeping up the pretense of separate bedrooms—because she was not willing to be *that* open—didn't give them much privacy.

"Should I be afraid?"

"How do you feel about a small cottage with a big back porch that faces west and looks out over a wide vista with hills and fields?"

He raised one brow. "And the inside?"

She shrugged. "Neat, organized, minimal, and contemporary."

He leaned over and kissed her. "As long as there is a comfy couch and a big bed, I'm in."

She leaned into his side. The final surprise would be once they moved in. There was a doggy door that led to the back porch. It was perfect for a rescue puppy. Neel was a man that needed a dog, and she wanted to give him everything. Always.

ACKNOWLEDGMENTS

I want to thank my parents, sister, and my family for their continued support. They've been my centering place while I worked on this novel. My paternal grandfather was a sugarcane farmer, and we grew our own vegetables when I was young, which inspired this work.

To my desi writing crew, thank you for the writing sprints, the spontaneous FaceTime chats, the help with solving gnarly problems, and for sharing in the doldrums that often come with crafting a novel for publication.

Thank you to all the writers and friends who held my hand as I navigated the release of my debut while working on this novel; you continue to inspire me with how generous you are with your time and expertise.

Thank you, Mr. Raman Patel of Custom Essence, for all your wisdom about perfume making and the business of it. Representation matters, and you are an inspiration for going out on your own and creating a company that is globally renowned.

To Colleen Battista and Kelly Skeuse, thanks for answering my non-stop questions about soils, flowers, herbs, and everything in between. (And for the roof deck garden.)

To my agent, Sarah Younger—thank you will never be enough.

My deep gratitude to my editor, Megha Parekh, along with Jenna Free, Kimberly Glyder, Jon Ford, Haley Swan, and Heather Rodino, I am in awe of how much you do to bring this novel to readers.

I hope this novel inspires anyone who is sitting with questions about how to honor legacy while pursuing your own dreams.

ABOUT THE AUTHOR

Photo © 2021 Andy Dean

Namrata Patel is an Indian American writer who resides in Boston. The author of *The Candid Life of Meena Dave*, she examines diaspora and dual-cultural identity among Indian Americans in her writing and explores this dynamic while also touching on the families we're born with and those we choose. Namrata has lived in India, New Jersey, Spokane, London, and New York City and has been writing most of her adult life. For more information visit www.nampatel.com.